"Damn it, Jenny, I don't know about the pledge. Just what the hell did we pledge, anyway?"

"I'm not so sure," she answered softly.

"Wasn't the pledge only for working hours?" Kerry's eyes were twin blue flames, scorching with want.

"I . . . I don't know."

"What do you want it to be, Jenny?" he murmured huskily. "What do you want from me?"

Jennifer knew she was casting caution to the winds. She let it go, let it drift beyond the point of no return. "I think," she said, staring deep into his eyes, "I want the same thing you want from me."

Then they were in each other's arms, and all the pent-up passion that had been mounting between them broke over them like a wave, wonderfully warm and totally enveloping. . . .

Dear Reader,

Sophisticated but sensitive, savvy yet unabashedly sentimental—that's today's woman, today's romance reader—you! And Silhouette Special Editions are written expressly to reward your quest for substantial, emotionally involving love stories.

So take a leisurely stroll under the cover's lavender arch into a garden of romantic delights. Pick and choose among titles if you must—we hope you'll soon equate all six Special Editions each month with consistently gratifying romantic reading.

Watch for sparkling new stories from your Silhouette favorites—Nora Roberts, Tracy Sinclair, Ginna Gray, Lindsay McKenna, Curtiss Ann Matlock, among others—along with some exciting newcomers to Silhouette, such as Karen Keast and Patricia Coughlin. Be on the lookout, too, for the new Silhouette Classics, a distinctive collection of bestselling Special Editions and Silhouette Intimate Moments now brought back to the stands—two each month—by popular demand.

On behalf of all the authors and editors of Special Editions,
Warmest wishes,

Leslie Kazanjian
Senior Editor

MAGGI CHARLES
Army Daughter

Silhouette Special Edition

Published by Silhouette Books New York

America's Publisher of Contemporary Romance

For Kathleen, with love.

SILHOUETTE BOOKS
300 East 42nd St., New York, N.Y. 10017

Copyright © 1988 by Koehler Associates, Ltd.

ISBN: 0-373-09429-9

First Silhouette Books printing January 1988

America's Publisher of Contemporary Romance

Printed in the U.S.A.

Books by Maggi Charles

Silhouette Romance

Magic Crescendo #134

Silhouette Intimate Moments

Love's Other Language #90

Silhouette Special Edition

Love's Golden Shadow #23
Love's Tender Trial #45
The Mirror Image #158
That Special Sunday #258
Autumn Reckoning #269
Focus on Love #305
Yesterday's Tomorrow #336
Shadow on the Sun #362
The Star Seeker #381
Army Daughter #429

MAGGI CHARLES

is a confirmed traveler who readily admits that "people and places fascinate me." A prolific author, who is also known to her romance fans as Meg Hudson, Ms. Charles states that if she hadn't become a writer, she would have been a musician, having studied the piano and harp. A native New Yorker, she is the mother of two sons and currently resides in Cape Cod, Massachusetts, with her husband.

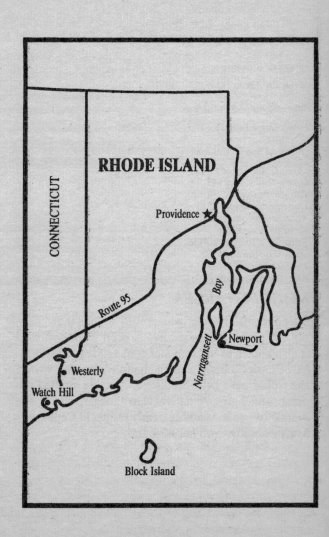

RHODE ISLAND

CONNECTICUT

Providence ★

Narragansett Bay

Route 95

Westerly

Watch Hill

Newport

Block Island

Prologue

Jennifer was frowning as she walked along the rutted dirt road baked dry by the intense Georgia heat. Her long auburn hair hung like a damp blanket around her neck. Her yellow voile dress was wet through and clung to her in a way that might have been considered revealing under other circumstances but at the moment was merely uncomfortable. Her delicate sandals had heels, so it was hard not to stumble. All she needed was to turn an ankle! If that happened, she might very well lie there in pain for days before anyone found her.

She'd been an idiot to come so far, she thought morosely. The worst of it was she'd totally lost her sense of direction. So much for seeking solitude! She had hoped to achieve the right mental state in which to make a crucial decision that would deeply affect the rest of her life, and look at the mess it had gotten her into.

She scowled at the red earth and scrub pine that stretched on all sides to a clear blue horizon and tried to remember the lessons her brother, Josh, had taught her years ago about navigating by the sun, whether on foot or asea. Unfortunately, *this* sun was directly overhead. The noon hour when, according to Noël Coward, only mad dogs and Englishmen ventured forth.

Suddenly, without warning, she heard artillery fire. Not a single shot, but a whole barrage. Instinctively, Jennifer flung herself flat into the dirt. Bullets whistled over her head as she lay prone, fright driving the breath out of her.

My God, what had she stumbled into?

Then, as abruptly as it had started, the firing stopped.

Jennifer was in such a state of shock that the jeep was almost on top of her before she heard it. Completely startled, she froze, and in a wild, frenzied instant the driver swerved, missing her by only the narrowest of margins.

The stubby khaki-colored vehicle lurched to a grinding stop, clouds of copper dust swirling up around it. Then a tall soldier wearing grimy fatigues leaped out, his boots landing on the hard ground with a resounding thud.

Obviously, he was furious. Despite her shock, Jennifer instantly became aware of that fury, and she shrank back. As he approached, his lean face was set in tight lines, and his eyes—a deep blue as clear as the Georgia sky—crackled with anger.

He stared down at her, his powerful muscles taut, his stance rigid. "Just what the hell do you think you're doing here?" he growled.

"I was taking a walk," she managed.

He snorted, then fired a few words that singed the already sizzling atmosphere. Forcibly restraining himself from exploding, he demanded, "Are you aware you're in a restricted area?"

She shook her head. "I wasn't, no."

"Did you think that was thunder you were hearing a minute ago?"

Jennifer, raised an army brat, knew the sound of artillery when she heard it. But considering the fib a form of self-defense, she hedged, "I wasn't sure what it was."

"Field practice," the soldier informed her, removing his dull green helmet and mopping his glistening forehead.

Jennifer saw that his hair was thick and wavy and such a light blond it was almost silver. She saw, too, that though he was still nearly vibrating with anger, he was a very attractive man. Even the baggy military fatigues couldn't conceal his excellent physique. He looked like a man honed for action, supremely self-confident about what he was doing. The type of man it wouldn't be too bad to be stranded with on a desert island, she thought mischievously. He'd be resourceful. He'd know exactly where to find the best coconuts and how to build a fire. And on those tropical nights when moonlight shimmered across the satin sea...

"Are you hurt?" he inquired abruptly, cutting off her fantasy.

"No, I'm not."

"Then will you kindly stand up and let me get you out of here?" He extended a lean brown hand as he spoke, which Jennifer clasped, only to feel herself yanked to her feet.

"Into the jeep," he said brusquely.

It was the telltale note of command in his voice that alerted her to the sergeant's stripes on his sleeve. Her chin tilted. So, he was a noncom. She, on the other hand, was the commanding general's daughter. She wondered how this belligerent soldier was going to swallow *that* bit of information.

"Come on, get in," he ordered, sounding totally exasperated. "You're holding up an important field exercise."

As she stepped toward the open vehicle, Jennifer was about to identify herself and tell this sergeant that she'd left her car somewhere in the area and would appreciate his help in locating it. But for some reason she paused and asked, "Where are you taking me?"

"To the military police," he informed her curtly. "I might add that they don't take kindly to people who crash our security, especially when they jeopardize their health in doing so. That's live ammo we're using. You could have been killed. Did that fact ever dawn on you?"

"No," Jennifer said soberly. It hadn't. Trying to humor her way through the dreadful thought, she added lightly, "It probably will in the middle of the night, though, and I'll wake up screaming."

He scowled and urged, "Get *in*, will you?"

Jennifer sensed that if she didn't do his bidding he'd simply hoist her into the vehicle. She settled into the dusty seat and sat stiffly at his side as the engine coughed several times before it whined into action. Only then did she say, "Look, there's really no need to turn me over to the MPs."

He favored her with a long, cynical glance. "Oh, really?" he commented coolly. "Well, then, Miss..."

"Smith," Jennifer supplied. She was suddenly glad she had a surname that wouldn't instantly register with him.

"Well, then, Miss Smith, just what would you suggest I do with you?"

"I have a car parked around here somewhere...."

He slammed on the brakes, bringing the jeep to a screeching halt that forced Jennifer to brace herself for fear of flying out over the hood.

"You what!" he exploded. "Are you telling me you got past the guards in a car?"

"No, not exactly," she hedged.

He glared at her. "You'll have to do better than that."

She drew a deep breath and stated, "I live on the post."

He snorted contemptuously. "That *is* a new one!"

"Seriously, I really do live on the post."

"Where?"

Jennifer quickly thought over the whole situation and decided it would be best if her father never found out about it. "I'd rather not say," she told him.

"You'd rather not say?" he retorted menacingly. His lips narrowed to a thin line as he jammed the jeep into gear and sped off.

They drove in stony silence, but when they approached the familiar periphery of the main post, Jennifer began to realize that this man was not going to let her off the hook. She sighed, dreading the upcoming confrontation, which, unfortunately, would prove embarrassing for both of them.

Her father's office was in the headquarters building. So were the offices of his two lieutenant aides, both of whom had been asking Jennifer for dates ever since she'd arrived in Georgia last month after her graduation from the Briarlee School in New York.

A week ago she'd celebrated her eighteenth birthday with both lieutenants in ardent attendance. One or the other always seemed to be off duty, and it was to get away from them—and everyone else—that she'd driven out into the boonies today in the car her parents had given her as a graduation present.

As it happened, she hadn't been able to do even a fraction of the in-depth thinking she'd set out to do. Her parents were expecting her to attend Greenridge College in

Connecticut, another exclusive educational establishment reserved for the privileged few. But she'd just about made up her mind that when September came she was going to elope with Andre.

She knew she'd be hurting her parents. But she also knew it was the only possible way she could be with the man she loved.

She worshipped Andre Perreault, her French instructor for the past year at Briarlee. And he claimed he adored her. Andre was undoubtedly one of the handsomest men in the entire world. Maybe even better-looking than this irate sergeant at her side.

College or marriage via elopement? It was a rough choice to make at the age of eighteen, and thus far Jennifer's future was a struggle, still unresolved.

Because she might soon be taking a step that would make her parents very unhappy, Jennifer was especially anxious to keep family affairs on an even keel. Thus, there was no point in upsetting her father simply because she'd happened to take a walk in the wrong place this afternoon.

"After all, all's well that ends well," she murmured.

"What was that?" her companion demanded.

"Sergeant, look, I'd like to strike a bargain with you," Jennifer began, deliberately giving him the full impact of her huge topaz eyes. "There's really no point in going any further with this."

He was climbing out of the jeep. Over his shoulder, he commented with exaggerated politeness, "You don't say." He strode around to her side of the vehicle and stood there, staring at her.

Jennifer reflected that only someone made of stone could be unmoved by this man's looks, his quiet power and the latent sexiness that emanated from him. But he was also very stern. She flinched as she met the steel in his blue eyes.

"Come along," he instructed.

"Sergeant, there's no *point*," she began again. And at that instant she saw her father's staff car pulling up directly in front of the jeep.

Her angry captor immediately came to attention. He executed a sharp military salute as General Ashley Sanderson Smith emerged from the car and approached the jeep, the set of his jaw matching the sergeant's rigid expression.

"You're blocking the entrance, aren't you, soldier?" the general observed caustically.

"Yes, sir," the sergeant snapped back promptly. "However, I'm delivering this individual to the MPs. She has violated post security, sir."

The general's eyes swept past the sergeant and fell on his daughter. "Jenny!" he exclaimed, "What are you doing here?"

Jennifer Smith hastily got out of the jeep and approached her father. "I got lost, Daddy, that's all," she said. "And," she simpered deliberately, not daring to look at the sergeant, "this nice man came to my rescue."

"Then what's this about violating post security?"

The sergeant was scrupulously polite, but Jennifer recognized the tenor of hostility in his voice as he said stiffly, "I apparently made a mistake, sir. Miss Smith didn't identify herself."

Only when she heard her name on his lips did Jennifer look at him. She saw the disdain in his eyes and easily read his message. He had her pegged as a spoiled army brat, taking refuge behind the gold stars on her father's uniform.

"Sir!" the sergeant snapped with another salute to the general. Then he climbed into the jeep and drove away, his back ramrod stiff.

Jennifer trailed along with her father, knowing that, once he'd had his say, it would be simple enough to enlist one of the lieutenant aides to help her reclaim her car.

Still, she was disturbed and vaguely unhappy throughout the balance of the day. And that night she dreamed not of artillery fire but of the irate young noncom whose blue eyes had blazed down on her with the intensity of the Georgia sun.

It was fortunate, Jennifer decided, awake in the wee hours of the morning and staring out at the moonsprinkled garden behind the house, that she and the sergeant would probably not meet again. Because on a scale of one to ten, she had little doubt that he'd rate her a zero.

Chapter One

"Mr. Gundersen will see you now, Mrs. Perreault," the receptionist said with a charming but impersonal smile.

"Thank you." As Jennifer got up and moved toward the office door the receptionist indicated, she took care that nothing in her manner revealed how very much she wanted the job she was about to make a pitch for.

She'd been cooling her heels in the austere atmosphere of Gundersen and Sonntag's reception area for the past thirty-five minutes, and Jennifer disliked few things as much as she did being kept waiting. But today she was not in the driver's seat, she reminded herself. So she would grit her teeth and smile and be gracious and thoroughly professional. Obvious annoyance wouldn't help convince Kerry Gundersen that theirs might be a mutually profitable business relationship.

The door she passed through opened into a wide foyer. The floor was carpeted in gray; the walls were painted a contrasting gray; the overhead lighting was silver-fixtured and discreet. Architectural renderings lined the walls, all depicting projects designed by this Providence, Rhode Island, firm that, in a few short years, had gained a national reputation for the originality of its exceptional work.

The decor, Jennifer supposed, was a calculated understatement. There were no visual distractions to lure a potential client astray. In the center of the room, a stunning woman with prematurely silver hair sat behind a sleek teakwood desk.

"Mrs. Perreault?" she queried, rising.

At Jennifer's affirmative, she led the way to a corner door, opened it and murmured, "Mrs. Perreault to see you, Mr. Gundersen."

Jennifer stepped across the threshold into an office that, like its surroundings, was stark in its simplicity. Her eyes immediately riveted on the enormous windows that formed right angles behind the outsize executive desk. Framed by nubby white silk drapes, they offered a panoramic view of Providence, punctuated by the white dome of the Rhode Island statehouse.

A tall, lean man stood at one window, looking out, his back to her. She was forced to admire the excellence of his tailoring, since his perfectly cut charcoal suit was, for the moment, the most visible thing about him. That and his hair, which was so light a blond it was almost silver.

Her breath caught. Once before—ten years ago—she'd seen hair like that glinting in the Georgia sun. Strangely, she'd never forgotten it.

The man swung around . . . and shock froze the soles of Jennifer's black pumps to the thick pile of the wall-to-wall oyster-gray carpet.

How could this possibly be the same man who'd turned his back on her and driven off in a jeep that awful afternoon in Georgia when, by her own stupid mistake, she'd stumbled into the middle of an artillery range?

And yet...it was. He was ten years older, but those same intense blue eyes blazed at her, the same tautness in the sculptured lines of his handsome face met her bewildered stare. If anything, the passage of time had made him even more attractive than he'd been a decade ago.

Kerry Gundersen. One of today's leading architects. Also, from what Josh had told her, one of the most sought after and wealthy bachelors around.

It was difficult, if not impossible, to equate his modern, professional image with that of the irate young soldier who, ten years ago, had wanted to hand her over to the military police at Fort McKettrick, Georgia...only to discover, to his extreme embarrassment, that she was the commanding general's daughter.

Jennifer saw his shock register and knew he must also be witnessing hers. She tried to speak but couldn't find a word to say.

He rallied first and said smoothly, "It's Mrs. Perreault now, is it?"

"Yes."

"Sit down, won't you?" he suggested, waving a hand toward the Scandinavian-designed chair by his desk.

Jennifer was glad to lower her trembling legs onto something solid. The veneer of composure she'd carefully applied before walking into the office was rapidly flaking away. She couldn't remember when she'd felt so confused—or so oddly vulnerable. Why, she asked herself, hadn't Josh told her this man was the same sergeant she'd had that emotion-stirring encounter with at McKettrick?

Because Josh didn't know, you imbecile, she answered herself sharply. Josh had been in the hospital ten years ago on that summer day when she'd come face-to-face with the angry sergeant. Her brother, just out of the Air Force Academy, had crashed in pilot training. He'd been in a military hospital in Texas, his own military career finished. The injuries he'd suffered in the crash had left him permanently lame.

She'd gone to Texas to visit Josh not long after the incident on the firing range. She'd sat by his hospital bed and regaled him with the story about wandering into a restricted area, making the whole episode sound quite funny. In fact, she'd even caricatured the stern, silver-haired, forbidding but devastatingly handsome sergeant with carefree exuberance. Josh, bless him, had laughed heartily, though she couldn't see how he'd been able to laugh at anything just then.

Now it was Josh who had recommended her to Kerry Gundersen. Josh who'd gathered the determination to get himself out of the hospital and work extremely hard to make his own way in a brand-new field—the world of magazine publishing.

Today he was an editor on the staff of *Architecture, American Style,* a highly respected trade publication. He'd met Kerry Gundersen while researching an article for the magazine several years ago, and the two men had become friends.

Jennifer suddenly wished that she had Josh at her side now to smooth things over in that marvelous way of his. "It's a question of looking at the lighter side," he'd said once, when she'd asked him how he always managed to present such a cheerful front, no matter how he might be feeling. She wished she were capable of looking at the lighter side right now. But there was nothing "light" in the mien of the man who'd taken his place behind his enormous desk and was facing her, his handsome visage a polite, cool, totally emotionless study.

"Josh never mentioned he came from a military family," he commented, momentarily betraying his surprise.

"Josh doesn't talk too readily about the past," Jennifer responded nervously.

Kerry Gundersen smiled faintly. "Well, he did allow that he had a sister," he said. "However, I didn't make the connection between your names. And I suppose that, even if I had, there must be more than one Jennifer Smith in the world."

"Many, I'm sure."

She was trying not to look at him, but it was impossible to avoid that bright sapphire blaze. He had the bluest eyes she'd ever seen, Jennifer thought as she had ten years earlier. She wished they weren't so distracting.

"Quite a coincidence, isn't it?" he said softly.

"Yes."

He cleared his throat, then frowned. "Look," he said, "I'm sorry I kept you waiting. I was on the phone with an associate in San Francisco."

She hadn't expected an apology. "That's quite all right."

To her surprise, he grinned. "Is it?" he asked. "Offhand, I'd say you're probably a person who hates to be kept waiting."

He reached out a lean hand—not as brown as on that long-ago day when he'd pulled Jennifer to her feet on that rough dirt road in Georgia—and shuffled a few papers on his desk. It was Jennifer's first indication that Kerry Gundersen, also, was uneasy.

This gave her a measure of confidence she otherwise might not have come by. She sidestepped his statement and got directly to the point. "Josh tells me you've bought a house for which you need a decorator. An investment property, perhaps?"

He shook his head. "No, I intend it as my home."

He muttered something else under his breath, and Jennifer thought he'd said, "The home I never had." But that didn't fit with the picture Josh had sketched of Kerry Gundersen.

He'd been featured, she knew, in all sorts of magazines, he was manna for the gossip columns, and he had appeared on television and radio talk shows to discuss his trend-setting designs. Had Jennifer been living in the States, there was no way she could have missed seeing his picture by now, or his face on a television screen. Nor was there any doubt that she would have recognized him. No other man in the world could look quite like him. As it was, though, what she knew about Kerry Gundersen came from Josh.

She'd lived in Europe for most of the past ten years—first in France, then in England—and had returned to the States only six months ago. Since then, she'd been staying at Josh's apartment in New York until she became, as her brother put it, "fully repatriated." In her case, that meant making a number of vital decisions about where she wanted to live and what she wanted to do with her life.

In London, she'd put together a variety of inherent talents and several acquired ones and had worked for a well-known interior designer. She had an excellent color sense and the daring to mix and match with exciting, eclectic results. She loved working with colors and fabrics, with textures and designs. But to do her best work, she needed a free hand, which meant she needed the client's utmost confidence in her.

For that reason, she liked to interview her clients in depth, ferreting out their most personal likes and dislikes.

She had a natural sensitivity toward people, and often in their conversations her "subjects" revealed much more than they intended. But that was always to the good. With her decorator's expertise, she translated her discoveries into creating environments appropriate to her clients' where they could relax, work or play in perfect comfort. Thus far, she'd yet to have a dissatisfied customer.

Given her work methods, she couldn't imagine coping with an assignment from Kerry Gundersen. For one thing, getting to know him so personally would involve too much intimacy. Furthermore, based not only on their brief encounter so long ago but also on his meteoric, highly innovative professional record, he was not a person who'd entrust any of his affairs to someone else. He would want to be in charge. He would want to call the shots.

She shook her head. It just wouldn't work out.

"You seem to be negating something," he observed, cutting through her thoughts. "What, may I ask?"

It was a question she couldn't logically answer. Here she was, on the verge of refusing a job he hadn't even offered her! At the same time, common sense reminded her that she desperately wanted the Gundersen account as a stepping stone. Were she to "do" this man's house, her mark would be made as a decorator. Josh had told her that, and she believed him.

"It's nothing, really," she said lamely.

His gaze was skeptical. He began to shuffle the papers on his desk again, then said abruptly, "I've bought a house here in Rhode Island, near Westerly. Watch Hill, as a matter of fact. Are you familiar with the area?"

"No, I'm not," she admitted, knowing she sounded vague. She was still thinking of what it would be like to work for this man and wondering if there was any way she could handle it.

Showing his irritation, he said none too patiently, "Mrs. Perreault, I'm not a mind reader, but I sense there's something bothering you about me. I'd appreciate knowing what it is."

"Well," she began, trying to rally, "I was thinking about your... taste. You seem to prefer a monochromatic color scheme, a variety of gray tones. I wondered about that, that's all."

"I like to keep my business surroundings neutral," he explained curtly. "It helps focus a client's attention on the projects we've done. You must have seen the drawings on the walls."

"Yes, I did."

"Well, if you're wondering whether I'd want my house decorated as these offices are, I can assure you the answer is no."

"I see," she said, feeling engulfed in the intense blue flames in his eyes.

"You come highly recommended by Josh," Kerry Gundersen stated.

Jennifer smiled softly. "Josh is my brother," she said, "and not entirely impartial." Then, deciding that hadn't sounded very professional, she quickly added, "I have a portfolio, of course... but I deliberately left it at the hotel."

"Deliberately?"

She nodded. "I find it better to simply talk to a prospective client the first time around, Mr. Gundersen. To see if we mesh."

"Mesh?"

"A decorator and a client don't necessarily have to have the same tastes," she elaborated, "but they do need to be on the same wavelength. Conflicting personalities create chaos in decorating. At least, that's my feeling."

"I see."

On surer ground now, her verbal skills returning with her convictions about her work, Jennifer continued. "I put a lot into what I do, with the goal of projecting my client, certainly not myself, into the surroundings I create. In doing so, I must become an extension of someone else's concept, if you follow me."

He arched an eyebrow and gave her a smile that easily could have been called wicked. "That sounds like a very interesting philosophy," he observed.

"It's a professional philosophy, not a personal one, Mr. Gundersen," she returned rather sharply.

"Oh, I'm sure it is, Mrs. Perreault," he answered smoothly.

Was it her imagination, or had he stressed the *Mrs.* ever so slightly?

"Well, then," he went on when she didn't speak, "about Watch Hill. I grew up...in Connecticut, for the most part. Near Hartford. Once, we were...that is, I was taken on an outing to the beach, one summer. A beach along the Sound." The oddly disjointed tempo to the way he was reporting his background alerted Jennifer's interest.

"They took us—took me, that is—to Watch Hill to see the carousel," he continued, still in that strangely hesitant way.

"The carousel?"

He nodded. "It's very famous, Mrs. Perreault. Over a hundred years old, and still with the original wooden horses, all painted in bright circus colors. I guess I was about five at the time. It was summer—did I say that already?—and someone bought us some saltwater taffy. I remember the blue water and the sunshine and the horses going around. It made a...very deep impression. Later, much later, I went back to Watch Hill, and not much had changed."

Jennifer sensed his mind's eye wandering backward and asked, "What's it like? Watch Hill, that is."

He gave her a totally disarming smile. "I guess you could call it a mostly Victorian-style summer resort," he told her. "Stuck way out at the end of a jutting point of land, so the water seems to be all over the place. Anyway, I made up my mind I wanted to own a house there someday...."

"And?"

"And it took a while to make enough money to achieve that goal," he confessed.

"So, you've bought a house?"

He nodded. "Yes. In fact, we closed just a couple of weeks ago. I was in New York right after that, and Josh and I met for a drink at the St. Moritz, where I was staying. That's when he said I should hire a good decorator to 'do the place in style,' as he put it. And he suggested you."

Jennifer glanced through the window behind him. The Providence panorama was dotted with trees dressed in autumn colors. "It's already the middle of October," she said. "Didn't you say Watch Hill was a summer resort?"

"For the most part, yes. Although there are definitely more year-round residents than there used to be. It's not that far from here, really. Less than an hour's drive. One could easily commute."

"Do you plan to commute?"

"I don't know," he admitted. "I haven't gotten that far."

"Is your house in good condition?"

"It's in excellent condition," he reported modestly. Riffling through the papers on his desk again, he added, "I took a couple of photographs on my last visit...but I seem to have mislaid them. It was a cloudy day, though, and they don't do justice to the place. Anyway," he finished, giving up his search, "I'd rather you see the place for yourself."

Jennifer's heart skipped a beat. Did that mean he was seriously considering hiring her? If so, what was she going to do about it? To her dismay, she realized that there was nothing the least bit professional in the questions she'd been asking herself about working for Kerry Gundersen. They were purely personal, as were her reactions to this entire situation.

That surprised her. But seeing him again so unexpectedly had totally rocked her. And if the truth were to be known, she was afraid of the emotional impact he was having on her. Scared to death of it.

Six years had passed since she'd left France and fled to England, where she'd endured a depressing transition period while getting a divorce. The love she'd felt for Andre Perreault had turned to ashes, and she hadn't been ready to face her family back in the States. So she'd stayed in England and found a new life in interior design.

Still, it had taken a long time for passion's original bonfire to extinguish itself. By the time the ash stage was reached, she was thoroughly wrung out. She slammed the door on love. She'd been *through* love, all the way through. The day her divorce decree was final, she knew only that she wanted to be free. She wanted to live her own life from then on, with no deep involvements.

She wasn't bitter; she was exhausted. Andre had been a very difficult man to live with once the courtship was over and she had committed herself to him by eloping. His ego had been boosted to the hilt when she'd risked alienating herself from her family forever in order to be with him.

That hadn't happened. Though she and her parents had yet to relate to one another again on the same trusting terms that had existed before Jennifer's "impulsive mistake," they still loved her. She loved them. But she'd hurt them deeply by moving overseas, and she feared there would always be a faint scar in their relationship.

Only Josh, bless him, had found room in his heart to accept her actions. Dear Josh, the one person in the world she'd always felt was one-hundred percent behind her.

Sometimes, since she'd come to stay with him in New York, they talked about love and romance. Usually the discussions ended with Josh laughing wryly and suggesting they drink a toast to their mutual hang-ups. He was painfully self-conscious about his handicap and very careful not to let any woman edge her way too deeply into his life.

Jennifer, on the other hand, simply didn't want any more fires. She liked men. She enjoyed going out with them. And there were always plenty of men around who sought her company. She'd had a couple of casual relationships in London, and she'd recently had a few dates with an attractive television newscaster in New York who plainly couldn't wait to get her into bed with him. No man had really moved her, though. And she wanted to keep it that way.

She tried to rationalize her reaction to Kerry Gundersen as the shock of seeing him again. Yet she hated phoney alibis—particularly when she was giving one to herself! This man sparked a disturbing chemistry, and Jennifer wondered if she possessed a sufficient antidote to dissipate it. For the first time in a long, long while, she wasn't sure.

She noted that he'd taken an executive calendar out of a drawer and was consulting it. Bound in sleek gray leather, it picked up the theme of the office. He was certainly a stickler for detail, she found herself thinking.

He looked up and asked, "Would you like some coffee?"

Jennifer swallowed, suddenly aware of her throat's dryness. "Yes, thank you."

He pushed a button and spoke into an intercom. Evidently his secretary had been waiting for the summons, because she appeared almost immediately, bearing a silver coffee set on a silver tray, plus two exquisite English china cups and saucers.

Jennifer had expected Scandinavian pewter. And she had the feeling Kerry Gundersen had read her mind when he said, "I bought this set in London about a year ago, in the underground silver vaults. Have you visited them?"

"Yes, I have."

Pouring coffee into both cups, he went on, "The china came from an antique shop in the West End. Too bad I didn't know that Josh's sister was living in London then," he added, handing her a cup and saucer. "That *you* were living in London," he amended. "Unfortunately, mainly because I've been traveling around so much the past couple of years, your brother and I don't touch base as often as I'd like."

"I'll tell him you said that."

He favored her with that disarming smile of his but only asked politely, "Cream or sugar?"

"Cream, please."

He handed her the miniature silver pitcher, and their fingers inevitably touched. That in itself told Jennifer that her antidotes weren't working! And her fear was compounded when she looked up and met his brilliant blue eyes.

An indisputable *something* flared between her and Kerry.

Clutching for her composure, she stirred cream into her coffee. "Tell me more about the Watch Hill house," she said.

"There's not that much to tell." He shrugged. "As I said, I guess I've wanted to own a place there since I was five years old. When Providence became my center of operations—about four years ago, now—I found myself driving down to Watch Hill one Saturday afternoon as if my car had been programmed. I didn't really intend to go—I just went, as if I were following some sort of compulsion. Which, I guess, is exactly what I was doing."

"Was that the first time you'd gone back there since you were five?"

He shook his head. "Once, when I was eighteen—just before I went into the service—I hitchhiked over from Hartford. I wanted to see the carousel."

"And you weren't disappointed?"

"On the contrary, I was very disappointed. It was just about this time of year. They'd closed up for the winter—the carousel, that is—and removed the horses for safekeeping. Even so, the memories surged back. That's when I made my resolution about owning a house there one day. At the time, it was like saying I was going to buy a chunk of the moon."

"And now it's a dream come true?"

He studied her skeptically. "You make it sound so saccharine, Mrs. Perreault," he chided. "The American dream, perhaps?" he scoffed. "It wasn't quite like that."

"No?"

"Maybe sometime I'll tell you about it."

He returned his attention to the calendar. "Thursday," he mused. "I don't want to keep you in Providence unnecessarily—not unless you'd planned on staying, that is. Where are you staying, incidentally?"

"At the Biltmore Plaza."

He nodded. "Well...I wish I was free to ask you to dinner tonight," he said regretfully. "Unfortunately, I have an engagement I can't break."

Jennifer fought back a surge of curiosity, hoping her expression hadn't given her away. Kerry Gundersen clearly wasn't about to enlighten her.

"Tomorrow," he said, "I'll be in conference all morning with a client who's flying in from San Francisco late tonight—that's what I was on the phone about when you arrived. Anyway, that's going to go clear through lunch. Then, in the evening, I have another dinner date...."

He sighed. "Could you possibly stay over till Saturday?" he asked unexpectedly. "Naturally, I'll assume the tab for your expenses. I could pick you up around eleven-thirty, and we could have lunch somewhere here in town, or perhaps in Westerly. Then we could spend as much time as you'd like going through the house."

"Is it furnished, by any chance?" Jennifer asked, masking her astonishment at this turn of events. She was also suddenly fearful that he'd bought a Victorian monstrosity stuffed with plush sofas, crocheted antimacassars and elephant-foot umbrella stands.

He shook his head. "There are a couple of things hither and yon, but basically the place is empty. It was sold by the heirs of an old man whose family had been summering in Watch Hill for almost eighty years. They had an estate auction before the property was put up for sale, and that took care of almost everything." He added, "I did buy a few things at the auction because I felt they really belonged in the place. I hope you'll agree."

He was watching her again, and she wished something else would divert that intent gaze. "Well?" he asked patiently. "Will you be free to stay over and drive to Watch Hill with me on Saturday?"

After a brief instant of hesitation, she nodded. "Yes, I think I can arrange that." And she wondered if he suspected there wasn't anything in the world she'd rather do.

Chapter Two

Saturday morning dawned bright and beautiful. Chilled-sauterne air, a sky as blue as Kerry Gundersen's eyes, vibrant colors greeted Jennifer through the hotel windows. This New England fall performance was the first she'd been fortunate enough to witness. Like all service families, the Smiths had traveled extensively during her father's career, but the closest he'd been stationed to New England was Fort Hamilton in Brooklyn, New York.

As she rode the elevator down, Jennifer firmly pushed aside her apprehensions about taking a job with Kerry Gundersen. Regardless of whether or not she made a bid to decorate his Watch Hill house, there was no reason not to enjoy today. The weather was perfect, and she was sallying forth to the shore with a singularly attractive man. Eligible bachelor that he was, he probably didn't want an involvement with a woman any more than she wanted one with a man.

"Gather your autumn leaves where you may," Jennifer quipped to herself as she stepped out into the hotel's black-marble lobby and looked around for Kerry.

He wasn't there.

Half an hour later he still hadn't arrived, and Jennifer, thoroughly annoyed, was on her way back to the elevator and her room—with intentions of getting the next train or bus to New York—when she heard her name called.

She turned to see Kerry hurrying toward her, crossing the lobby with long strides. He held up his hands in mock self-reproach when he saw her face. "Hey," he said, "please...hold the firing squad until you give me a chance to explain."

She made no comment, but she didn't pull away when he took her arm and propelled her toward the front doors.

"Textbook excuse," he pleaded en route. "I had a flat tire on the way over."

"A likely story," she scoffed, remembering that he'd had a dinner date last night. No doubt he'd extended it, spending the night somewhere with someone. She glanced up at him, searching for telltale signs of a sleepless night, but she'd never seen anyone look healthier or more rested.

Thursday's tautness had vanished from his face, and without that hint of tension he looked younger. He was wearing a heather-toned sport jacket and burgundy shirt, and the combination was outrageously becoming. No man had a right to be so...so devastating!

He led her to a beige Mercedes parked at the curb. "Let's beat a hasty retreat," he suggested, "or I'm apt to get a ticket. This space isn't exactly legal, and even though I tipped the doorman, his patience may wear thin."

So he sometimes greased palms to get his way, she mused. On the other hand, she also suspected that he got his way a good bit of the time without having to offer any incentives.

She wondered if he'd get his way with her—concerning the decorating of his Watch Hill house. It seemed logical to assume that he wouldn't be taking her to see the place if he wasn't seriously considering asking her to work for him.

They started off, and Kerry quickly turned onto the expressway that ran through the heart of the city. Traffic was heavy, so for a time he concentrated on driving. Then, when the pace eased somewhat, he glanced at Jennifer and asked, "Hungry?"

"Yes, I am. It must be this wonderful fresh air."

He smiled. "I thought we'd have lunch at a place just outside of Westerly. The food is very good, but it's the decor I think you'll find most interesting. The building dates back to the middle of the eighteenth century, and there's an enormous stone hearth that should be blazing brightly at this time of the year. There's also a fascinating beer stein collection—"

"Are you a collector, Mr. Gundersen?"

"I haven't started yet," he said seriously, "but I intend to." He flashed her an appealing grin. "I keep expecting you to call me Sergeant instead of Mr. Gundersen," he confessed, "and in exactly that peremptory manner you used ten years ago."

So, he remembered how long it had been since they'd first met. Jennifer digested that, then said, "I didn't think I was peremptory."

"Well, let's say that as a general's daughter you were accustomed to getting your way," he retorted lightly. "Anyway, I wish you'd call me neither—Sergeant *or* Mr. Gundersen, that is. Would it be too hard to say Kerry?"

"No."

"Do I need special dispensation to call you Jennifer? Or do you prefer Jenny?"

Had he also remembered that her father had called her Jenny? More stiffly than she'd intended, she said "I prefer Jennifer."

"Very well. Anyway, I brought along a camera. I thought you might like me to take a few shots of the house for you—both interior and exterior—so you'd have them for reference."

Jennifer tapped the briefcase in her lap. "I prefer to do my own sketches," she informed him.

"Well, whatever you wish. I only thought photos might help."

She unbent a little. "They wouldn't hurt," she informed him.

As she spoke, she was trying to fit together some of the puzzle pieces of this man—that statement he'd made yesterday, for one. The more she thought about it, the more she was sure she'd heard him correctly, sure that he'd muttered, "The home I never had." What did he mean by that?

Just now he'd said that he'd never collected anything but intended to begin. Somehow these revelations gave Jennifer the crazy impression that Kerry Gundersen—at the age of about thirty-five, she guessed—was just starting his life.

What *had* he been doing all these years? Certainly he was no amnesia victim. His memory of their first encounter proved that. But what of his life before the service, and in the years since, when he'd gained such renown as an architect?

She asked cautiously, "Where do you live now?"

"I have a condo not too far from the office," he answered readily enough. "Actually, it's a large studio apartment in an old building up by Brown University. I live alone, and I'm not there that much anyway, so it suffices."

"You seem to like older residences," she observed.

"I hadn't thought of it that way, but...I suppose maybe I do," he admitted.

"Why's that?" Jennifer persisted.

His brow furrowed. "I've never really analyzed it. Does there have to be a reason?"

"There usually is for most things," she answered carefully. "In your case, it strikes me as sort of an anachronism."

"I don't think I follow you."

"Your office is as contemporary as a spaceship—"

"And just as sterile?" he queried with a smile. "No, don't apologize. I can appreciate how my office must have appeared to you. Josh says you have a fantastic eye for color, and the headquarters of Gundersen and Sonntag could hardly be more colorless, right? But I explained my rationale for that to you."

"Yes, I know you did."

More slowly he said, "You made it clear the other day that you don't take on a client unless you mesh with him. Added to what Josh has told me about your work, and what you yourself said about how you approach each job, I gather that you probe rather deeply into a person's background. Is that right?"

"Yes, that's true, although I don't especially like the word *probe*. It implies prying, and I've never done that."

"I wasn't being critical, Jennifer," Kerry said quietly.

It was the first time he'd used her name conversationally, and she felt an odd little thrill, like a sixteen-year-old on her first date. Crossly, she told herself to grow up. To Kerry, she said, "I learned early on that the more I know about my clients, the better my chances of creating the right surroundings for them. Still, I avoid getting personal, if you know what I mean."

He smiled slightly. "Aren't you talking in riddles?"

"I don't think so," she shot back defensively. "Look, Kerry—" She stumbled over his name and came to a sudden halt.

Into the small silence that followed he said, "Perhaps I'm pressing the issue, because . . . I'm afraid I'm going to disappoint you."

"Oh? How so?"

"I have no background, Jennifer."

"Don't be silly," she reproved him. "Everyone has a background."

"I don't."

"What do you mean?"

"I hate this," he said by way of answer. "That's why I never talk about it to anyone. Josh has no idea, I might add. But then, your brother's not an inquisitive type." He took one hand off the steering wheel long enough to hold it up admonishingly. "Don't jump to conclusions," he instructed. "That doesn't mean I think you're overly inquisitive. I know what you're getting at. I know what you want. I can't give it to you, that's all."

He was staring straight ahead. They'd turned off the highway and were driving along a less traveled country road. Jennifer said unhappily, "I have the feeling we're getting into territory you'd rather avoid."

He slanted the briefest of glances at her. "You're so right," he said bitterly. "I suppose what I'd hoped was that you could . . . well, that you could simply create a background for me—through my house, that is. But I can see it doesn't work that way. Can't work that way. I've been in homes—since I've been successful—where the background's all there. Even the furniture and the silver have that special patina that spells heritage. Know what I mean?''

''Yes, I know what you mean.''

''The portraits on the wall depict real ancestors. They're not just faces acquired at an estate sale . . . as my portraits would have to be, if I owned any.'' He paused, then added ruefully, ''Oh, sure, like everyone else, I must have ancestors. The thing is, I don't know who they are.''

She stared at him, appalled. ''What are you saying?''

His mouth twisted into a pained smile. ''You've heard about babies being found on doorsteps?'' he asked rhetorically. ''Well, one day I was found in a field on a farm in western Connecticut, up toward the Berkshire Hills. That's right,'' he agreed, hearing her gasp, ''in a field. In fact, it was just about this time of year. The crops had been harvested, except for the pumpkins. And there I was, so I was told, among the pumpkins.''

''Kerry!''

''The main reason I don't tell this story is that I don't like bleeding-heart sagas,'' he said tersely. ''I've never felt sorry for myself, and I don't want anyone else feeling sorry for me. But that's the way it was. The name of the farmer was Gundersen. He didn't want to keep me, but he did let the authorities label me with his name. A sort of reference, you might say.''

''What about your first name?'' Jennifer managed.

''One of the cops Mr. Gundersen called was named Kerry. This was a small community, you understand. Everyone knew everyone else. The cop said why not give me Kerry for a name? So they did, sort of like you'd tag a suitcase.'' He chuckled dryly.

''You mean, this farmer simply called the police and gave you to them?''

"Exactly," Kerry stated. "Of course, the police couldn't keep me, either, so the welfare people were called in. I was placed in a home. Another word for orphanage. Naturally, they searched for my parents, or whoever it was who'd left me in the field. I was about six weeks old."

"Did you ever find out when you were born? I mean, there must be hospital records somewhere."

"There weren't," he said. "So... I've always considered Halloween my official birthday. Me and the pumpkins—get it?" He laughed again.

When she remained silent, he drew a long breath. "For someone who hates making sympathy bids, I guess I'm doing a pretty good job of it, huh?"

"I don't consider it a sympathy bid, Kerry," Jennifer said sincerely. "And I appreciate your being so honest with me."

"I don't really have a choice." That sad smile twisted his lips again. "Believe me, when you walked into my office the other day, I would have bet a million dollars I wouldn't be telling you this today. Not because it was *you*, you understand. Though that didn't help."

"Why do you say that?"

"When I saw you, I was jolted back ten years in time," he admitted. "And it *was* a jolt. I don't think I ever experienced class distinction more clearly than I did that day when your father loomed up as I was about to turn you over to the MPs. I asked around about you afterward. I found out that you'd just graduated from some posh girls' school in New York, that you were the general's only daughter, and that he—and that was pretty obvious—doted on you. I'd judged for myself that you were spoiled rotten and an unmitigated little snob."

"What miserable things to say!" Jennifer fumed.

Kerry actually laughed, incensing her further. The laughter still in his eyes, he observed, "Well, you said if we were going to work together, we needed to know each other. Scuttlebutt, at the time, revealed that your father had married into a very wealthy family. Your mother was a Rutherford of the New York Rutherfords, and, to put it succinctly, she was loaded. Your father came from a very good but not quite so rich Virginia family. Of course, until you walked into my office yesterday, I didn't know that General Smith's daughter had become interior decorator Jennifer Perreault. Once that registered, I knew I had the right person to do my house for me."

"Oh, really?"

"Let's just say I'm sure your family silver has the right patina, your Oriental rugs are hand-woven, and your ancestoral portraits are genuine." He noticed the fire in her eyes and added, "Hey, don't look at me like that. You're making me feel like a monster."

"Not a monster," Jennifer corrected. "Just extremely gauche."

To her surprise, he chuckled and said, "Well, what can you expect of a man who comes from nowhere?" When she didn't reply, he teased, "You haven't lost that temper, have you? That afternoon in Georgia, you looked as if you'd like to shoot me on the spot when I told you I was going to hand you over to the MPs."

"You," she said coldly, "were extremely high-handed!"

"And now I'm being extremely gauche. Well, excuse me, Jenny—Jennifer—but you wanted me to level with you, and I have."

That was true enough. She rolled down her window and took a deep breath of fresh October air. Then she asked, "Do you really have no idea who you are? No idea who left you in that field?"

"No idea whatsoever."

"Since you've had the money to do so, have you tried to find out?"

He shook his head. "Once I was out of the eternal red and into the black, financially, I gave it serious thought. And . . . I decided it was past the time to know. If whoever abandoned me had later wanted me, I would have been easy to find. The authorities left a path a mile wide for them to follow. Whereas my parents left no trail at all."

"I don't think I could stand not knowing," Jennifer said, her voice nearly failing her.

"When you don't have a choice—" Kerry began. He broke off, then continued, "Last year it got to me pretty badly. I even thought about hiring a private investigator and making a last-ditch attempt to find out *something*. It was my thirty-fifth 'official' birthday. And that sort of hit me. Thirty-five years being no one, with no family and no past."

"You've never married?"

"No. The few times I've even thought about becoming that involved with anyone, I've taken a good look in the mirror, and my intentions have changed dramatically. When you get married, there's always a chance of having children. When my kids started to grow up and get curious, what could I tell them? That their grandparents—at least one of them—abandoned me when I was a few weeks old? That would be a hell of an ancestry to offer a child, don't you think? Any kid of mine would have an awfully lopsided family tree. No branches at all on one side."

"Even so . . ."

"Then consider this," he said gravely. "I have no idea what might be in my genes. Insanity, perhaps? Or some disabling hereditary disease? Who knows? There's no absolute guarantee, even with the most sophisticated tests.

All in all, too many issues that can never be resolved. So I've sidestepped marriage and will probably continue to do so."

Jennifer felt like scolding him. There were many uncertainties in this world, and not taking chances was a weak excuse for not living life to the fullest. Still, he was entitled to his opinions, and she wasn't quite ready to dispute them.

"Anyway," he said, "to go back to last October. I almost hired a detective, but then I sat down and drank the better part of a bottle of Glen Morange. Maybe it was the Scotch, I don't know. In any event, I reached the conclusion that I should shut the door on the past, lock it, bolt it, then forget it. I was through torturing myself over something I could do nothing about. If they'd wanted me when I was young, they could have found me. If my parents hadn't wanted me all along, why would they want me now? Even if I could have found one parent or the other, the confrontation would have come as a terrible shock to both of us. So I decided it's better to go with visions."

"What visions?"

Kerry's expression turned nostalgic. "When I was a little kid," he said, "I used to have visions of a beautiful mother dressed in pink. She'd come and sit on the side of my bed at night and sing me to sleep. I could imagine her kissing me good-night, to the point where I could feel the warmth of her lips on my forehead and smell the scent of her perfume—"

He broke off and stared at Jennifer, clearly horrified. "Why in *hell* am I telling you all this?" he demanded.

It wasn't the first time someone had told her he'd revealed too much about himself. But nothing anyone had ever said to her before had had the impact on her that Kerry's story was having.

"Damn! Talk about being maudlin! It's not my usual style, Jennifer," he added hastily.

She smiled at that. "I believe you."

"I hope so. Believe me, I've never gone on like that to anyone."

"Then I'm flattered, Kerry," she said softly.

"After that sickening soliloquy?" he growled. "God, I won't blame you if you turn this job down flat." He glared out the windshield and waited for her to reply. When she didn't, he asked, his voice curiously vulnerable, "*Are* you going to turn down this job, Jennifer?"

"Let's wait till I see the house before we talk about that," she temporized.

"Fine," he agreed. "And over lunch we can talk about things like the weather and the World Series and the general state of the nation," he promised. "We'll be at the restaurant in another few minutes."

When they pulled up in front of the old tavern he'd selected, though, they found it closed. Kerry read the sign on the door in disgust. "Damn, I didn't realize they only opened for dinner."

"Well, maybe we can have dinner here," Jennifer found herself saying.

"Maybe," he agreed, brightening. "Meantime, there's a Chinese place down the road. It's not the greatest, but it'll keep us from starving."

Over a lunch of egg rolls, barbecued ribs and jasmine tea, Kerry determinedly kept their conversation on neutral ground. But as he spoke, Jennifer saw, to her distress, that those telltale lines of tension were once again etching his handsome face.

She could only dimly appreciate how difficult it must have been for him to come to terms with his past, as he insisted he'd done on his thirty-fifth birthday. She wondered how a person could cope with the idea of being rootless. Not to know who you were, who your parents were, must leave one feeling so hollow, so empty.

How unlike her own life, with her rock-solid ancestry. There were times when she'd even accused her mother of ancestor worship, because genealogical research was such a hobby of Caroline Smith's. She'd relished the times when her husband had been stationed in or around Washington and had spent hours using the genealogical facilities of the Library of Congress.

Even though Jennifer had never been ancestor happy like her mother, she felt her heart going out to Kerry. She quickly tugged it back, however. She could sympathize with him, but she could not afford to lend him her heart.

At the conclusion of their meal, a smiling waitress brought the check and two fortune cookies.

"Close your eyes and pick a cookie," Kerry instructed.

"What superstition!" she groaned. Nevertheless, she did as he asked. She reached for a crisp cookie, broke it open and laughed. "What a lot of nonsense!" she exclaimed.

"May I see it?"

"Of course."

He read aloud. "Romance moves you in a new direction." Grinning, he commented, "Any likely candidates in your life at the moment?"

She laughed. "I'm afraid not."

"Good."

"What about your fortune?" she countered, having noticed that he'd folded the slip of paper and put it into his coat pocket.

"Classified information," he told her.

"Come on," she chided. "Fair is fair."

"Later, perhaps," he informed her tantalizingly. "Not now." As they got into his car again, he said, "Watch Hill is only a few more miles. Funny, but now that we're almost there, I'm developing a case of stage fright over showing you the place."

"Why, for heaven's sake?"

"I suppose because I wish I could know in advance what your reaction will be," he admitted. "I want to warn you, Watch Hill, on the outside, at least, is a real summer resort. Most of the shops run along a waterfront street that winds up at the carousel. This time of the year, there are only one restaurant and a couple of shops open. The majority of the businesses have either closed for the season or are open on very sporadic schedules. So prepare yourself for a rather deserted village air."

She nodded. "All right, I will."

They came to a fork in the road, and a large sign pointed to Misquamicut Beach in one direction and to Watch Hill in the other. Kerry took the requisite right turn and concentrated on the curves in the road.

Suddenly he said, "You know, I've pulled out all the stops for you, but you've told me nothing about yourself. And Josh is one of the most closemouthed individuals in the entire world."

"You already know quite a bit," she said.

"About your family, not about you."

"There's not that much to tell about me," Jennifer hedged.

"Isn't there? I don't buy that. You've been *somewhere* for the past few years. In London, a part of the time, I seem to recall hearing. And since I last saw you, you changed your name." Kerry went on. "Which does bring us to the big question, doesn't it? Is there a Mr. Perreault, Jennifer?"

She told herself she should have known this was coming, and she reluctantly admitted, "Yes."

"Where is he?"

"In Paris." It was an automatic answer and not one to which Jennifer gave a second thought.

Chapter Three

Kerry grew silent. Jennifer sensed a decided shift in the mood between them, but before she had time to analyze it, she noticed they were entering an area of widely spaced, very attractive homes. Many of them were imposing enough to be classified as genuine mansions, she realized, her excitement mounting.

She had envisioned a community of old and probably somewhat dilapidated Victorian frame houses standing side by side along narrow streets. On the contrary, these homes occupied small estates and were set back from the winding road and separated from one another by spacious lawns and gardens in which the last chrysanthemums of the season, and even a few late roses, still bloomed brightly.

"Watch Hill," Kerry commented taciturnly.

"It really *is* a hill, isn't it?" Jennifer murmured.

"Yes, and quite steep in places. During the Revolutionary War it was a coastal lookout point for spotting British privateers. Hence, the name. That's Block Island Sound to our left, and the mouth of the Pawcatuck River to our right. Makes you feel as if you're surrounded by water, doesn't it?"

"Aren't we?"

Kerry smiled faintly. "I'll give you the short grand tour first," he said, "along the waterfront." At that, he took a right fork in the road, and they swooped downhill to the main street of the village.

"There's not too much to see at this time of year," he conceded. "Not many people around, even on a Saturday. Want to get out and stretch your legs?"

Jennifer did. She was still aware of the difference that had crept between them, and it was making her uncomfortable. Why had Kerry so suddenly shifted mood and tempo?

He pulled into a parking lot at the edge of the water and gestured toward a boxy shingled building with blue awnings that sat offshore on the end of a low wooden pier.

"The Watch Hill Yacht Club," he said. "Different, isn't it? The only access to the place is by that long dock or by boat."

"Where's the carousel?"

"Down to our left. It doesn't look like much with the horses gone, but I'll drive by it on our way back up the hill. I can't blame them for putting the horses in storage during the off-season," he added. "A winter storm could play havoc with them, even though the carousel is covered and fairly well protected, as you'll see. It's been around a long time, built in 1867."

Listening to Kerry, Jennifer was again aware of his fondness for the past. His attitude was almost reverent.

She wondered if this was because he felt so keenly that he had no past of his own.

There were still a few boats moored around the yacht club or tied up along the dock that connected it to land. Walking back to the car, they passed a small grassy park where Jennifer paused to examine the poignant statue of a small boy perched atop a fountain turned off for the winter. Nearby, a life-size cast-iron Indian crouched atop a boulder. He held a large fish in each hand and peered intently toward the west, keeping watch over the harbor.

"The little restaurant on the corner's still open, I see," Kerry observed. "Would you like a cup of coffee?"

"I wouldn't mind."

They crossed the street together...yet not together. Jennifer's perplexity about this atmosphere change was reaching the peak of her tolerance point as they were seated across from each other at a tiny table in the restaurant. She waited for Kerry to order their coffees, declined a piece of homemade pie, and listened to him choose apple pie with ice cream for himself. Then she sat back and eyed him levelly.

"What's bothering you all of a sudden?" she queried.

He'd been staring out the window abstractedly. Now his blue eyes swerved to focus upon her face. "What do you mean?"

"Please, Kerry, maybe I don't know you very well, but I know you well enough to realize that something made you change all of a sudden. Was it anything I said?"

He shook his head ruefully. "I didn't realize I was so obvious," he admitted. "No, it wasn't anything you said. It's merely that I can't help but wonder how your husband lets you traipse around as you do in the course of your work, from London to New York and I don't know where else. I don't think I could possibly be so... liberal, were I in his shoes."

"My husband?" Jennifer echoed, honestly baffled.

"Yes, your husband," he said, the tightening of his mouth giving a clue to his irritation.

"But I don't have a husband."

"What about Mr. Perreault?"

"Andre? Andre and I have been divorced for nearly six years."

"But you said..."

"You asked me if there was a Mr. Perreault, and I said yes. Then you asked me where he was, and I told you."

"It was a very present-tense statement you made, Jennifer," Kerry informed her.

"I certainly didn't mean it that way. Andre hasn't been present in my life for a long, long time."

"And?"

"And even if he were..."

Kerry grinned. "Let's just say I'm glad he isn't," he said. "Maybe it's old-fashioned of me, but I'd be uncomfortable at the thought of... well, of keeping a man's wife away from him."

"That's absolutely ridiculous!" Jennifer sputtered. "Women's careers often take them away from their homes and husbands these days. And modern men cope."

His grin deepened. "Would you like a soapbox?"

"What?"

"Sidewalk orators used to stand on old wooden soap crates." He laughed at her expression. "Look," he said, "I'm not a male chauvinist, if that's what you're inferring. I respect the right of women to have careers or anything else they want in their lives. Also, I know it's absolutely none of my business whether you're married or not. If Mr. Perreault was a part of your present, rather than your past, whether you stayed in Paris or not would be his problem, not mine. Nevertheless," he finished, "I'm glad you're free."

Kerry Gundersen had not purchased a mere summer home, Victorian or otherwise. He had acquired an eye-boggling mansion. His magnificent home stood atop a hill with a commanding view of the water. The ground sloped away on all sides, leading to a bluff on the east from which a steep flight of steps descended to a narrow beach.

The main part of the house was built of fieldstone, while the wings and ells were covered with shingles that, caressed by the salt air over the years, had turned soft gray. There was a porte cochere on the left. And the dark brown roof, highlighted by numerous gables and a prominent round turret, was set off beautifully by barn-red wood that trimmed the windows and eaves.

Tucked beneath the highest gable was a window with a character all its own. Fashioned of stained-glass medallions, it looked as if it belonged in a cathedral. Far below, on the right side of the house, an archway framed in stone led underneath a wide porch to the back lawn, overlooking the water.

Kerry drove up the winding driveway and parked under the porte cochere. But before taking Jennifer inside, he led her around the front of the house and through the arched passageway. The view that greeted her was dazzling—the sea sweeping past the horizon to eternity. The intense color of the water instantly reminded her of Kerry Gundersen's eyes.

He was standing so close beside her that she could almost feel his warmth. She wondered if she was imagining the current that vibrated between them or if he felt it, too. The thought made her shiver.

"Is it too breezy for you out here?" he asked quickly.

"No, no," she said, shaking her head. "It's wonderful," she added honestly. As it was. Not only the view or the possible challenge of decorating the imposing mansion behind her or the stimulating tonic of this perfect October day... but being with him.

Expressing that, even to herself, was a revelation powerful enough to make Jennifer shake. She couldn't remember when she'd last felt so vibrantly alive. The fact that this unusually fascinating man at her side was making her feel that way was very dangerous. She, who had thought herself immune to men, suddenly knew how entirely vulnerable she really was.

Kerry glanced toward the beach below them and at the steep flight of steps that led to it. Gazing pointedly at her feet, he said, "We won't attempt to navigate those steps today. Maybe another time you could wear a different pair of shoes."

Another time.

Would there be another time? Jennifer wondered. There was always the chance that, by the end of today, they'd come to the decision that she wasn't the person for the job he had in mind.

"Jennifer?" Kerry prompted.

She looked down at her feet, having forgotten about her high-heeled sandals in her mental absorption. Smiling sheepishly, she managed, "They're not very practical, are they?"

"No," Kerry agreed rather huskily. His eyes lingered on her slender feet, then slowly traveled up her slim legs. "No, but they go perfectly with that outfit you're wearing. Josh was right when he said you have a great eye for color."

She'd combined camel and gray in her plaid skirt and jacket and blouse. Worn with chunky gold and silver jewelry, a vivid yellow handkerchief that peeked from her jacket pocket, and a matching leather band on her wrist-watch, the effect was attractive and fun. To complement the style, she'd worked a strand of yellow yarn through her chignon. Josh was right. Color coordination and a novel way of blending colors effectively came naturally to her.

At her side, Kerry, that husky note still in his voice, observed, "In the sunlight, your hair looks as if it's on fire. Funny, in the shadows it's quite dark. But I saw you first in the sunlight, and I still remember your hair—maybe because it matched your temper," he teased.

Jennifer was about to retort when she looked up at him. Despite his raillery, he was gazing down at her very seriously, a baffled expression clouding his eyes. She recognized the expression and knew that he, too, felt the current flowing between them—and was as dumbfounded by it as she was.

Sadly, she also knew that if she had any sense at all, she would refuse the job of decorating his house if he made her a firm offer. He'd made his views about commitment to a woman very plain. She'd formed her own conclusions years ago about ever again making a commitment to a man.

It would be one thing if the two of them could have a casual affair in the course of her decorating his house. But Jennifer knew, deep inside, that it would be impossible for her to remain casual with this man. An involvement, she decided, could bring nothing but hurt in the long run. And they'd both had enough of that.

As Kerry led her inside his imposing house, her mind was made up. She'd go back to New York tomorrow, explain to Josh that handling Victorian mansions just wasn't her style, and that would be that. What she failed to anticipate was the overwhelming love she felt for Kerry Gundersen's home the moment she crossed the threshold.

The mansion had been built in an era when building costs were a relatively minor concern. Obviously, no expense had been spared in its construction. If the exterior hadn't clued her to that fact, one glance at the interior did. The spacious, high-ceilinged rooms were, for the most part, empty. But Jennifer's imagination immediately began to run riot, and visions of these rooms restored to their original elegance and beautifully furnished to the last detail raced through her head.

Josh had said that if she "did" Kerry Gundersen's place, her reputation as a designer would be assured, and he'd come to that conclusion solely because of Kerry's reputation, not because of the house he'd bought. Had Josh known very much about the house itself, he would have forewarned her that this would be no ordinary task.

For the next two hours Jennifer wandered from room to room like a child in an enchanted toyland. Her sketchbook emerged from her briefcase, and with it one of the fine-pointed black pens she used for sketching. Kerry withdrew discreetly to let her roam, sketch and indulge in her personal and professional daydreams.

Finally, when she'd gone through each of the many rooms on the house's several different levels, she shook herself out of her absorption enough to realize that it was quite a while since she'd seen Kerry.

A curving stairway descended into a spacious foyer graced by an enormous stone fireplace. Jennifer couldn't help but imagine a fire blazing on the hearth and a towering Christmas tree glittering in one corner. Then she remembered that this mansion had been used primarily as a summer home, and she envisioned guests being greeted at the door while the strains of cheerful music emanated from the huge drawing room, the home's focal point.

An odd lump filled her throat. Then she saw Kerry.

He was standing in the center of the foyer, gazing up at her, and she had never seen a more wistful expression on a man's face. He came toward her slowly, reaching the stairs as she reached the last tread. It seemed natural and inevitable to step right into his arms. It was like living out a dream that had been planted in her subconscious and was now being transformed into reality.

He bent his silver-blond head to her face, and she willingly drowned in his eyes. Then his mouth descended to touch her lips gently. A feather kiss. It was she who wordlessly pleaded for more, kissed him back, the kiss deepening as their lips parted, their tongues explored.

Finally, the need to breath set them ever so slightly apart. But even then they clung to each other, and tender seconds passed before Kerry gently released her.

His voice shaking, he said, "While you were looking around I drove up the road till I found a place that sells coffee. I seem to have a thing for coffee today. Anyway, there are two cups in the kitchen."

Clearly, he was trying very hard to get back to normal. So was she. But as Jennifer walked with him toward the kitchen, she knew that it was going to take more than a cup of coffee to restore her equilibrium.

As they drove back toward Providence, there was an uneasy silence between them. Finally, sounding as if he were wrestling with himself, Kerry said, "I didn't intend for that to happen."

"I know," Jennifer told him, her voice almost a whisper. "I didn't intend for it to happen, either."

"So what do we do about it?" he demanded, as if they had a business question under discussion that had to be settled.

"I don't know," she admitted.

They lapsed into silence again and, by mutual consent, decided not to stop in Westerly for dinner. Though the dinner hour was at hand, neither of them was hungry.

It was pitch dark outside when Kerry suddenly said, "I want you to do my house for me, Jennifer. I can't imagine entrusting the job to anyone else, nor do I have the time or talent to do it myself."

"I dispute that," she countered, glad the silence was broken. "You may not have the time, but surely you have the talent. Josh raves about your work."

"Architecture and interior decorating are only tangentially related," Kerry said frankly. "You said my office is as contemporary and sterile as a spaceship. Well, in a way, so are the buildings I design. Of course, I try to make them truly beautiful. And my partner, George Sonntag, is quite a genius. He's the one who goes off on the flights of fancy, while I tend to pull him back to earth, toward the more plausible and practical."

"Don't you ever go off on flights of fancy of your own, Kerry?"

"In architecture, or in life?" he asked.

"Both, I guess."

He thought for a moment. "In architecture, yes. I get caught up in some pretty esoteric concepts, I admit. But the bottom line is doing something not only innovative and ahead of its time, but something that's also possible. Do you follow me?"

"I think so, yes."

"In life . . . my life," he continued more cautiously, "I gave up the flights of fancy way back. I think my last were . . . the boyhood visions I told you about. To tell you the truth, my work occupies so much of my time and energy that there's not much room for daydreaming. Today was the first time I . . . I've indulged myself in that direction."

Was he trying to pass off their embrace as an ephemeral will-o'-the-wisp that would float away as quickly as it had appeared? Would that it could be so easy!

"Look," he said after a moment, "you've only known me for a few days out of both our lives, yet I've told you more about myself than I've ever told anyone else. Did anyone ever mention that you'd make a great shrink? I suspect you always have that way of drawing people out without their being aware of it. No, you don't have to answer that," he added quickly. "I'm not asking you to give away any trade secrets."

"I won't," Jennifer assured him.

"I do, however, think it's important that you and I make a pact."

"What kind of pact?" she asked edgily.

"Maybe we should only permit kissing on Saturdays and Sundays," he said, trying for a quip and grimacing at his failure. "Oh, hell, Jenny—I mean, Jennifer. We *are* both adults, you know. Don't you think we should be able to handle this?"

"Put that way," she said slowly, "I suppose the answer is yes. My question is, *will* we be able to?" She shook her head. "I really don't know, Kerry. Something's . . . happened."

"Tell me about it." He nodded. "The cliché for it would be 'chemistry' or something akin to that. What it comes down to, though, is that I should have kept my hands in my pockets."

"Maybe."

"Only maybe?" He arched an eyebrow. "That, Mrs. Perreault, could be considered encouraging. Except," he added seriously, "I don't want to be encouraged by you."

That stung. Jennifer said stiffly, "Believe me, I am not about to get out my seven-league boots and chase you."

He chuckled softly, "Temper, temper," he warned. "I admit my word choice is lousy sometimes. *Want* isn't right. I'd love to be encouraged by you, but I think we both know it would be...crazy. I get the impression you've made a life for yourself since your divorce. You seem to be doing what you want to do. Once you're better known in your field, you'll be going exactly where you want to go."

"What about you?" Jennifer asked.

"I've also made a life for myself, and it's a very good one," Kerry allowed. "Professionally, socially...I have no real gripes. I've come a long way from the pumpkin patch," he added with that slight, sad smile that tended to turn Jennifer inside out. "All I need, at this point, is a home. I need to put down roots. In order to do that, I need someone to create a background for me that I can believe in."

"That's a strange way of putting it."

"I can't think of a better way. I want to be surrounded in that magnificent house by the kind of beautiful things that should be there. I want an atmosphere that gives me a sense of completion. No ordinary decorator could possibly do that for me. I think you can."

"I'm not so sure—"

"Think of it as a challenge," he cut in encouragingly. "The type of challenge you might never face again. If you succeed, I'm willing to let the house be photographed and publicized from top to bottom. You'll be so busy that you'll be turning down lucrative commissions all over the place." He paused, then added modestly, "I've reached that career point, and, believe me, it's a great feeling."

"I can imagine."

"Meantime," he said, "I swear I'll give you free rein, Jennifer. You can work things out however you want, and name your price. I won't bother you."

Why should that promise give her such a sinking feeling? Jennifer asked herself ruefully, knowing he'd considered all the angles she'd been worrying about. Briefly, she wished he weren't quite so efficient.

"We're well into fall," she temporized. "And winter, of course, isn't the best of times for construction work in New England. Still, there isn't very much work needed on the exterior, is there?"

"A few things here and there," he diagnosed judiciously. "They fall more within my province, so I'll take care of them. But I see no reason why the interior work shouldn't start as soon as possible and progress right through the winter. What do you say?"

"Well, I..."

"Please, Jenny," he said, this time not correcting himself in his use of the diminutive. "Don't make a barricade out of a lot of buts. I won't be a problem to you, I promise."

A strong emotional tug told Jennifer that she didn't *want* him to keep his promise, but she had the discipline to remain silent. After a moment she said, "This desire of yours for roots is puzzling to me, Kerry."

"That's because you've never been rootless."

"Maybe, but...do you intend to have children?"

He sat bolt upright. "Children?" he blurted. "My God, no. I thought we talked about that."

"You talked about possible hereditary problems because you know nothing of your family history. I personally think that's borrowing trouble. None of us can guarantee that our children are going to be perfect; I think you'd have as much chance in that as anyone.''

"It's not a chance I'd care to take," he said tightly.

"So you've said. Which brings me back to my question. If you don't intend to have any descendants, why the preoccupation with roots?''

He frowned. "I suppose it's purely a personal thing with me. A very real need, or I wouldn't be so intense about it. I want to put down roots more than I can possibly explain to you. I want a home of my own that's all a home should be.''

"What, eventually, are you going to do with this home, if there's no one to pass it along to?'' Jennifer queried.

"I've already planned that," he assured her. "I've left provisions in my will for the foundation of an organization that will provide what might loosely be called halfway houses for kids, like me, who were brought up in orphanages or foster homes and then turned out into the world with no real sense of direction, no real place to go.

"The military was the answer for me," he went on. "You can acquire an excellent education free of charge in the service, which is what I did. After I was discharged, I went straight to graduate school, ready to complete my architectural studies. But that was me. It's not the answer for everyone. I'd say a lot of kids—maybe most kids— need something and someone to turn to. Thus, my foundation. And in case you haven't already guessed, the Watch Hill house will be its headquarters.''

She looked at him curiously. "Do you always work out all the details in your life so completely?'' she asked.

"I try to," he said simply. But there was an odd expression on his face, noticeable even in the car's subdued light, that made Jennifer wonder how sure of himself Kerry really was.

The same thought plagued Kerry Gundersen as they drove through the outskirts of Providence. Usually he was totally in control. Today, he'd lost control completely when he saw Jennifer walking down the stairs in *his* house. He'd had the sudden vision of her coming down that stairway in a gorgeous satin evening gown, ready to stand with him in front of the fireplace and greet their guests. It was a vision far more real than any of his childhood visions of an ephemeral mother or a house by the sea.

There was nothing ephemeral about the way Jennifer had approached him. She was warm and alive and wonderful—and certainly not a figment of his imagination.

Suddenly he'd wanted her with an intensity that clutched at him like physical pain. He'd been a man in a trance as he'd taken her into his arms and stared down into her lovely face with its gentle, cameolike features. Their mouths had meshed so naturally, and when she'd deepened the kiss he'd been thankful there were no beds in the house. Had there been, he knew he would have swept her back up those stairs and into a chamber where he could make ardent love to her as daylight faded to dusk and dusk to darkness.

Fortunately, he'd brought himself back to reality, and Jennifer along with him. Because this burgeoning attraction between them seemed entirely mutual.

She, Jennifer Smith Perreault, was the last person in the world to whom he could offer a permanent place in his life. And the thought of offering her anything less than something permanent was unthinkable.

Maybe he was crazy to still remember so acutely the class distinctions that had been so evident ten years ago be-

tween Jennifer Smith, privileged resident at Fort Mc-
Kettrick, and Sergeant Kerry Gundersen, soldier. Lots of
the old demarcation lines had faded or disappeared, he
knew, and yet . . .

These days he moved in the top echelon of society. But
at heart he was still the boy who'd been found in a field.
As such, he had no place in the social stratosphere of a
general's daughter.

Nonetheless, two blocks from the Biltmore Plaza, he
almost suggested they have dinner together. He was
tempted to invite Jennifer to his apartment, where he could
fix her one of his innovative omelets. Casual cooking was
a hobby he excelled at, and he rarely had the chance to
show it off.

But a candlelight supper for two in the close quarters of
his studio would offer far too much proximity, he realized. Maybe Jennifer would be able to handle it. It was
himself he couldn't count on.

As he pulled up to the curb in front of the hotel, he
wondered what his next move should be. He wanted Jennifer to decorate his home. And he suddenly realized that
if that happened, he'd always have something of Jennifer
herself to keep with him.

Chapter Four

That night Jennifer dreamed she was wandering through a field of daisies. It was a cloudy day, about to rain, and she was frantically picking the flowers and plucking their white petals. As she discarded each petal, instead of chanting, "He loves me, he loves me not," she was moaning, "Yes...no...yes...no."

Suddenly a strong wind arose, swept across the field and blew the flowers away. Jennifer was left staring at acres of endless green, no answer having been given to her question, which echoed in her mind as she sleepily opened her eyes and blinked.

Should she, or should she not, accept Kerry Gundersen's commission? Yes...or no? This question, the question about which she had dreamed, kept repeating itself as she dressed. Yes...or no?

She had agreed to meet Kerry for brunch at L'Apogee, the popular rooftop restaurant in her hotel. This time he was ahead of her. He was sitting at a window that offered an eagle-eye view of the city, dressed conservatively in a gray plaid jacket, gray slacks, a white shirt and dark tie— a combination that might have appeared staid on someone else, yet looked terrific on him.

He was as handsome and unruffled looking as ever from a distance, Jennifer saw, but up close she could tell that he hadn't slept any better than she had. Shadows of fatigue smudged those intensely blue eyes, and there were grooves around his mouth that she didn't remember seeing yesterday.

"Is something wrong?" she demanded, honestly concerned by his appearance.

"Why do you ask?"

"Well..."

He grinned. "I think any astute observer would conclude that we're both a little the worse for wear after yesterday. After last night, maybe I should say. Even counting sheep didn't help. What about you?"

"I was picking daisies in a field, and a terrible wind came up and blew them all away," Jennifer confessed.

A waiter appeared to take their order, preventing Kerry from questioning that remark. After the waiter left, he leaned back and surveyed her. A few long seconds passed before he asked, "Does the prospect of doing my house really upset you so much?"

"On the contrary, the idea of decorating your house intrigues me. It isn't the house, Kerry...." Flustered, she stopped.

"I upset you, is that it?"

"Well," she said, beginning again and proceeding more cautiously, "I'd say that we upset each other. Yesterday, I think it was partly the mood of the house."

A smile curved his lips. "Do you really?" he teased. "I think I was more honest in my on-the-spot definition: chemistry. That's precisely what it is, wouldn't you say? When I looked up just a few minutes ago and saw you walking toward me, my pulse didn't exactly lie still."

Jennifer shook her head reprovingly. "I thought we made a pact."

"We never got down to details," he countered. "In fact, the purpose of our meeting this morning—one of the purposes—should be to draw up guidelines. Unless you've already made a decision against getting involved."

Involved? What exactly, Jennifer wondered, did that mean to him? As for a decision . . .

She remembered the quandary she'd experienced in her dream. Yes . . . or no?

"Jennifer," Kerry said gently, "don't struggle so. It *is* your decision, you know. No one's going to force you to go one way or the other, least of all me. If you enter this challenge unwillingly, it will only compromise the job—for both of us. Believe me, that's the way I am myself when it comes to accepting an architectural commission. Unless I'm one-hundred percent in my enthusiasm for a prospective job, I can't give a top performance. I feel sure the same thing applies to you."

"Yes, it does."

He expelled a deep breath. "Look, I'll admit I'd hoped you'd give me an affirmative answer this morning, but I can see that's too much to expect." He shook his head in self-reproof and added, "I could kick myself."

Jennifer had been staring at the tablecloth, but she looked up at that. "Why?" she asked curiously.

"Because I should have clenched my fists yesterday and kept my distance," he stated grimly.

Jennifer remembered that moment when he'd claimed her lips with his. In all honesty, she couldn't say she wished it had never happened. She had wanted his touch, his kiss. Worse, she wanted more than just a fleeting kiss from this man.

The realization swept over her like the strong wind in the field of her dreams, and she quickly averted her eyes to keep from staring at the mouth that had aroused such a surge of feeling in her the day before.

She was not a child, she reminded herself tersely. Suppose she and Kerry Gundersen decided to embark on an affair? Suppose they decided they didn't want to resist each other, despite all these initial protests? Maybe there *was* no valid reason to resist each other. They were both adults. Neither of them had someone else in the wings who would be hurt by their actions. So... what would be so terrible about giving in to honest desire?

Terrible? Having an affair with Kerry would be wonderful, Jennifer admitted frankly, wringing her napkin with agitated fingers as she gave free rein to her thoughts. Being with Kerry, being close to him in that way, would be unforgettable, she knew. That was the problem. She felt clear to her bones that if she let herself go with Kerry, the result would be something she'd never be able to get over. Should she indulge in a relationship, its ending would leave deep wounds to deal with.

Kerry had been open about not wanting a permanent relationship. He simply wanted a home that could provide the surrogate roots he felt he needed. He didn't want anyone to share that home with him—not on a permanent basis, anyway—and he certainly didn't want any children. Jennifer, on the other hand, liked to think that sometime in her future she might have children....

She drew in invisible reins, pulling her thoughts to a halt. She was jumping her fences much too fast. Still, the image had been engraved in her mind, and it was difficult to erase—a little boy who would be a replica of Kerry, with silvery blond hair and those astonishingly blue eyes. And maybe a little girl who would look something like her. . . .

Whoa! She nearly said the word aloud. Then she swallowed hard.

The waiter brought the delicious breakfast Kerry had ordered, but Jennifer could only toy with her food. Quite suddenly she had absolutely no appetite.

"Jennifer?" Kerry said gently.

Reluctantly, she looked up from her plate. "Yes?"

"I have the impression you've been going around in mental circles," he told her. Forcing a smile, he commented, "So both of us lost a little sleep last night being foolish about each other."

Foolish? Was that what he called it?

"I yielded to a very natural impulse," he continued, "and you responded. But I assure you I'll give you no cause for worry if you accept my commission. I'll keep my hands off the job except for whatever consultations you might want to have with me. And...I'll keep my hands off you."

The tone of his voice changed radically on those last words, and Jennifer had the satisfaction of knowing that they hadn't come easily to him. But she also knew, deep down inside, they weren't the words she wanted to hear.

She sighed as Kerry added, "You can believe that."

She was sure she could. He wasn't the type to give his word, then retract it; she felt certain about that.

Jennifer reflected briefly on the old saw about getting hooked on the horns of a dilemma, and, frustrated, she bit her lip. She was dismayed at herself, painfully aware that she was handling this situation very badly. It was ridiculous for a woman her age, a woman approaching thirty, who'd been married, divorced and had come to terms with a lot of things in her life, to be thrown off base so completely by any man.

She wished she had Josh to talk to. Her brother had always been such a helpful confidant, especially since the accident that had taught him the meaning of patience and how to deal with incredible frustration. He'd done very well, except for a single hang-up.

Thinking about Josh's emotional problem, Jennifer realized that Kerry shared it. Both men had vowed never to allow a woman into their lives on a permanent and total basis. Kerry's rationale was his lack of knowledge about his origins. It seemed incredible to think that this handsome, successful, charismatic man had an inferiority complex, but obviously he did.

Josh's problem stemmed from a physical handicap, though Jennifer had long ago decided his leg hampered him far more psychologically than it did physically. Josh, like Kerry, was an extremely attractive man, with so much to give. He even knew Kerry....

Suddenly the need to see her brother, the need to talk with him about Kerry Gundersen, was nearly overpowering.

"Jennifer?" he asked softly.

She looked up, drawn into his sea-blue gaze. "I'm sorry," she told him. "I've been woolgathering."

"So I've noticed."

She tried to sound calm. "Kerry...when do you need an answer from me?"

He drew back slightly, his expression taut. But, matching her calm, he said, "There is no deadline, per se, Jennifer. I *would* like to get any exterior work on the house started as soon as possible, simply because of the weather factor. The weather should be okay for the next few weeks, but then it gets pretty cold, not to mention the likelihood of winter storms. As for the interior, I would think that work could continue straight along, unless we run into a real blizzard or something that causes power outages or keeps the workers from getting to the site."

He drew a breath, then added carefully, "So, while there's no actual deadline, I think you can understand that I don't want to let things hang fire indefinitely."

"Of course not," she agreed quickly.

Kerry stared over Jennifer's head, thinking. Then he looked directly into her eyes. "I must tell you, Jennifer, I'll really be disappointed if you turn me down. I saw your reaction to my house. Even if Josh hadn't spoken to me about your work, my feeling would be—my feeling is— that you're the right decorator for the job. Of course, the decision is yours. If you've already made it, I'd rather you didn't spare me. I'd rather you come out and tell me."

Kerry looked away. Jennifer's lovely topaz eyes were clouded by confusion, and that was the last thing he wanted to see. Not knowing what would happen was tormenting him. Though he'd let her know her decision meant a lot to him—he'd been quite frank about his faith in her ability—she had no idea how *much* it meant to him. Nor did he want her to know. This entire situation was making him feel more and more foolish by the minute.

Jennifer Smith Perreault wasn't the only competent interior designer in the world. He realized that. There were many others—many with more experience, in fact—who would assess the potential of the Watch Hill mansion as quickly as she had, come to similar conclusions, even fall in love with the place, and do a very good job for him.

Yet he wanted Jennifer to bring his house to life. Even though he'd known her only a few days, he was certain she would bring a special caring to her work. He liked to think that she'd care because the house was his, even though common sense told him that she'd do superb work on any job she undertook. She struck him as that kind of person—a deeply involved professional dedicated to excellence. Her performance would have nothing to do with the sensual vibes that had rocked them yesterday.

Actually, Kerry recalled, their sensuous dance had started ten years ago, back on a hot dusty road in Georgia.

He rarely indulged in the thought, but General Smith's daughter had made one hell of an impact on him that broiling afternoon on the artillery range. She'd nearly talked him out of taking her to post headquarters! He'd been mesmerized by her topaz eyes, her assured attitude.

Jenny Smith—Jennifer Perreault, Kerry corrected himself—was naturally self-assured because she knew exactly who she was, where she'd come from, where she stood. In short, she knew things he could never know. He'd had to build a tower of self-esteem and confidence for himself, brick by brick. Until now, he'd had no idea how flimsy a structure it was, or that the bricks might suddenly collapse under their own weight. If that happened, the gains of all those years—the struggle to achieve success, to be someone—would symbolically vanish in a cloud of dust as red as the dust in Georgia.

He dared to look at Jennifer again and saw that her lovely face mirrored unhappiness. He hated to hold himself responsible for that mood, yet he knew he was. Again he felt like kicking himself. Over the years he'd learned how to rationalize his discontent, how to accept himself. But meeting Jennifer after all these years had somehow put him right back in that desolate field that had marked his beginning.

A tumult of mixed feelings swirled around inside him, making him feel very much as he had that day when he'd taken Jennifer to post headquarters, only to discover that she was General Ashley Sanderson Smith's daughter. It was as if she'd suddenly been framed with blinking lights that spelled *OFF LIMITS. UNOBTAINABLE.*

Jennifer hadn't said a word, he suddenly realized. Did that mean she'd already made a negative decision?

"Jennifer?" he prompted, drawing her intense topaz gaze. The impact was shattering. He saw her draw in her breath sharply, and his mouth twisted in a wry smile.

His voice very low, he said, "I do need to know... if you've made up your mind, that is."

"I haven't," she told him honestly. "I... well, after I moved from London and got settled in, I put a few irons in the fire, in New York," she explained.

"And?"

"And at the time I met with the various people about their decorating projects, I had no idea about your place."

"Have you made any firm commitments to anyone?"

"No, but..."

"You don't need to look for an out, Jennifer," he stated curtly.

"I'm not looking for an out. I honestly did talk to some people."

"So you feel you have obligations."

"Not obligations, no," she hedged. "But I do think I should touch base. That's only right."

"And if something has jelled since you've been up here, you may decide that's what you want to do, rather than tackle the house in Watch Hill?"

Jennifer felt her nerves beginning to fray. "I don't know what I'll decide," she admitted.

Silence stretched between them before Kerry said, "All right, then. As I've already indicated, I don't want to pressure you. On the other hand, I'll need your decision within a reasonable time. Shall we say two weeks?"

Jennifer was contemplating her fingernails as if she'd never seen them before. Now she looked up quickly and had the weird impression that she was suddenly seeing a total stranger. This was Kerry Gundersen, the highly successful, sought after architect she was sitting across from, not the man who had held her in his arms only yesterday, evoking unprecedented explosions within her as they kissed.

This man was all business. And he retained that business facade as he paid their check, rode the elevator down to the lobby with her, and then bade her goodbye.

"I take it you'll be going back to New York today?" he quizzed.

"Yes," she answered unhappily.

"Say hello to Josh for me."

"I will."

Very briefly, Kerry's features softened. "Take care, Jennifer," he said, looking down at her with those dazzling blue eyes. "I'll expect to hear from you within two weeks, okay?"

"Okay." She nodded. Then, her heart sinking, she watched him walk out of the hotel and, very possibly, out of her life.

Josh had a large, comfortable apartment in an older building on Riverside Drive. The view of the Hudson River was magnificent, the sunsets spectacular. But Jennifer had little more than a vague appreciation for nature's beautiful spectacle as she turned away from the window late that Sunday afternoon and faced her brother.

"I'm ambiguous about taking the commission," she reported carefully, answering Josh's question about Kerry's proposal.

"Why, for heaven's sake?" he demanded.

Josh was seated in his favorite easy chair, his bad leg propped on a hassock, the single crutch he needed tossed on the floor by the side of the chair. He looked tired, and Jennifer wondered if his leg had been bothering him more than usual. At times he had bouts of severe pain. Once, such a bout had necessitated further surgery. Jennifer prayed that wasn't going to happen again. Josh had spent more than his share of time in hospitals.

She surveyed him with affectionate eyes. Though not as tall as Kerry, he was still above average height. Like Kerry, he was lean, well proportioned. He kept himself fit by swimming regularly and following a regimented program of isometric exercises.

Often, Jennifer thought, Josh looked younger than his thirty-four years. Almost boyish, in fact. But at other times, like now, fatigue and pain etched lines on his face that made him look older. His eyes were gray, and his hair was considerably darker than hers, but she liked to think their features would clue people to the fact that they were closely related.

He said now, rather irritably, "Stop looking at me like that, will you?"

"Like what?" Jennifer asked innocently.

"Like an anxious nursemaid! And kindly answer my question."

"What question?"

"Why you'd even think about refusing Kerry's commission," Josh growled.

"I'm not sure it's the right thing for me," she evaded.

"That," Josh informed her, "is the most ridiculous statement you've ever made. Don't you realize who Kerry Gundersen is, Jenny?"

"Of course I do," she stated. She had a sudden vision of silvery hair, deep blue eyes and a handsome, rugged face that was also strangely vulnerable. "Oh, yes. I realize who he is, all right."

Josh frowned. "Do I get the feeling that somehow Kerry turned you off? That's not the way he impresses most women."

She gritted her teeth. "No," she managed, "I'm sure it's not the way he impresses most women. And he didn't turn me off. On the contrary, he was very charming."

"Didn't he offer you the job?"

"Yes, Josh, he offered me the job."

"Then why—"

"There's more to it than that," Jennifer cut in, feeling color rise to her cheeks. Silently, she counted to three. Then she asked, "Would you care for a drink? I'm going to have a glass of wine."

"Scotch and soda," he answered brusquely, wincing as he shifted position.

Jennifer nearly came out and asked him about his leg, but she knew only too well that Josh hated any talk of his handicap. She busied herself at the small bar in a corner of the living room, fixing Josh's Scotch and pouring a glass of blush zinfandel for herself. After handing him his drink, she settled on the couch across from him.

After a moment he said, "Before you make any negative decisions about the Gundersen job, Jenny, you should really think it through. You should realize that doing work for Kerry will open up all kinds of doors for you."

"I'm sure that's true," she agreed. "We didn't discuss money, but I'm sure he's well prepared to pay the tariff for what he wants."

"I wasn't talking about money," Josh rebuked. "I meant professionally. Professionally, you shouldn't let this opportunity get away. And before I say any more about that, I should tell you that two of the people you met with before you went to Providence called. The job decorating that Beekman Place penthouse is yours if you want it. So is redoing the Park Avenue duplex."

"Great," she responded. "When it rains, it pours."

"Maybe so. But you'd be an idiot to turn down Kerry to accept either one of them."

The two commissions he'd mentioned were very good jobs. If either had been firmly offered to her a week ago, Jennifer would have jumped at the chance. Reflecting on this, she fleetingly wondered if either job might actually be as useful to her in augmenting her portfolio as doing Kerry Gundersen's Watch Hill mansion.

"You're aware, I know, that my company publishes *Living, American Style* as well as *Architecture, American Style*," Josh said suddenly.

"Yes."

"*Living*'s the bigger of the two, obviously. And…well, I've been asked to combine an editorial post there with my job on *Architecture*."

Happiness for him made Jennifer forget, for the moment, her problem concerning Kerry Gundersen. "That's absolutely terrific!" she enthused.

"Yes, and it's also going to mean a helluva lot of work," Josh grumbled. Still, judging by her brother's expression, Jennifer knew he was pleased, no matter how he might downplay this milestone in his career.

"Anyway," he continued, "I've sold the editor in chief of *Living* on the idea of following the Watch Hill project step by step. Did Kerry say anything to you about that?"

"Not precisely. He did mention that he'd be willing to have the house photographed and publicized."

"Exactly." Josh nodded. "We'd start in almost immediately with 'as is' photos, then follow through as the place is transformed. Kerry wants to make a real showplace there, and he has the money to give carte blanche to whoever does the interior.

"This is the kind of feature story our readers will eat up," he continued. "Most of them know they're never going to own a mansion like Kerry's, but they can watch what's happening as a clever decorator—that's you, I sincerely hope—brings it back to life. Each step will give them ideas about changes they can make in their own homes. Let's call it high-level inspiration. I admit that for most people it will be like substituting rhinestones for diamonds, but look at the vogue rhinestones have right now. Am I making sense?"

Jennifer nodded thoughtfully. "Yes, you're making very good sense. I can see exactly what you're driving at. You want to present the ultimate in dream homes, using a house that is potentially magnificent but at the moment lacks vitality. By seeing a fantastic atmosphere and decor develop in every corner of the Watch Hill mansion, your readers will learn—even as they drool with envy—about various decorating basics they can incorporate in their own homes or apartments. So, provided the Watch Hill mansion becomes all it should be, there will be a very happy ending for everyone concerned. Am I right?"

"Exactly," Josh agreed. "You've grasped the concept, and you have the talent and ingenuity to do it. Not only will *Living*'s circulation soar, you'll be so firmly established as an interior designer that you'll be pushing away commissions by the dozen."

"You make it sound so easy."

"It's a great opportunity, Jenny," he repeated. "And you'd also be fulfilling the dream of a very decent guy. Kerry's a pretty terrific person, and I'd say he's earned his success more than anyone else I've ever met. Worked for it the hard way. I doubt he ever had anything handed to him on a silver platter, you know?"

She did know. Kerry had told her his story. How could there be platters, silver or otherwise, when there were no parents, no ancestors? Josh, she suddenly realized, didn't know any of this. Nor did he know that she and Kerry had been acquainted many years before, on a hot and dusty day in Georgia.

"You didn't turn him down, did you?" Josh asked abruptly, cutting a swath through her thoughts.

She was thinking about the abandoned baby, and it took her a moment to assimilate Josh's question. "No," she said, shaking her head slowly. "I didn't turn him down. He's given me two weeks to make a decision."

"That doesn't sound like Kerry," Josh mused suspiciously. "Usually he demands his answers on the spot. Snaps his fingers and gets what he wants. I've seen him in action."

"Well, he gave me two weeks."

"Then I can only say you must have made an impression on him, little sister. He must want very badly for you to do his house. He did take you to see it, didn't he?"

"Yes."

"What did you think?"

"I thought . . ." Jennifer tried to speak, but her throat went dry as she remembered Kerry waiting for her at the foot of the curving staircase. He'd looked so compelling, yet so wistful.

"Yes . . . you thought?"

"I thought his Watch Hill mansion could be transformed into an absolutely beautiful home. Even though it's so big, I can envision it as a warm and wonderful place, a real home." Jennifer looked up as she finished speaking to find Josh staring at her.

"If you feel like that about the place," he asked, clearly perplexed, "what's holding you up?"

When she didn't answer, Josh pleaded, "Take Kerry off the hook, will you? Do it for me, Jen. . . if only because he's a good friend of mine. Please, call him and tell him you'll do his house for him."

Chapter Five

Despite Josh's pressure, Jennifer didn't rush to the phone, call Kerry and say she'd decided to accept his commission. Instead, she did a lot of brooding.

Monday morning she made an appointment with the people who were interested in having her redecorate their Beekman Place penthouse. They were delightful people, and the penthouse was already beautiful. Jennifer guessed their reason for wanting her services was simply that they were bored with what they had—spacious rooms overlooking the East River that three-quarters of the city's residents would have given their eyeteeth for!

That was all right, though. They obviously had money to burn, and the way they spent it was their business. Still, Jennifer had the feeling that if she did the whole place in sky-blue and pink they'd probably be satisfied, as long as it was different from the present color scheme. In other words, there was no challenge involved in the job.

On Tuesday Jennifer met with her other potential clients, people who had bought a Park Avenue duplex. They'd had the interior gutted and now wanted the place transformed into a sophisticated setting where they could entertain in a highly cosmopolitan style. This couple wasn't as pleasant as the Beekman Place pair. In fact, Jennifer disliked their rather patronizing attitude toward her. It was suddenly easy for her to tell them that she'd really hoped to do their place, but a priority project had intervened.

Their faces were still registering disbelief as they ushered her to the front door, and Jennifer felt an odd sense of satisfaction in being able to say no. But again, the Park Avenue job offered no real challenge. She'd only be "manufacturing" the settings they required. Creativity and originality were unnecessary ingredients in this case.

The more she thought about it, *challenge* became the key word in her whole situation. Kerry had told her that his job would be a challenge for her. Josh had thrown down a challenge, too, when he'd reported that his magazine intended to follow the Watch Hill project step by step, featuring the interior designer. If the project turned out as successful as everyone hoped . . .

The idea of restoring Kerry's terrific old mansion to full glory was a tremendous challenge. It would require considerable research, a keen appreciation for a bygone era, imagination and creativity—the list went on and on, Jennifer realized. Also, both Kerry and Josh had assured her she wouldn't be hidebound by a strict budget. Although she was never cavalier about a client's finances and always sought the best values she could get, it was nice to know that if she discovered exactly the right piece of furniture for a room or exactly the right painting to adorn a certain wall, she wouldn't have to quibble about the price.

Best of all, Kerry had promised he'd give her free rein with the project. He'd told her he'd stay out of her way, wouldn't be constantly peering over her shoulder, as so often happened with clients. She could do as she saw fit without having to seek his approval every inch of the way. Unless, of course, she wanted to consult with him.

It was a dream job, and she'd be doing it for a dream man. Therein lay the rub. The professional challenge was great. The personal challenge was even greater. Could she possibly work on Kerry Gundersen's house and still keep her feet on level emotional ground? Would he really keep the distance he'd promised?

It was hard to imagine him not coming regularly to Watch Hill to see how things were developing. It was rather nice to think that he might also want to see her. After all, they'd admitted to the chemistry between them. The question was, what to do about it?

As she walked along East Sixty-sixth Street to Fifth Avenue, then turned south, Jennifer was reliving her afternoon in Watch Hill with Kerry. She was descending the curving stairway, moving naturally into his arms....

She stumbled on a crack in the sidewalk, then nearly collided with a woman laden with shopping bags before she snapped herself from her reverie. The vision of Kerry's handsome face, the memory of his touch, evoked wonderfully provocative feelings in her, feelings that were apt to lead her right out into traffic if she weren't careful.

On Fifth Avenue, many of the stores she passed were featuring Halloween themes in their window displays. She paused almost unconsciously in front of a card shop and scanned its featured merchandise. Then, on an impulse, she walked inside and bought the biggest card she could find. It was a huge haunted castle complete with ghosts, bats, spiders, cobwebs and black cats. The doors and windows revealed eerie yellow lights.

Jennifer bought the card before she could change her mind. Soon after, she ducked into a tearoom and, seated at a small corner table, took the card out. She'd been thinking of how Kerry had adopted Halloween as his official birthday, and she'd intended this as a birthday greeting, nothing more. Instead, she found herself writing, "Maybe I can achieve this effect with your Watch Hill home. Happy Birthday! Jennifer."

Quickly, she addressed the envelope to Kerry's office and finished her tea. Then, after buying a postage stamp at a corner cigar store, she dropped the card into the nearest mailbox. Only after the metal chute closed with an echoing thud did she stop to think about the absolute enormity of what she'd just done.

Kerry received the outsize envelope Thursday morning. He noted the New York postmark, but the handwriting was unfamiliar to him. Opening the Halloween card with a mounting sense of curiosity, he read—in sheer astonishment—the message Jennifer had written to him.

Jolted, he sat down abruptly, his elbow inadvertently hitting the intercom. Within seconds his secretary appeared in the doorway to ask, "Did you want something, Mr. Gundersen?"

Kerry, in a private daze, shook his head. "Thanks, no," he said, then chuckled inwardly at what a lie that was. Well, not a lie exactly. He didn't want *something*; he wanted some*one*. Specifically, a redhead named Jennifer Smith Perreault.

He suddenly wondered what Jennifer's French husband had been like, and why they'd divorced. Then it occurred to him that, although he felt he knew her so well, there was an awful lot about her that he didn't know.

He reread her message and wondered if she might be playing a joke on him. He couldn't picture her as the type who would raise his hopes, then laugh as they crashed. No, that wasn't Jennifer at all. Still, it was a crazy way to convey that she'd decided to accept his commission.

He reached for the phone and dialed Josh's apartment, hoping she would be there. He let the phone ring ten times, hung up, dialed again. Still no answer. He thought of calling Josh at his publishing company but decided against it. This was Jennifer he was dealing with, not her brother.

It was nearly six that evening before he finally connected with her, having dialed Josh's number a dozen times throughout the day. By then he was convinced that he'd somehow misinterpreted what she'd written, though he couldn't fathom what else her words might mean.

When he heard Jennifer say "Hello?" he was so surprised at the sound of her voice that he couldn't speak for a moment.

Then Jennifer asked impatiently, "Who is this? Is there someone there?"

"It's Kerry," he finally managed.

"What's the matter with your voice?" she asked him. "Do you have a cold?"

"No, no. I'm fine. I got your card, that's all. Thank you."

She laughed. "You're welcome. I couldn't resist it."

"It's quite a card."

"Yes, it is, isn't it?"

"Yes." Kerry's voice was still oddly subdued, almost halting, as he added, "I read your message."

Jennifer didn't know what to make of him. This strangely inarticulate role was totally unexpected from a man who might easily be nominated bachelor of the year.

Time spun a small web between them. Then Kerry, his voice nearly hoarse, said, "Am I to assume that you've decided to say yes to my offer?"

He sounded so bewildered that a surge of emotion swept over Jennifer. A hot tidal wave stung at her eyes, and she knew she was about to cry.

"I talked to Josh," she told him, her voice quavery. "Yes, I want to do your house for you."

"Bless Josh," Kerry said. "I owe him one."

She started to tell him that Josh hadn't talked her into anything, that she'd made the decision entirely by herself, but she knew she'd be risking her emotional neck if she did so. And right now tears were enough to handle.

"I think it would be best if I rent you a place in Westerly, or as close to Westerly as possible," Kerry stated.

They were sitting in Josh's living room sipping after-dinner liqueurs. Kerry had come down to New York from Providence in the afternoon, and Josh had suggested dinner at his place, telling Jennifer he'd cook. Jennifer had quickly vetoed that idea. Josh was great in the kitchen, but she'd discovered that tonight she'd wanted to do the cooking.

She'd prepared a stellar gourmet chicken dish served with fresh greenhouse asparagus—bought for an outrageous price—and a potato souffle of her own invention. For dessert she'd made a delicate pumpkin chiffon pie, which both Josh and Kerry complimented lavishly.

Kerry had insisted on helping clear the table and in the kitchen admitted, "I wouldn't have believed you could cook like that."

Jennifer, stashing cutlery in the dishwasher, had looked up over her shoulder and regarded him suspiciously. "Why not?" she'd asked.

"Well, when I first met you..."

"In Georgia, or in Rhode Island?" she'd teased.

"Let me rephrase that," he'd suggested. "As we both know, back in Georgia, I didn't really 'meet' you properly at all. We had an encounter. But I did find out that you'd just graduated from a very fancy girls' school up north, not to mention the fact that you were an army brat."

"So you had me pegged, right?"

He'd had the decency to flush slightly. "I suppose so."

"Sergeant," she'd reproved, "won't you ever learn that you can't always judge a book by its cover?"

"Or a general's daughter by her father's stars?" Kerry had countered.

They'd both burst out laughing, and Josh had appeared in the doorway, demanding to be let in on the joke. Finally Jennifer had managed to shoo both males out of the kitchen.

Now, in the living room with the two men, Jennifer felt absurdly content. Just looking at them was enough to make her feel good. She loved Josh so much. As for Kerry...

She stopped herself when it came to expressing such strong feelings for Kerry. Yet... it would be easy to love him. Real love, too, she found herself thinking, not the phony variety she'd experienced when she'd let herself be lured into eloping with Andre Perreault.

She'd paid for that mistake through four years of a very bad marriage. She'd gone through the trauma of divorce. She liked to think that she'd healed her crushed emotions with a gradually mounting strength—first in London, now in New York where, thanks to Josh, everything had been going so well for her from the moment she'd landed at Kennedy.

She couldn't imagine a relationship with Kerry disintegrating as it had with Andre until only resentment, anger and disappointment remained. No, life with Kerry would be entirely different—not that it wouldn't bring a fair share of disagreements. Jennifer was fully aware that she flared easily into anger, but she forgave just as easily. She suspected that Kerry was slower to anger. But was he also slower to forgive? That she didn't know.

There was so much she didn't know about him. She became aware that her thoughts were straying toward dangerous ground, and she vaguely heard Kerry say something about getting a place for her to live in a town called Westerly.

"Why can't I commute from New York?" she asked. "If and when I need to stay in the area, why not book a room at the Biltmore in Providence?"

"It's a fair drive to Watch Hill from Providence," Kerry answered practically. "A good hour, remember? Maybe an hour doesn't sound like much now, but we'll be running into winter weather soon. I wouldn't want to think of you on the road in the snow, especially after dark."

"I second that," Josh opined. "It'd be a lot better to be closer to the house, Jenny."

"Wait a minute. Are you two suggesting that I need to be in Watch Hill that much of the time? I expected maybe one or two full days a week after things get off the ground. Perhaps more often during critical phases. But if we have good workers, surely they can carry out my instructions."

"I want you there to supervise," Kerry stated with a stubbornness that surprised her. Then she reminded herself of Kerry's meteoric business success. Certainly he'd had to cultivate something of an iron will to get where he'd gotten in such a short time.

"It'll also be necessary from my point of view," Josh put in. "The photographer I assign for the job should probably make Westerly a base of operations, too. We won't need a photo session every day, but if something special comes up, I want you to alert us right away, Jenny. Missed opportunities lead directly to failure, you know."

Jennifer glanced at Kerry and found him looking incredibly smug. Somewhat discomfited, she asked what she immediately realized was a stupid question. "Who's the architect involved in the actual renovation?" she queried.

Josh laughed outright. "Who do you think?" he asked wickedly.

"Sorry," Jennifer retorted, "but I really didn't think a Victorian house would fall within Kerry's field of expertise."

"Ouch!" Kerry protested.

"That wasn't meant disparagingly," she quickly assured him. "It's simply that, from what I've seen of your work, you tend to be extremely avant-garde."

"No respect for tradition, you mean?" It was a double-edged question.

"I didn't say that." She looked him straight in the eye and elaborated, "You've established yourself in your own metier, that's all. There's no particular reason you should backtrack, is there?"

"You call respecting tradition backtracking?"

"I didn't say that, either. But on the other hand, maybe you tend to go overboard when it comes to respecting tradition, if you know what I mean. It can be more exciting to have new origins."

"New origins? Now there's a phrase!"

Josh looked from Kerry to Jennifer, obviously puzzled. "You two are actually bickering," he informed them. "And you scarcely know each other. Think you can work together for the next six months, starting out like this?"

"It's healthy bickering," Jennifer said defensively, and was rewarded by an honest chuckle from Kerry. But then something else Josh had said struck her. "Six months, did you say?" she asked him.

"I estimate it will take a good six months to do the whole house as it should be done," Kerry answered quickly. "I'm not trying to bind you into a firm finishing date, Jennifer, so I've instructed my attorneys to draw up a contract that will state your term of employment will be six months, more or less, from whatever date you can actually start."

"Have you really?" Jennifer commented quietly. Her brother glanced at her in alarm. With Jennifer, Josh knew very well, absolute calm more often than not really did precede a storm.

"Yes." Kerry nodded.

"Well, you can have your contract amended," she informed him. "I don't like contracts drawn up in which I have no voice. As a matter of fact, I don't want a contract, anyway. It seems to me that we could have a gentleman's agreement, so to speak. Our mutual word of honor should suffice, wouldn't you agree? If we don't have that much faith in each other, we shouldn't be doing business together."

"You're absolutely right," Kerry agreed unexpectedly. He spoke solemnly, yet there was a decided twinkle in his deep blue eyes as he added, "Of course, you'll be the most unusual gentleman I've ever affiliated myself with."

Jennifer stared at him, ready to spark. But just as abruptly, she felt herself melting, wrapped up in his charm.

She loved his warmth and humor. This man tugged at her heartstrings—there was no denying it. He touched her now in an entirely different way than when he'd evoked such a fierce surge of unadulterated desire. He was sensual as ever, yes. Sexy as hell. Yet something else was reaching out to her, something she couldn't define.

She wished Kerry would take her in his arms and let her lean her head against his strong shoulder. She wished he would gently stroke her hair, and whisper soft sweet things into her receptive ears.

She felt herself flushing. She was acting like a smitten sixteen-year-old. She'd had more common sense the first time she'd encountered Kerry Gundersen ten years ago. Or had she?

Theirs had been such a brief encounter on a hot, dusty road in Georgia. Had it lasted a little longer, Jennifer couldn't guarantee what her response to him would have been. As it was, the memory of those blue eyes had blazed for a long, long time.

At the door of Josh's apartment, Kerry turned. "Lunch tomorrow, Jennifer?" he asked.

Why did she hesitate every time this man put anything to her? Before she could give him an answer, he said, "Well, if you're tied up for lunch, how about dinner? Or even afternoon tea, if that would suit you better. I understand they serve tea at the Plaza."

"Look, give me a minute, will you?" she protested, flustered by his persistence, but smiling. She expelled a deep breath, then told him, "Okay, lunch will be fine."

It was Kerry's turn to hesitate. "Just this once," he said, "I'd like to have a lunch-lunch with you."

"What's that supposed to mean?"

"A date," he conceded, "without discussing business."

He looked deceptively innocent, prompting Jennifer to say, "Uh-oh. I think you're forgetting our pact again."

"The pact doesn't begin until the day you start work in Watch Hill," Kerry declared. "Anyway, I think it could use a spot of revision."

"Kerry!"

"I'm not going back on my word," he promised solemnly. "Once you start work for me, I swear I won't be a nuisance. But right now...well, I took a couple of days off to come down to New York. You could say it's a mini-holiday for me. So I'd just like to relax, roam around the city with you, get to know you a little better—if that's agreeable to you. I do find you a very interesting person, you know. Even on an intellectual level."

"*Even* on an intellectual level?" she echoed. And she burst out laughing.

"I think we already established where we stand on more primitive levels," Kerry stated blandly.

"Kerry," she warned again.

He grinned. "You're being repetitive, Jennifer," he teased. "Anyway, I sincerely want to get to know you better, and there are no seductive strings attached to that remark. Okay?"

"Okay," she agreed, pushing back a vague sense of disappointment.

"So you'll have lunch with me tomorrow?"

"Yes."

"Great," he said, visibly satisfied. "I'm staying at the Essex House," he went on. "I usually do. I like the view of Central Park, especially from the upper floors. You know..."

"Yes?"

"Well, I'd suggest you come straight to my room," Kerry told her, "but in all honesty, I don't think I'd better. Let's say we meet in the lobby at twelve-thirty."

He swayed very slightly in her direction. Noticing this, Jennifer nearly swayed forward herself. Then he straightened. And when he leaned forward again, it was deliberate. He bent slightly to kiss her cheek in just the kind of way Josh might have.

"Till tomorrow," he said.

Jennifer closed the door behind him, then suddenly realized her pulse was racing out of control. She was still not entirely steady as she walked back into the living room, to find Josh speaking on the phone.

He hung up the receiver and nodded almost complacently. "She's going to do it," he announced.

Jennifer, settling into the chair Kerry had vacated just a short while before, could smell the faint blend of his after-shave lingering in the air, combined with the masculine scent of Kerry himself. Her brother's words registered slowly. Then she asked, "Who's going to do what?"

"Marta Brennan's going to photograph Kerry's project."

The name was familiar. Josh had spoken of Marta Brennan before. She was a first-rate photographer, very much in demand by a variety of magazines. She'd won a number of prizes for her work, Jennifer remembered Josh remarking enthusiastically.

"You and Marta," he mused now, his eyes glowing. "Now that's a winning team! You'll like her, Jen. She's really terrific."

Jennifer's senses were on red alert as she heard her brother praise the woman. There was an unusually personal note in his voice, a certain exuberance that just wasn't there with Josh, normally.

"Marta's the best photographer who's ever worked for either of our magazines," he added. "Everyone on the staff agrees about that. She's at the stage in her career now where she can literally call her own shots. I wondered if she'd consider the Watch Hill project her kind of thing, but fortunately for us, she went for it. She wants to meet with you sometime in the next few days. Maybe Kerry could meet her, too."

"Well, I'm having lunch with him tomorrow," Jennifer admitted, having learned long ago that there was no point in even trying to keep secrets from Josh. "I'll mention it to him then. Did she have a particular time in mind?"

Josh didn't answer at once. He surveyed his sister speculatively. Then, to her surprise, he said, "Tell me if I'm out of line, but I get the impression there's something more than a job commitment between you and Kerry, isn't there?"

Jennifer sat up straight. "There really isn't," she denied. "I mean, there are vibes, yes. But to tell you the truth, they scare both of us equally, Josh. Kerry doesn't want a real involvement with anyone, and I certainly don't. So, we're wary."

"I hope so," Josh said simply.

"Why do you say that?"

"Because much as I like Kerry, I happen to know he's a loner. Don't misunderstand me. I'm not saying women don't interest him, because I'm sure they do. He certainly interests women. You only have to go out with him somewhere and watch all the female heads turning in his direction. But . . . well, I don't know that much about Kerry's past, but I suspect he got burned pretty badly at one point. And you . . . well, you've had your share of disappointment, little sister. I don't want to see that happen again."

"Neither do I," Jennifer agreed fervently. Then, thinking about Kerry, she decided to share one small secret with her brother. "Remember when you were in the hospital while Dad was still stationed at McKettrick?" she asked.

"All too well," he said grimly.

"Remember I came to see you," she persisted, "and I told you a story about having wandered out onto an artillery range and this high-handed soldier came after me and nearly had me arrested?"

Josh frowned, then slowly nodded. "As it happens, I remember that particular story very well. At the time, I laughed. I thought it was hilarious. But after you left, I reviewed the scene in my mind, and it scared the hell out of me. It occurred to me you so easily could have been killed."

"That's what Kerry told me," Jennifer confessed.

"Kerry?"

"Kerry was the sergeant who whisked me off to post headquarters to have me arrested."

Josh grinned widely. "No!" He contemplated what she'd just told him and shook his head admiringly. "Ten years ago, Kerry was an army sergeant. Today he's one of the wealthiest, most successful young architects in the country. You have to hand it to him. That's really a success story."

"Kerry took advantage of everything the service had to offer," Jennifer found herself saying. "He studied, got his bachelor's degree while he was still in the army—"

Just that quickly, she stopped herself. But Josh's discerning gaze told her she'd already revealed too much.

Chapter Six

We seem to be making a habit out of meeting in hotel lobbies," Kerry observed as he and Jennifer left the Essex House and walked out onto Central Park South.

"Think of the thousands of people all over the world who must meet in hotel lobbies," she reminded him.

"That doesn't mean I find them a favorite trysting place," he growled.

"Not one to follow the crowd, huh?"

"Not when I can help it." He smiled down at her. "Any idea where you want to go?"

"Not really."

He glanced toward Central Park, across broad Fifty-ninth Street, and saw that most of the trees had lost their leaves. The few tenacious hangers-on were withered and brown, soon to become prey to a gusting November wind. The sky was a uniform gray, the air cold and damp. Under ordinary circumstances, Kerry would have labeled this a miserable day. But with Jennifer at his side, he could as well have been in paradise.

He remembered the words of an old song and paraphrased them whimsically. He couldn't say that he had Jennifer's love to keep him warm, but certainly she made him *feel* warm.

A couple of hansom cabs hugged the curb on the opposite side of the street. Two coachmen were stamping up and down, blowing on their hands to ward off the cold. Their horses were garlanded with paper leis in a riot of colors.

Watching the horses, Kerry asked, "Have you ever ridden through the park in one of those?"

Jennifer shook her head.

"It's supposed to be a romantic New York tradition, isn't it?"

"Maybe on a warm night when there's a full moon," she said. She looked up at him. "Are you suggesting that's what we do?"

"No, no, not today," he answered hastily. "You'd freeze to death. You don't even have a coat."

She was wearing a smart dark green suit fashioned of heavy wool, so she hadn't felt she needed an outer coat. Actually, she was quite warm . . . especially with Kerry at her side.

He was wearing a cashmere overcoat a few shades darker than his hair. It was open in front, revealing a conservative charcoal gray suit. All in all, he looked terrific.

"Well," he said. "Let's first of all find a good place for lunch. Any ideas?"

"Do you like Japanese food?" she queried.

"Very much."

"Then you're in luck." She led him to a sushi bar on Fifty-sixth street that Josh had taken her to not long ago.

They feasted on a sampler of sushi and sashimi, then had shrimp tempura accompanied by crisp vegetables also deep-fried in the delicate tempura batter. With this they drank sake, hot rice wine, served in individual porcelain bottles.

The sake was smooth, pleasant to the taste, and went down easily. After drinking three tiny cupfuls, Kerry observed, "I seem to be getting my chopsticks crossed all of a sudden. This rice wine is heavy-duty stuff, isn't it?"

"Didn't anyone ever tell you that?"

"No, but then I have a confession to make, Jenny," he admitted, lapsing into the use of her nickname.

Jennifer had always restricted its use to family, but now she discovered that she loved the sound of the diminutive on Kerry's lips.

He leaned forward slightly, seductively enmeshing her in an invisible silken web of desire. "Want to hear a confession?" he murmured.

"I love to hear confessions." She tried to brush away those allegorical strands while at the same time wishing he'd draw the net of attraction even tighter.

"This is only the second time I've been in a sushi bar."

"But you said..."

"That I liked Japanese food very much. Well, the one other time I had it, I did. But the real reason I wanted to come here was very simple."

"And why was that?"

"I just wanted to get to a place where I could sit across from you and stare into those lovely topaz eyes of yours."

Jennifer refrained from answering that and poured herself another cup of sake. Sipping it, she mused that most men would have sounded inane, or at least insincere, saying something like that. Kerry, though, got to her. If there was ever such a thing as lessons in how to make a woman fall in love with you, Kerry must have been a very adept pupil, she decided. It wouldn't take much more prompting from him to make her tumble over the edge of a cliff she'd been trying desperately to avoid.

After lunch, they walked out into an afternoon that had turned even colder, even grayer. Jennifer assumed that Kerry had business to conduct in town, perhaps another appointment, and she turned to say goodbye to him.

To her surprise, he complained, "I thought this was to be our afternoon together."

"You invited me to lunch," she reminded him.

"To lunch and to get to know each other better," he shot back. "But if you have something else to do . . ."

"No, nothing special."

"Up for a walk?"

"Sure."

As they strolled north along Fifth Avenue, he said, "We didn't get into anything very personal over lunch, Jenny."

"Probably because the food was so good," she quipped lightly.

"You're hedging, Jennifer. After all, you know practically all there is to know about me."

She smiled straight ahead. "I doubt that."

"You know what's important," he insisted. "And you're the only person who does."

Jennifer digested that bit of information. "The only one?" she asked doubtfully.

"Oh, maybe there's still someone on that small-town police force up in Connecticut who remembers. Or someone at the orphanage where I grew up who might have some recollections about me. But they deal with so many kids, I doubt it. Anyway, by the time I got into the military I'd become more of a number than an individual. With my service in the army, I gained a whole new identity. So you see," he finished quietly, "you're the only person I've ever told the whole story to."

"Kerry," she chided, "you just turned thirty-six."

"So?"

"Through all those years, there must have been other people, other women."

"Lots of people and enough women," he agreed readily. "But that doesn't mean I sat down and spelled out the entire story to anyone. I guess I've always considered my background classified information. So now the secret is in your hands," he said with deceptive airiness.

She gazed up and met his eyes. "You don't have to worry about my ever telling anyone anything you don't want known," she said seriously. "Not even Josh."

"I know that."

They walked for a while in silence. Then Kerry said, "As I pointed out, you know all about me. I'm not asking you to tell all, but I have to admit I wish you'd fill me in on a few things."

"Something specific?"

"Yes, something specific. I'll be frank. I wish I knew more about your marriage. I know that's treading on very personal ground, and you have every right to tell me to bug off, but—"

"It's not that," Jennifer said carefully. She didn't want to hurt Kerry's feelings or shut him out in any way. But she wasn't ready to admit him into that personal inner vault where she'd locked up the failure of her marriage. She liked to think she'd triple-locked that particular emotional compartment and thrown away the keys.

She glanced at him and noted his face had become a mask of indifference. "It's okay," he said. "I'll drop the subject."

She marveled that apparently no one else had ever re-alized what a fragile ego this man had. An American suc-cess story—much more so than people knew—yet so very, very vulnerable. Over all those years, hadn't anyone touched him deeply enough so that he'd reacted as he was reacting now with her? The answer to that question ap-peared to be no. And realizing that, Jennifer was stunned.

If Kerry was vulnerable only to her...

Too much, too soon. Jennifer heard the inner warning, tried to heed it. But she couldn't push away the greater need to get through Kerry's present inscrutability.

"Do you always take everything so personally?" she asked more abruptly than she'd intended.

"Would you care to elaborate on that?"

"Kerry, I don't like to talk about my marriage simply because it was a mess. That's all. It has nothing to do with you. That is to say, there's nothing personal in my reluc-tance to discuss Andre with you."

"I think if you and I are going to be... good friends," Kerry said carefully, "then you need to let down the fences a little."

"Good friends?" Jennifer repeated. She had to repress a smile, even a chuckle. She wanted very much to be Ker-ry's friend. But deep in her heart she knew that friendship alone was not going to be enough. Not for her, not for him. Just walking along by his side was affecting her in ways mere friendship did not. She felt desire for him; she felt desired by him. It would be a miracle if she and Kerry could get through the next six months without going to bed together. She wasn't about to delude herself on that issue.

What did concern her, increasingly so, was not so much making love with him, but the aftermath of that lovemak-ing. The consequences. If they yielded to the strong tug of desire, if they capitulated to each other, could they later pick up the pieces and continue with their individual lives?

We've both been bruised enough, Jennifer thought. Neither of us needs another major trauma.

Rather automatically she said, "Let's cut over to Madison Avenue, find a coffee shop and get something hot to drink, okay?"

"Sure."

They found a small café, ordered cappuccinos and sat at a window table where they could people-watch while they sipped. Kerry was being polite. Scrupulously polite. Keeping his distance. But he couldn't entirely erase the hurt from his blue eyes.

So, it meant that much to have her confide in him!

Jennifer said slowly, "I was honest when I said my marriage has nothing to do with anything between you and me. When I met you back in Georgia . . . well, I was wandering out there in the boonies that day because I was trying to decide what to do. Andre had been my French instructor at Briarlee, here in New York."

"Don't tell me anything unless you really want to," Kerry told her. "You don't have to go into this."

"That's all right. I want to go into it. I don't want you to have any misconceptions." She paused to draw a deep breath. "I started dating Andre on the sly early in my senior year," she stated. "He was the prototypical handsome, dashing Frenchman every girl dreams about. Continental charm, continental manners. He bowled me over, Kerry."

"Honestly, Jennifer, you don't have to tell me."

"Look, you wanted to hear about my marriage, and now I want to tell you." When he didn't say anything, she went on. "As I said, I started dating Andre on the sly. I would have been expelled if the headmistress had ever found out about us. It was absolutely forbidden for faculty and students to mix socially—or romantically, I should say. So in the beginning our relationship had that added excitement because we were doing something forbidden. He made me feel like a real femme fatale. When I think about it now and admit what an absolute kid I must have been, that seems rather sad to me."

"Stranger things have happened," Kerry put in.

Jennifer continued. "Anyway, I went to Georgia during Easter vacation. To McKettrick, where my dad was stationed. At Andre's request, I returned to New York a day early. I fibbed to my parents about the date I had to be back at school. Andre met me at Penn Station. He'd booked a hotel room for us. I hadn't really thought it through—can you understand that?"

Kerry smiled disarmingly and said, "It depends on what you're going to tell me."

"I'm telling you that once we were at the hotel, he ordered champagne sent up to the room, he had a gardenia corsage there waiting for me, and...he made love to me."

"That was the first time?" Kerry asked, his voice curiously hollow.

"Yes."

"The first time with Andre, I mean?"

"The first time with anyone, Kerry. I won't go into it...except to say that I didn't rise to the kind of emotional heights I'd heard about. Andre explained that was because it was my first time."

"Jenny...look, I had no intention of pressing you for details," Kerry said hoarsely. "What you're telling me is your own private business."

"Isn't that what you asked me about?"

Kerry pushed back his chair and surveyed her, his blue eyes pained. "I had absolutely no right to ask you anything," he conceded.

"Look, we're into this now. So . . . just let me talk. Just let me say that for all his social finesse, Andre was not the world's greatest lover. Of course, I was too inexperienced to know that. He was a marvelous con artist. He knew how to promise, how to tantalize. He had me convinced I was absolutely mad about him and couldn't live without him. When graduation approached and he told me he'd decided not to return to Briarlee in the fall, I was crushed."

"Then what happened?"

"Well, I'd been admitted to a college in Connecticut, so I thought he and I could sneak away together on weekends. But then he told me he'd decided to return to France. A couple of months later, I found out that actually the school had dropped him. Told him they didn't want to renew his contract for a number of reasons.

"Anyway, just before graduation I met Andre in a little cocktail lounge that we'd been having our rendezvous at."

"You were old enough to drink?"

"Not quite, but they never carded me. Anyway, I don't think I ever had more than a glass of wine. But to get back to the story, I met Andre at this place, and he begged me to marry him and move to France with him. Believe me, he could be very convincing."

"I believe you," Kerry said dully.

"I couldn't give him an instant decision. I'd always been close to my parents, and Josh had just had his terrible accident. He was in the hospital at the time I graduated. I was devoted to Josh, and I could imagine what my marrying Andre would do to my family. For one thing, he was so much older than I was."

"How much older?"

"He said he was forty. I was eighteen. A twenty-two-year discrepancy that he and I dismissed very lightly at the time. Later, I found out that he'd lied about his age, too, as he did about most things. He was closer to forty-five. Not that it mattered.

"Anyway, I went to McKettrick for the summer. And I was brooding about what to do the day I met you. Later...I know this sounds insane, but even when I was making plans to elope with Andre, I somehow couldn't get you out of my mind. For a long, long time, I kept remembering your face."

Kerry sat statue still, statue silent.

"Andre kept calling. I kept fibbing to my parents, telling them the calls were from classmates who wanted to come down to Georgia and visit me. Finally, it got to be the zero hour. And...well, I left a note for my parents, caught the bus to Atlanta and flew from Atlanta to New York. We got married a few days later and left almost immediately for France. From that moment on, everything went downhill."

"Jenny, really..." Kerry said gently.

"I'm going to finish this, Kerry, once and for all. I discovered that I was married to a self-centered, totally conceited individual to whom the only thing in the world of importance was himself. I discovered he knew my mother was an heiress. He even thought I received a far larger allowance than was actually the case. I could go on and on. He was never a good...lover," she sputtered. "Nor was he a good friend or a good companion. I became more and more miserable until finally I got the courage to take my own destiny in my hands. It wasn't really courage, though, because all I did was run away—again. I'd run away from my parents and what I thought were the stringent restrictions they imposed on my life when I eloped with Andre.

I ran away from Andre by flying to London. It was quite a nightmare, really."

"Then you got into interior decorating?"

"In London, yes. I was fortunate to make a very good connection in that field, and later I got an English divorce. From then till now, things have slowly but steadily gone uphill. My parents have never entirely forgiven me for what I did, though Josh, bless him, has always stood behind me. During a visit to London last spring, he finally said, 'Jenny, I think it's time for you to come home.' He invited me to live in his apartment until I got my feet on the ground. So I came."

Kerry asked softly, "And are you glad you did?"

"Very much so," she told him. "I don't think I've ever been so glad of anything."

"And are you comfortable, at this point, about having accepted the commission to do my house?"

"Yes. Yes, I am."

Kerry sank back in his chair, knowing he should be satisfied with that. But he couldn't help thinking about something Jennifer had freely admitted. When faced with crisis decisions, she had run away. First from her parents, later from her husband.

Jennifer was different from any woman he'd ever known. She was special, in so many ways. Kerry, normally wary about deep involvement, had melted considerably where she was concerned. Still, the nagging thought persisted that, should something negative happen between the two of them, should Jennifer then run away from him, the bottom would drop out of his world.

"Most of the motels around Westerly are closed until late spring," Kerry reported, "but I found an old inn in the area that stays open all year. I've booked two suites there—

one for you, one for Josh's photographer. I hope that will be satisfactory."

His voice sounded especially deep and mellow over the phone, and Jennifer was in something of a trance listening to him.

"Jenny?" he asked.

"That sounds terrific," she told him quickly.

"Good," he approved. "In that case, when can you move up here?"

Only three days had passed since he'd left Manhattan. He'd worked fast! She said, "I'm not quite ready...."

"Any particular reason for a hold-up?"

"I guess you could call it trying to get my act together, that's all."

"Jenny," Kerry pointed out, "you're not about to be isolated in Siberia. When I told you I didn't want you commuting to Watch Hill on a daily basis from Providence, I was thinking primarily of really bad winter weather when the driving would be dangerous. That doesn't mean the weather's always going to be terrible or that you're not free. It's just that I'm eager to get started with the project."

"I know you are."

"So I'd like to meet you at Watch Hill tomorrow, if you could possibly make it. You can check out the accommodations I've booked for you, too, just to be sure you like the place. Then you can return to New York tomorrow evening or stay over at the Biltmore Plaza. That's up to you."

"Tomorrow?" she queried, honestly dismayed. True, Kerry wasn't asking her to make the actual move. Still, she wasn't ready to bridge what loomed as far more than a physical gap between Manhattan and Watch Hill, Rhode Island.

"I want to meet with you alone before anyone else gets in on the act," Kerry continued. "I want to go over the house with you in detail. I have a few structural changes in mind that you should know about before you plan your strategy."

"What kind of structural changes?"

"The kitchen, to cite just one example. I'm going to have a wall knocked out to open the area up. One of the bedrooms, too. I'm going to add skylights, knock out another wall—things like that. I'd like to go over them with you, for obvious reasons."

"Kerry?"

"Yes?"

"You did promise, if you'll remember," she said carefully, "that this was to be entirely my project."

"I pledged to keep my hands off it—is that what you're saying?"

"That's what I recall."

"My recollection is that I primarily pledged to keep my hands off *you*," he remarked dryly. "However, I'm not denying that your memory may be better than mine. The fact is, I was so damned eager to have you say you'd take the job, I was ready to pledge almost anything."

"And now you're reneging?"

"I didn't say that. I've simply decided to do a few internal modifications that I hadn't dreamed up when we first talked."

"I'm sorry," she said. "After all, it is your house, and you have every right to do what you want."

"Architecturally speaking, you mean?"

Jennifer drew a deep breath. Kerry was teasing her, she knew, but she wasn't quite sure how to respond. "Yes, architecturally," she managed unconvincingly.

"I could always hire another architect, if that's what you really want."

She sighed. She knew perfectly well that structural changes in a mansion such as Kerry's would require a competent architect's expertise. She certainly wouldn't feel comfortable okaying an idea and then entrusting the actual details of the design to a local builder, even a good one.

Evidently tired of waiting for her answer, Kerry said stiffly, "This is one area in which I'm going to have to make the decisions, Jennifer. Yes, I know I told you that you'll have free rein at Watch Hill, not only with decorating but with interior design. Meaning, structural changes you might envision. Even so, the mechanics for changes like that fall within the realm of my profession rather than yours, and I'm damned if I'm going to hire another architect to work on my house. I hope you'll accept that."

He was cool and assured, aggressively so. Jennifer had heard him use that tone of voice only once before, and like that other time, it gave her a glimpse of an entirely different Kerry Gundersen. This was not the vulnerable, passionate Kerry she'd come to know, but the hard-as-nails Mr. Gundersen of Gundersen and Sonntag.

Now she was dealing with the man who had climbed to the top of the ladder in his profession. She could almost feel his determination, could almost see a certain brand of ruthlessness. She'd glimpsed that man the day she'd first walked into the austere offices of Gundersen and Sonntag, and she'd spotted him once more the day he'd pressed her into a deadline on her decision to accept or decline his commission. But for the most part he'd been the charming, warm, approachable male who lit unwanted fires deep inside her.

Well, from now on, Jennifer decided, she'd have to have a stiffer spine where Kerry Gundersen was concerned. Matching his coolness, she said, "I wouldn't think of suggesting that you hire another architect, Kerry. I know as well as you do how ridiculous that would be."

"Do you?" he challenged.

"Of course I do. I suppose I simply hadn't thought out the fact that there might be some structural alterations."

"That's precisely why I want to make an on-the-scene survey with you," Kerry said, still behaving like a formal stranger. "So is tomorrow convenient?" He asked the question politely yet managed to convey the impression that only a yes would suit him. That, in short, he was her employer.

Jennifer fought a rising tide of resentment. She didn't want to begin this important assignment feeling hopelessly at odds with the man she loved.

Loved?

She gasped, admitting that love was the emotion she felt toward Kerry. Love, like a blooming flower, filled her mind with wonder. Love, like a glorious sunset, filled her heart with the tender ache of wanting.

"What is it?" he asked abruptly.

At least she'd driven the ice out of him! He couldn't have sounded more concerned.

"Nothing," she hedged.

"Whatever that sound you just made was, it didn't sound like nothing. Did you have a sudden pain?"

"Just a stitch in my side."

"Have you had your appendix out?"

Jennifer's laugh bubbled forth, loosening the tension that had been building up between them. "When I was ten," she told him. "Honestly, it was just a stitch. Kerry?"

"Yes?"

"You threw me a slight curve, asking me to come to Watch Hill tomorrow. I wanted to have some definite ideas committed to paper before we met."

"You weren't in the house long enough to get any definite ideas about it," he pointed out.

"I wouldn't say that. I remember the house very well."

"I remember, too," he said huskily, and that silken thread of desire began to weave its way across the miles that separated them.

"Promise me something, Kerry," Jennifer said suddenly.

"What's that?"

"Promise me we won't repeat our little scene on the stairs. At least, not for a while."

"I made the pledge, remember?" he teased.

"Yes, I remember."

But as they hung up, having agreed to meet at Watch Hill at two o'clock the following afternoon, Jennifer was wondering if she'd be able to keep that pledge herself.

Chapter Seven

The following day was gray and raw, with a cold east wind blowing in from the Atlantic. As Jennifer cruised up the driveway of the Watch Hill mansion, she was relieved to see Kerry's car already there. He'd considerately left the space under the porte cochere for her, and she took advantage of it. Nevertheless, she was shivering as she pushed the buzzer beside the heavy oak door and heard chimes echo through the empty house.

She'd half expected Kerry to be keeping an eye out for her. Evidently he wasn't. After what seemed to Jennifer a considerable wait, she pushed the bell again.

Abruptly the door opened. Kerry stood in front of her, wiping his hands on an old cloth. Jennifer caught a whiff of smoke and, looking beyond him, saw that the huge foyer was filled with a blue haze.

"My God, what happened?" she exclaimed.

"I was trying to get the chimney to work," he said, looking disgusted. "I should have gotten hold of a chimney sweep first. I'll have one over here tomorrow to clean out all the chimneys in the place. As it is, I've got a fire going in the dining room, and it seems to be drawing all right. Let's go in there and get warm. The rest of the house is colder than a tomb."

It *was* cold. Cold and dank, the emptiness especially pronounced on this gray November afternoon. Had the weather been like this on her first visit, Jennifer thought as she followed Kerry across the smoky entrance hall, she would have received an entirely different impression of the mansion.

The crackling fire in the dining room was the only bright note to be found. Kerry looked totally glum and absorbed in thoughts he wasn't sharing. Jennifer felt at a loss. Suddenly, the enormity of the project pressed heavily on her shoulders. Where to even begin? she wondered dismally, looking around as she warmed her hands in front of the hearth.

"The electric company was supposed to be here this morning to turn on the juice," Kerry complained. "Obviously they never arrived, which means we have no lights and the furnace isn't working. The telephone company didn't get here either."

"Sounds as if we're really out of touch with the outside world," Jennifer said, trying to smile.

"Wait'll I get back to civilization and speak to those damned utility companies," Kerry warned. "I certainly didn't intend to have you walk into a situation like this."

So that's what was worrying him! Jennifer had wondered if he was burdened by something considerably more critical. Relieved, she slanted a genuine smile at him and said, "It comes with the territory, okay? Now, for the moment at least, I'm warm. Would you like to start in the kitchen or upstairs?''

"Damned if I know," Kerry admitted abjectly.

Jennifer burst out laughing. "You should see your-self," she told him.

"Am I that funny?" He scowled.

"Funnier, really. This isn't a tragedy, Kerry."

"It will be if you come down with pneumonia."

"That's not going to happen, I assure you. Why don't we start with the kitchen, the pantry and those rooms out back? They're what one might call the center of opera-tions, especially in a house this size. Anyway, you men-tioned knocking out a wall. Why don't you show me where that's going to happen? Then we can share our ideas on how the kitchen can best be organized and decorated."

"From a woman's point of view?" he asked mischie-vously, his sense of humor returning.

"From the decorator's point of view," she countered.

"Touché."

Appraising the kitchen objectively, Jennifer deter-mined it was very much outdated but had terrific poten-tial. It was large and rectangular with a high ceiling. Beyond it were a pantry and two small storage rooms. Be-yond those were two studio-type rooms with baths, evi-dently quarters for the help.

Jennifer and Kerry became thorough professionals as they concentrated on planning the general layout of the kitchen. To her delight, Jennifer found that they worked well together. Kerry was quick to grasp her concepts as she envisioned the finished "center of operations," as she called it. She brought out her sketch pad, Kerry produced one of his own, and very quickly ideas took shape on pa-per.

"In the old days, this house had quite a staff of servants," Kerry reported when finally they paused for a break and went back to the dining room to warm their hands by the fire. "I know those two rooms behind the kitchen were used as servants' quarters, and I think the third floor was for the staff, too. There are six more bedrooms up there. I thought of converting them into dormitories."

"Dormitories?"

"Remember I told you I eventually want this place to be a halfway house for homeless kids?"

"I thought that was way in the future," Jennifer said, slightly distressed that he was thinking in such terms already. She'd equated the halfway house—the foundation, he'd called it—with his will. And his will with...a very remote date. Even the thought of a will in connection with Kerry gave her a chill. He was thirty-six years old, the picture of health. Why was he thinking about putting dormitories in the house now?

"I'm not sure how far in the future it's actually going to be, Jenny," he said slowly.

Fear clutched her. Was there something about Kerry he hadn't told her, despite his claim that she knew more about him than anyone else? Was he suffering some fatal illness and keeping the fact hidden? She felt sick and dizzy at the thought and actually swayed.

"Hey there, what's wrong?" he demanded, gripping her arm. "You've gone white as a sheet."

"Is there something you haven't told me?" she asked weakly.

He looked at her with those blazing blue eyes as if he didn't have the faintest idea what she was talking about. Then suddenly he put two and two together and came to the right conclusion.

"I'm as healthy as a horse," he said huskily. But the way his pulse was beating, he wondered if maybe his heart wasn't developing a problem at that. Not a physical problem, but a problem centered upon this lovely woman who was looking up at him as if...

As if she loved him.

Kerry, staggered by the poignant message in Jennifer's eyes, warned himself sternly not to be a damned fool. She was a warm, caring person, that was all. He'd scared her a minute ago. It would be folly to read more than that into her expression.

"What I mean was...I know you're going to do the best possible job in the world on this house, Jenny," he said gently. "I know you intend to draw on my personality, my life-style, my inner self—call it what you will. You explained to me that first day in my office how you mesh space and people, how homes are extensions of their owners. The problem is, no matter how well you do with this place and me, I'm not sure I can live up to it."

Jennifer frowned. "I'm afraid I don't understand you."

"We were talking about the servants' quarters a few minutes ago, about possibly refurbishing those rooms for a housekeeper and maybe a cook. I started imagining myself dealing with a cook and a housekeeper, to say nothing of a butler, an upstairs maid and gardener all living on the third floor. Frankly, I can't see myself playing lord of the manor. I've never had anyone wait on me in my life. An elderly woman comes in and cleans my apartment one afternoon a week, does a little ironing, but that's it. She has a key, and I'm seldom there when she is. When we do run into each other, she treats me more like a son than an employer."

Kerry chuckled and put another log on the fire, then poked at it, scattering embers. "This place," he com-

mented, "was meant for gracious living, sumptuous entertaining. When I saw it, my imagination went wild. Now
I'm beginning to think my mind was playing tricks on me."

This was the last sort of development Jennifer had contemplated. She asked slowly, "Are you saying you don't
want to live here?"

Kerry thrust his hands into his coat pockets and stared
at the fire. "I guess I don't know what I want," he admitted glumly. "No, wait a minute. Don't misunderstand me.
I'm very excited about this project of ours. I intend to see
it through no matter what, so have no fear on that
ground."

"If you're not going to live here, what point would there
be in totally redoing the house?" Jennifer asked reasonably. "Whoever bought it might have entirely different
taste."

"They'd have awfully bad taste if they didn't like what
you'd done."

"You don't know that," she pointed out. "Taste is an
extremely subjective matter, not necessarily good or bad.
It's merely a statement of preference. I might choose to do
an upstairs bedroom in a color the new owner would
hate."

The *new* owner? Jennifer thrust that thought aside before it had time to germinate. Still, she had to be honest
with Kerry. "If you feel you've gotten in over your head,"
she said, "now's the time to pull out, you know."

He shifted uncomfortably. "I think maybe we've had
enough for one day," he evaded. "Anyway, it's starting to
get dark in here. Let's head back to Providence, shall we?
I took the liberty of booking a room at the Biltmore for
you."

"I appreciate that," Jennifer told him, "but I'd planned
on driving back to New York."

"There's something you have to do?"

"Well, no. I told Josh I'd be home, that's all."

"You can call him. We can drive up to Providence in my car. Yours will be okay here for the night. I can phone the police and ask them to keep an eye on it if you're worried."

"I'm not worried about my car, Kerry."

"If you're worried about me . . . just remember the pledge, Jenny."

"I'm not even worried about the pledge."

"What, then?"

"Well, I think you should be absolutely sure about what you're planning to do here."

"Fair enough," he agreed reasonably. "We'll discuss that over dinner."

They were approaching Providence when Kerry said, "You cooked for me in New York. How about my cooking dinner for you tonight at my apartment?"

She grinned. "You mean you really can cook? Or are you a canned foods connoisseur?"

"You'll eat that remark," he warned.

Jennifer was surprised when they pulled up in front of the interesting old building Kerry lived in. She was more surprised when he ushered her into his studio apartment. At some point walls had been knocked out of two or three smaller rooms to create this one oversize room. A fireplace with a beautiful marble mantelpiece had been retained. An intricate, scrolled plaster frieze bordered the high ceiling.

Despite its size, the room was cluttered. A king-size daybed—Kerry's sleeping place, obviously—took care of one corner. An assortment of beautiful antiques filled the rest of the room. Vying for space were several tables, a lovely old mahogany pie stand, an elaborate, glass-fronted cabinet, chairs representing several decorative eras and a small rolltop desk. As a final touch, a magnificent crystal chandelier hung from the center of the ceiling.

Gazing up at the chandelier, Jennifer observed, "Surely this didn't come with the apartment?"

Kerry was standing in his small alcove kitchen, splashing Cinzano over ice. "No, it didn't," he called over his shoulder. "I bought it at an estate sale. Looked it up, since. It's a good one."

"Indeed it is. Am I to presume you also bought most of these other pieces?"

"At estate sales, auctions, flea markets—I love 'em."

Kerry crossed the room toward her, a glass of the red vermouth in each hand. Just looking at him displaced Jennifer's heart treacherously. She would have sworn it slid up in her chest and then back down again.

"You surprise me," she said, taking the glass from him, then slowly walking around the room, surveying each piece in turn. "You've really done your homework."

"I like furniture with a history to it," he admitted. "I'll never know the true history of these pieces, of course, but I've imagined little stories for each. The homes they were part of, the people who owned them. They all look as if they've been used, cherished."

He paused. "I know you'll think I'm crazy," he confessed, "but I keep a special eye out for auctions and estate sales over in Connecticut, in towns near where I was found. Several of these things have come from there. I like to fantasize that perhaps they were in my own family. After all, I must have had a family."

He broke off, and Jennifer saw that he was biting his lip. "There I go again. I must sound like a soap opera to you," he said disgustedly.

On the contrary, he'd moved her tremendously, as he always did when he spoke of the past he'd never know about. This was another unplanned speech, she realized, and a tribute to her that he opened up as he did.

At the same time, he tore at her heartstrings at moments like this. Kerry didn't want her sympathy; he was much too strong a person for that. Still, Jennifer wished once again that there was something she could do for him. It was frustrating to accept the reality of the situation, to admit that there was nothing anyone could do for Kerry where his past was concerned. He'd gone that route, come to a dead end and was wise enough to accept the facts as they were.

But that didn't help Jennifer. It was hell not to be able to ease the pain of someone you loved.

That word again. *Love.*

Jennifer's feelings were a plainly written message to Kerry. Her lovely, expressive face was a study in the sympathy she knew he didn't want. He turned away abruptly, went back to his tiny kitchen and started busying himself with the ingredients for gourmet omelets.

They dined by candlelight at an antique table Kerry pulled out from the wall. He served a consommé first. The clear soup had a special flavor Jennifer couldn't identify, and he teasingly refused to tell her what his secret spice was.

His omelet, laced with a mushroom sauce, was a real creation. So was the salad that accompanied it. The dinner was light and tasty, and Jennifer was glad she had room for a dessert of delicate sorbet and crisp brown sugar cookies—a present from his cleaning lady, Kerry told her.

As they relaxed over coffee, Jennifer said, "I could purr, I'm so content. Don't be surprised if I fall asleep."

Kerry nodded toward the huge bed. "Be my guest," he invited.

Their eyes locked. Desire rose between them, twisting like a spiral staircase. Kerry murmured, "Damn it, Jenny, I don't know about the pledge. Just what the hell did we pledge, anyway?"

"I'm not so sure," she answered softly.

"Wasn't the pledge just for working hours at Watch Hill?" His eyes were twin blue flames scorching her with want.

"I...I don't know."

"What do you want it to be, Jenny?" he murmured huskily. "What do you want from me?"

Jennifer knew she was casting caution to the winds. She let it go, let it drift beyond the point of no return. "I think," she said, staring deep into his eyes, "I want the same thing you want from me."

Neither of them was aware of standing up. Neither of them was conscious of edging out from the table and moving toward the other. Then they were in each other's arms, and all the pent-up passion that had been mounting between them broke over them like a wave, wonderfully warm and totally enveloping.

Kerry caressed Jennifer, his touch making every cell in her body throb with sensual vibrancy. It was as if she'd been totally unaware of her body until she felt Kerry's hands sparking her to life. Her hands fluttered over his shoulders, then roamed restlessly down his broad back, following the contours of his firm, masculine body until she could no longer bear merely the feel of cloth. She wanted the feel of him. She wanted to touch his skin, feel him, arouse him.

Despite their initial haste, they undressed almost languidly. Then they were on his bed. Jennifer didn't know when he'd paused to throw back the heavy, hand-loomed coverlet, but she felt the smoothness of cool percale sheets under her and Kerry's heated body beside her, then atop her.

They explored each other with their hands, with their mouths, leisurely at first until gradually the pace quickened of its own accord and they were caught up in a whirlwind of passion.

Kerry, in those magic moments that followed, became the lover Jennifer had never had. He led her along the delicious path of sexual abandonment, and she needed no coaxing to follow him. Ultimately, they reached its end in unison, exploding together in love's blazing triumph.

For a timeless interval they lay quietly side by side, their arms, their legs entwined. The room was in darkness except for the two candles peacefully flickering on the dinner table. Finally Jennifer whispered in wonder, "Has there ever been anything like that before?"

Kerry chuckled. "I don't think so."

"Will there ever be anything like that again?"

She felt his fingers on her chin. He tilted her face toward his. In the dim light, his eyes looked darker than night. And his voice was profoundly tender as he said, "The answer to that, Jenny, will be up to you."

Later, Kerry drove Jennifer to the hotel. As they stood in front of the elevator, he handed her the overnight bag she'd brought and complained, "This seems crazy. Why wouldn't you stay at my place?"

"I don't recall your asking me."

"Come on, lady! You know damned well you didn't need an invitation."

"Well..."

"Well?"

"I think we need a little time apart."

"For reflection?"

"I suppose so."

"That scares me," Kerry confessed.

"Why should it?"

"Sometimes it spoils everything when you think too much. It's better to let things happen."

Jennifer smiled. "I'd say we followed that prescription, wouldn't you?"

"Damn it!" Kerry threatened. "Stop looking at me like that or I'll never let you go upstairs by yourself."

One of the elevators reached the lobby, and the door slid open. Jennifer said, "I'd better get in before we change our minds. Good night." Just as the door closed, she whispered, "My dearest love." But she didn't think he heard that.

Actually, Kerry heard something. He thought she said "dearest love," but the closing door had muffled her voice. And even if he were sure, he warned himself not to take it too seriously. A woman could say anything in the aftermath of a night of passion.

Kerry had always been a loner. He'd often thought wryly that, since he'd been born alone, loneliness had become his natural inheritance. You could get used to almost anything, he'd philosophized.

But back in his apartment later that night, he discovered a new kind of loneliness—an empty feeling that gnawed at him until he hurt inside.

He'd wanted Jennifer so desperately. Well, tonight he'd gotten what he wanted—and more. So, he knew, had she. They'd satisfied their tremendous physical need for each other, only to make their situation worse instead of better, he was discovering. Being without Jennifer now was like having possessed the world, only to lose every last drop of water, every last grain of sand.

Kerry paced the floor, his familiar companion, loneliness, becoming a terrible force that tore at his guts. He wanted Jennifer again.

Eventually, morning arrived. Kerry, hollow-eyed from his meager snatches of sleep, had already consulted with his partner, George Sonntag, and verified that there was nothing on the agenda that couldn't wait a day. He'd told Jennifer he'd pick her up at nine o'clock. By the time they reached Watch Hill, both the electricity and the phone should have been connected.

Again, he and Jennifer met in the hotel lobby. They stared at each other solemnly. She looked as harried as he did, Kerry saw with no particular sense of satisfaction.

"You had a rough night, too, I see," he commented.

"Yes."

They were both silent as they headed out of Providence.

Workers from the telephone company were still at the mansion when Kerry and Jennifer arrived. They finished their work almost immediately and took off. The electricity had been turned on, but again it was a gray November day. The bare bulbs in most of the rooms glared into the grayness, the effect anything but cheerful. Every blemish in the paint and wallpaper showed up starkly.

"There's a lot to be done, isn't there?" Kerry observed.

"You knew that when you bought the place."

"Yes, I did." He didn't know why he felt so disgruntled, out of sorts. What was he kicking about? Last night, this beautiful woman—now walking around the enormous dining room as if she were in a trance—had shared his bed with him for an interlude of pure rapture he would never forget.

The problem was, he wanted her back in his bed. Again and again and again. For the rest of his life.

He shut off the thought. The mere idea was idiotic.

Remember who you are, Gundersen, he cautioned himself silently. *Rather, remember who you aren't.*

Jennifer, surveying the walls, said, "My guess is that these were panels once, probably wallpapered. In an even earlier era I'd suspect they were done with brocade or tapestry. If you want to be very elegant, I think we should go with a panelled fabric. And a lovely soft tone for the paint, picking up the lightest background in the fabric pattern. How does that strike you?"

"I don't know," Kerry said dejectedly. "I've never pictured myself as an elegant type. I can't see myself presiding over a banquet."

He hesitated, having almost said, "Unless you were sitting at the other end of the table, Jenny." He nearly choked, realizing this. Abruptly he said, "I think you'd better stick with a good paint job."

"What?" Jennifer was sketching out an idea. She couldn't believe what she'd just heard.

"When this place is a halfway house for kids, they won't want brocaded walls in the dining room," he announced.

She stared at him silently as she assessed the implications of what he'd just said. It was a shock, just as his remarks about turning the place over to homeless youngsters had been yesterday. She'd thought those plans were a long, long way down the pike. Now... now there was an imminence in Kerry's tone she didn't like.

She said firmly, "I'm stopping right now, Kerry. Not another line will I draw, not another thought will I permit myself to have about this house, until you and I have talked this out. I didn't contract to do a home for kids—I contracted to do a home for you!" she blurted, looking away from him. When he didn't answer, she glanced over her shoulder.

He was standing in the center of the big empty room, looking so terribly alone that it took all her willpower not to run to him and throw her arms around him. His agitation showed in the way he was running his fingers through his striking silver-blond hair. But he sounded calm as he said, "Okay. You're right. Look, why don't we pick up some sandwiches and wine, take them over to one of the beaches and have a picnic?"

A picnic on a raw November day with that cold wind blowing in from the east? Jennifer would have scoffed at the suggestion had it come from anyone else. To Kerry she said, "That sounds great."

They ate in the front seat of Kerry's car, sipping their wine from paper cups while the waves crashed against the beach and the wind howled. Kerry had also brought a thermos of coffee. Finally he said, "A hot cup of coffee would really be in order, but there's something I'd like to do first."

"What's that?"

"Walk the beach to clear my head of the cobwebs that seem to be cluttering it up," he said. "I always find it good therapy. You don't have to join me if you don't want to. I know it's cold out."

She slanted a reproachful look at him and said, "Race you to the sand." She slipped off her shoes and got out of the car before Kerry quite realized what was happening.

She was nearly at the tide line when he caught up with her. He swung her around, clutched her in his arms, then stared down into her laughing, upturned face and groaned, "Invoke the pledge, Jenny. Quickly, invoke the pledge!"

Chapter Eight

Jennifer and Kerry walked along the beach for nearly an hour. They walked vigorously, staying close to the tide line where the sand was firm. At Kerry's insistence, the first leg of their walk was with the wind in their faces. It was cold and wet, and Jennifer was ready to plead for mercy when he suggested they turn back. The return trek was considerably easier. Even so, Jennifer was thoroughly chilled by the time they reached Kerry's car and more than ready for the cup of hot coffee he poured for her.

The coffee, though it nearly scalded their throats, wasn't enough to keep them warm. Surveying their situation, Kerry frowned. "This isn't exactly cozy," he observed. "We need to talk, and we have no place to go."

"How about the inn?" Jennifer suggested.

Kerry smiled wryly. "I'm not sure I trust myself to be alone with you where there's a bed," he confessed. "But there's also a parlor in your suite, and an uncomfortable looking couch," he added humorously. "Maybe if we stick to the parlor . . ."

"You're on," Jennifer told him.

The inn was on a pleasant, tree-shaded street in Westerly. The charming main house was over two hundred years old and had been completely restored. The decorator in Jennifer admired the choice of wallpapers, trim colors and furnishings. In fact, she doubted she'd change a thing. It was perfect.

The suite Kerry had chosen for her was quiet and comfortable. Both the parlor and bedroom were spacious and nicely appointed. And the couch looked comfortable enough to sleep on, as far as she was concerned. To sleep on *alone*, she amended hastily. Large windows, framed by country curtains, looked out over a garden that was no doubt ablaze with flowers and blossoming shrubs in late spring and summer.

Jennifer wondered if she'd still be around Westerly and Watch Hill when spring swept away the last traces of a winter that had barely begun. There was a chance she might not be around long at all, should Kerry admit that he didn't plan to live in the Watch Hill mansion. He certainly seemed to be veering in that direction, and she didn't want to decorate the place unless she was doing it for him. She wanted to think of him as living in a setting she'd created, a setting that would suit him perfectly.

She turned away from the window, faced him and smiled. "This is really lovely. I doubt you could have found anything nicer—or more convenient."

Kerry didn't answer right away, and Jennifer caught her breath when she translated the expression in his eyes. He was looking at her with such naked longing that it jolted her. He quickly rearranged his expression, though, and smiled back at her. "Glad you like it," he said simply.

"I love it."

"There's a kitchenette, so you can fix coffee in the morning or have a warm snack when you don't feel like going out to dinner. The inn only serves meals on weekends this time of year."

"I'm not surprised."

"Anyway," he continued, "the suite across the hall is about the same as this. It's not quite as large, and it looks out on the street, so I thought you'd rather have this one. Josh's photographer will take the other one. As I understand it, she'll be coming up the first of the week."

Jennifer hesitated, then ventured, "Doesn't that depend?"

"Depend on what?"

"On you, of course. Take your coat off and sit down," she urged. "You take the armchair. I'll take the couch."

"Yes, ma'am," he agreed easily.

Jennifer glanced at his grinning face suspiciously.

"I promised," he reminded her.

She moved to the couch, trying to quell her rebellious emotions. If she was going to work successfully for Kerry, she needed to keep a much tighter rein on her feelings. But *was* she going to work for him?

She came directly to the point. "Kerry, our agreement as I understood it was for me to decorate the Watch Hill house as your permanent home. Am I right?"

"That's the way this started out, yes."

"But now you've changed your mind?"

"It isn't that I've changed my mind, Jenny," he said uncomfortably. "I just don't know. Being in the house with you yesterday and again this morning made me feel different about it. I told you, I simply can't see myself playing lord of the manor. Frankly, I think I'd make an absolute ass of myself."

"To hear you, you'd think that you ate peas with a knife," she muttered, "whereas actually you have the most impeccable table manners I've ever seen."

"I learned them the hard way," he reported grimly. "Lots of observation."

"So? We all learn by observing others. You're no different in that respect."

"I think you know what I'm saying."

"I think it's time you knocked that chip off your shoulder."

Kerry stood and wandered over to the window. With his back turned to Jennifer, he said, "I got rid of any chips that might have attached themselves to my shoulders a long time ago, Jenny. By the time I was in the army, all the old doubts and frustrations and fears were behind me."

"Were they really?" she queried skeptically.

"I don't like the way you say that."

"Then why don't you be honest with yourself, even if you won't be with me?"

He swung around. "I've been completely honest with you!"

"Kerry." She nearly added, *darling*. "Look, you may think you got rid of all your hang-ups, but it seems to me you still spend a lot of time torturing yourself."

"Only since I've met you," Kerry stated.

He couldn't add that way back in Georgia, ten years ago, it had been made abundantly clear to him that Jennifer Smith and Kerry Gundersen were light-years apart. It was a lesson that had been quickly learned and had clung to him ever since. When she'd walked into his Providence office, where ostensibly he'd been the one in command, she'd somehow stolen his show, though he knew she was unaware of that.

Ever since, he'd been only too conscious that Kerry Gundersen hadn't been good enough for Jennifer Smith, never would be good enough for her. He was convinced of that to the core of his being, even though he could imagine how she would deny it were he to come out and tell her so.

As it was, she was taking his comments in exactly the way he hadn't intended. "I'm sorry I'm the one who raked up a lot of painful memories for you," she said stiffly.

"I didn't mean that, Jenny."

"Never mind. Listen, Kerry, I worry about the way you keep edging into your past. Why don't you slam the door on it?"

He turned away again and studied a small tree that had a single brown leaf still clinging to a slender limb. She didn't know what she was saying, of course. She'd never had his kind of ghosts to lay to rest.

Maudlin, maudlin, maudlin! he told himself in disgust.

He turned back to her and said gently, "I don't blame you for being tired of hearing me talk about myself."

"That's not what I said."

"Okay." He sat down in the parlor's overstuffed armchair and stretched his legs. "Am I correct in my impression that you want me to guarantee to you that I'll live in the Watch Hill house once you've finished decorating it?"

Jennifer thought carefully, then said, "Yes, I guess I would like to have that guarantee from you."

"Can you understand that I simply can't promise you it would be my home forever?"

"Then why bother getting into the project at all?"

"Because I bought the property. I own it."

"Oh, it's 'property' now. And you feel you're stuck with it."

"Not at all. I'm sure I could easily resell it, but . . ."

"You want it, and yet you don't want it?"

"That about sums it up," he admitted ruefully.

After a moment of consideration, Jennifer said, "I think, with that attitude, it would be better to drop the whole thing. Close the house up and let it sit for a while. Maybe after a couple of months have passed you'll be able to come to a decision more rationally."

Kerry shook his head stubbornly. "No."

He was being downright exasperating! "I thought not being able to make up one's mind was supposed to be a feminine characteristic."

"Now you're being sexist," he teased.

"No, I'm simply trying to get you to face reality," she countered. "It would be foolish to begin major renovations in that house unless you want to keep it."

"Not true, Jennifer. Restoring the interior and sprucing up the outside will increase the value of the property and make it considerably more salable."

"Will you kindly stop referring to that beautiful home as 'property'? You sound like an entrepreneur, not the man who claimed he wanted to establish some kind of permanence in his life," she said crossly. "Anyway, I'm not interested in making that house more salable."

"Then just what is your interest in it, Jenny?"

"Damn it!" she exploded. "You know very well what my interest is!"

"Your temper's showing."

"Kerry, why? Why are you being so..."

He held up an imploring hand. "I know, so spare me. I think I also know what your interest in my house is. But spell it out for me once more, will you?"

"You told me you never had a real home. You always wanted a real home. I gathered you fell in love with the Watch Hill mansion and thought you'd want to live in it.

I thought that's why you'd bought it. And I wanted to make it into a real home for you, okay?''

As Jennifer's words tumbled out, she felt herself getting edgier and edgier and knew it would be easy to burst into tears. That was the last thing she wanted to do!

Kerry said gently, "Thank you."

"What are you thanking me for?"

"For being such a warm and generous human being, and for caring that much about my interests." As he spoke, Kerry was wondering how he could possibly keep his hands off Jennifer much longer. How he could refrain from taking her in his arms and kissing her passionately. He knew she was fighting to hold back her emotions, sensed that she could easily let the tears spill over. And he loved her for caring so much about making a home for him.

Suddenly his decision was made. "I won't renege," he said steadily. "In all honesty, I can't promise you I'll live in Watch Hill forever, but I can promise you..."

"Yes?"

"How long do I have to promise you that I'll live there in order to get you to do the job?" he queried, smiling.

She considered that. "A year," she decided. "It seems to me that one year would be a fair test period. After a year in that beautiful home—and it will be beautiful, I assure you—you should know what you really want to do with it."

"You've got yourself a deal."

Jennifer packed two suitcases and moved to Westerly the following Monday. Marta Brennan arrived the same afternoon, and Jennifer immediately took to her.

Marta was tall and thin, with a shock of black curls and eyes nearly as dark. She wasn't exactly pretty, but her personality and zest for life overflowed and took charge of her less than perfect features.

It was dusk when Marta arrived, and Jennifer suggested she cook a light supper for both of them. Over dinner Marta said, "Josh has told me so much about you."

Marta waited, and Jennifer suspected that Josh's photographer friend wished to hear her say something along the same line. Josh *had* spoken of Marta's professional accomplishments with unusual enthusiasm, she recalled. At the time, she'd thought she deciphered a certain undercurrent in his comments, but . . .

Cautiously she said, "Josh thinks very highly of you."

Marta laughed. "You don't have to hedge with me, Jennifer. Josh is the original Mr. Wary. No one knows that better than I do. I practically do somersaults every time I'm around him," Marta admitted ruefully, "and I don't think he even notices."

"Don't be too sure of that."

"I wish I weren't, Jennifer, because . . . well, I think Josh is a very special person. Somehow I get the feeling that some woman burned him a long time ago, and he honestly believes he can never fall in love again."

Marta slapped a hand over her mouth, her dark eyes wide with horror. Then she said, "Here I've just met you, and I'm telling you things about Josh that I've never said to anyone. And you're his sister!"

Jennifer smiled. "You can relax, Marta. I'm not about to report your confidences back to Josh. You should know, though, that Josh's problem doesn't really have much to do with women. He had his share of youthful romances, and he was semicommitted to a girl when he was in the Air Force Academy. But she didn't break his heart."

Marta looked puzzled. "Then what's his problem?" she asked. "Sometimes I think he comes very close to asking

me out, but he never does. As far as I've been able to de-
termine through the office grapevine, he never dates. And
believe me, the office grapevine is an extremely efficient
gossip machine. So if Josh does date anyone, he's incredibly secretive about it."

"Josh has had women friends," Jennifer conceded.
"The thing is, he's never allowed himself to get seriously
involved. He'd kill me if he knew I was telling you this,
Marta, but I'm rather surprised you don't realize what
Josh's problem is."

"You mean he's that sensitive about his leg?" Marta
asked incredulously.

"Definitely."

"But that's absurd. Josh is one of the most attractive
men I've ever met. He's pure dynamite—or he would be if
he'd let himself loosen up a little. At a couple of the office
parties, when he had a drink or two, he relaxed just enough
so it was easy to see the potential. Aside from that, every
time I've done a job for him, he's been the easiest person
in the world to work with."

"I'm sure he is," Jennifer agreed.

"And another thing about Josh," Marta went on, "he's
not given to flattery, like some men are. When he pays me
a compliment about a photograph I've taken, I know it's
for real."

"His handicap doesn't bother you?" Jennifer asked.

"Of course not. I feel sympathetic toward him once in
a while, but only because I can imagine what a bore it must
be for someone like Josh to have to clump around with a
crutch."

"I wish he'd see it that way," Jennifer mused softly.

After Marta had gone back to her own suite, Jennifer
thought about their conversation. She didn't want to let
Josh in for any traumatic experiences where women were

concerned, but she suspected that Marta really cared for him. Cared for him from the heart. If she could only get Josh to tear down the fence and welcome Marta's interest in him...

She was just out of the shower and slipping her nightgown on when Kerry called. As usual, her heart skipped several beats when she heard his voice.

"Did the photographer make it all right?" he asked.

"Yes, Marta's here. We had dinner tonight. She's a terrific person, Kerry."

"So Josh has told me," Kerry said. "So, suppose I pick up both of you at the inn tomorrow morning?"

"Were you planning on coming to Watch Hill?"

"I'd like to see Marta's first impression of the place," he said easily. "Also, I thought maybe she might want to get a couple of shots of the two of us conferring. Maybe out on the lawn, looking up at the house. Maybe in the dining room. That's up to her."

Kerry spoke casually, camouflaging his emotions. All day, sitting above Providence in his glass-walled office, he'd been thinking about Jennifer driving up from New York. Thinking about her moving into the inn at Westerly.

"I think that's a good idea," she said, surprising him. "For you to come out to the house in the morning, that is. Why don't we meet you there, though? You might want to get away before we do."

"I was going to suggest I take you two to lunch afterward," he said quickly. "I'd like to get acquainted with Marta."

Jennifer agreed with that, too. As he hung up the phone, Kerry breathed a sigh of relief. Then he made himself a whiskey and soda, hoping it might calm him and help him sleep, and sipped it as he watched the late news before turning in.

In the morning, the sun was shining. Kerry felt as if the old mansion was being given a golden benediction as he pulled up under the porte cochere. Marta was beside him. Jennifer was in back, having insisted that Marta sit up front so she'd get the best view of the scenery, all of which was new to her.

Marta stared at Kerry's house in awe. "It really is something," she breathed. "I expected it to be impressive, but I wasn't planning on having my eyes knocked out. What else can I say but . . . wow!"

While Kerry helped get her camera gear out of the trunk, Marta asked, "Would you two mind if I wander around the grounds by myself for a little while? I'd like to take a few preliminary photographs to get the feel of this setting before I start including people in the pictures."

Jennifer had hoped Marta would tour the house with them first. Every time she was alone in the mansion with Kerry, her emotions threatened to run away with her. But like Kerry, she only nodded to Marta's request.

"When you get cold, wander back and we'll have some hot coffee waiting," Kerry promised.

Inside, Jennifer discovered to her surprise that he was all business today. He'd brought along a briefcase. He placed it on the kitchen table—a venerable old oak table, the only piece of furniture in the room—and withdrew several architectural renderings.

"This is how I envision the kitchen," he began. "Nothing radically different here, except for knocking out one short wall to open up that corner. I thought of converting the pantry, which is behind that wall, into a walk-in refrigerator-freezer area. The two small storage rooms can serve as the new pantry. Then, if we scatter the other new appliances I'm planning on buying around the perimeter, there'll be plenty of room for a four-by-ten, waist-high work counter right in the center. You know, with a large chopping block, state-of-the-art gas burners and a stainless-steel exhaust hood. We'll really have a nicely organized, uncluttered kitchen for your 'center of operations.' What do you think?"

Jennifer was admiring the perfection of his renderings. His work was not only precise, it was exquisite. "These are terrific. And yes, I agree. I'm glad you didn't feel the whole area needed to be torn apart and turned upside down."

He smiled faintly. "Is that your impression of how architects usually work, Jenny?"

"I've seen it happen more than once," she admitted.

"Well, I don't feel that anything in this house should be torn apart or turned upside down," he assured her. "What we need here is not a brutal change for the sake of new concepts, but an enhancement of the quality designs that have withstood the test of time and proven themselves beautifully."

Kerry was surveying his drawings as he spoke, and, as she studied the strong line of his profile, Jennifer ached with love for him. At that instant he glanced up into her eyes, his own as deep a blue as the North Atlantic on this sunny November day. Jennifer swallowed hard, knowing her vulnerability to him was fully exposed this time. That it was she who was in danger of breaking their pledge, not he.

"Do you agree with my theory about the house, Jenny?" he asked gently.

"Yes, but I think you must be unique among architects."

"I wouldn't say that. We don't all want to change things just for the sake of change." He paused, then added, "Okay, if you agree, I think we can get started on the kitchen renovation almost immediately. I have an excellent contractor on tap, and he's ready to bring his crew in the moment I say the word. We'll need to have your colors, of course, for the appliances and such. Which reminds me, I'd like you to approve all selections along that line before I actually buy them. I'm going to deal with an outfit in Providence. We can meet there this Thursday, if you think you can be ready with your color schemes by then."

"I can't see why not."

The kitchen faced south, as did the adjoining pantry, the storage rooms and a laundry room. The two studio bedrooms faced south and east, respectively. Jennifer wanted to unite them all with a basic color theme.

"I like a cheerful kitchen," she said. "But your southern exposure means lots of sun, and it would be easy to make things too bright. Also, the vogue in appliance colors changes from year to year, so you should go with something pleasing, something you'll like living with regardless of style."

"What would you suggest?" Kerry asked.

"A pale lemon background, beige trim and copper-toned appliances." Jennifer laughed. "It will look considerably better than it sounds, believe me. Attractive yet subdued. Copper and lemon can be nicely matched with decorative terra-cotta pieces, copper pots on the walls, tile, baskets, even wrought iron. And if you would think of pushing out that large window over the sink, you could have some wonderful greenery there. The soft natural greens could be picked up in cushions on the kitchen chairs. I'd love to have this old oak table refinished. It's a gem, and we should find four chairs to go with it. Also, we might have an old-fashioned rocking chair painted in a moss green, and a braided rug that picked up all the colors. As a final touch, I'd like to see a wood stove installed, pale moss enamel.''

"How about the cat in front of the stove? Copper-colored, I presume?"

Jennifer looked up and saw Kerry's eyes twinkling. "Of course," she agreed lightly. Glancing out the window, she saw Marta strolling across the back lawn. Marta paused to gaze down at the water, then focused her camera. After taking several photographs, she turned toward the house, completely absorbed as she studied angle after angle, took shot after shot.

"Marta's really getting into it." Jennifer smiled.

"You sounded pretty into it, too."

"Totally," she told him. In fact, Jennifer had fallen in love with the house. Even though she tried to be an objective professional in choosing and coordinating the interior design of the mansion, she found herself pretending this was her house.

It was a dangerous pretense, she knew.

Later in the morning, Marta photographed Kerry and Jennifer on the front lawn. Kerry was holding his renderings while they both pretended to study them. Afterward, they moved to the dining room for another photo session, then to the foyer with its magnificent stone fireplace. As if by silent accord, Jennifer and Kerry avoided the curving stairway where their passion had first flared.

For lunch, Kerry took them to a charming year-round restaurant back in Westerly, where they feasted on linguica rolls and clam chowder.

Marta, disconcerted by the chowder, asked, "No tomatoes in it, just milk and potatoes?"

"Plus clams, clam juice, butter and spices," Kerry told her. "You're thinking of Manhattan clam chowder. This is the way chowder's supposed to be."

After only a few spoonfuls, Marta concurred.

Over a dessert of Indian pudding topped with whipped cream, Marta said, "I need to go back to New York tomorrow to finish up another assignment. I can come back up on Friday, if you think the work in the kitchen will have progressed to the point of warranting more photographs."

"Well, I'd say that if you've made plans for the weekend in the city, you might as well stay down there," Kerry answered. "I'm going to call my contractor later today, so my guess is the beginning of next week might be more productive from your point of view."

"That's fine with me," Marta assured him.

"I've been thinking of going down to the city for the weekend myself," Jennifer said suddenly. "Maybe I'll take the bus down, if I could drive back up here with you on Monday, Marta."

Before Marta had a chance to speak, Kerry said, "You can drive to New York with me, Jenny. And back, too, if you'd like."

"Were you already planning to go, Kerry?"

"I'm planning to now," he evaded.

Jennifer felt certain he was planning the trip for her sake. One inner voice told her to be careful, but another said, "Go for it!"

She decided to plunge further. She didn't know how Josh would react, nevertheless she said, "Do either of you have any plans for Sunday dinner?"

Both Kerry and Marta shook their heads.

"Then why not come over to Josh's apartment?" Jennifer dared to ask. "By then, I'll be in the mood to cook up something special."

Chapter Nine

"It would be nice if you consulted me before you set up dinner parties in my home," Josh said gruffly.

Jennifer was glad to set down the two heavy bags she had just carried from the corner grocery. She stared at her brother in disbelief. "What's with you?" she demanded.

Josh, leaning on his crutch, scowled as he surveyed the bags on the kitchen counter. "Maybe I had something else planned for tomorrow," he suggested.

"Did you?"

"Not exactly."

"So?"

"I'm not much for unnecessary socializing, that's all. Command appearances for the company at banquets and cocktail parties are bad enough."

Jennifer planned to spend the balance of the afternoon making a succulent bouef bourgignonne, which would marinate overnight. She put the meat to be cubed to one side and refrigerated the rest of the perishables.

Over her shoulder she asked, "Would your sudden antisocial feelings have anything to do with the fact that I asked Marta to join us?"

Dead silence answered her question.

She heard Josh's crutch thud and turned to see that he'd moved to the kitchen window and was staring out at the alley behind the building.

"Enjoying the view?" she taunted.

His indrawn breath hissed between his teeth. "You can be a real . . ." He stopped himself. "Actually," he said, "I love studying concrete."

"Of course you do."

Josh smiled sheepishly. "So I'm behaving like a clod," he admitted in an abashed way that made her want to hug him instead of chastising him further. "Okay, you're right as usual. When I think about Marta coming here for dinner, I begin to sprout feathers—chicken feathers!"

"Listen, Josh . . ."

He held up a restraining hand. "Please, Jenny," he said seriously, "I already know what you're going to say. You've said it before. It won't help to hear it again."

She could have cried for him. But she gritted her teeth and said, "What might help, then?"

"Nothing you can do anything about. Nothing anyone can do anything about."

She got out a butcher knife and a cutting board and began working on the meat. Carefully she said, "May I ask you a leading question?"

He grunted. "I've never known you to hesitate before."

"Well...suppose Marta would really like to get to know you better?"

"Why should she?"

"I think she does."

"What makes you think that?"

"Come on, Josh, must you be so difficult?"

"I don't think I'm being difficult, Jenny. I'm being realistic. Look, you've already asked her here, so there's no point in talking about it anymore."

"I could call her and say you're having an attack of social panic."

"Very funny."

As deliberately as possible Jennifer finished cutting up the meat, put the pieces into a bowl, covered the bowl, then put the bowl into the fridge. She was counting to ten in order to curb her mounting impatience with her brother. Long ago, damn it, Josh should have broken out of this shell!

"You *will* be here tomorrow, won't you?" she asked.

"Huh?"

"Tomorrow," she repeated, wanting to throttle him. "You'll be here, won't you? I told Kerry and Marta to come over around five. I thought we could have a fairly early dinner and then play four-handed Rummikub. I told them you and I play it frequently, and they want to learn."

"I'll just bet," Josh retorted skeptically. "Hey, no! Don't throw that wet sponge at me, Jenny. I'll behave." He actually grinned at her. "I'll be here," he stated quietly.

"Promise?"

"Promise."

Josh was definitely in evidence the next afternoon as five o'clock approached. Wearing dark slacks, a maroon turtleneck sweater and a plaid sport jacket, he looked terrific. He hung around the kitchen, snitching tidbits from the platter of hors d'oeuvres Jennifer fixed.

Though Jennifer was afraid he'd be tense, on the contrary, he seemed surprisingly relaxed. She had a sneaky feeling he was actually looking forward to having Marta in his apartment, now that the die had been cast.

Munching, he asked, "Is there anything I can do?"

"Yes. You can put these napkins on the coffee table."

At the precise instant Josh picked up the napkins, the doorbell rang. He promptly dropped them, and Jennifer suspected he would have dropped whatever he was holding, even the most valuable of the family heirlooms.

As she hurried to answer the door, she gave him one last long look and advised, "Calm down."

It was Kerry at the door, not Marta, so it was Jennifer's turn to go weak at the knees. Especially when she saw the bouquet of long-stemmed red roses he was carrying. Red roses . . . a symbol of love.

"They're beautiful, Kerry," she said, accepting the flowers shakily. "Why don't you hang your coat in the closet and head into the living room. I'll go put these in water."

She hurried back to the kitchen while Kerry shrugged off his overcoat and said hello to Josh. Jennifer took advantage of the interlude by trying to follow the advice she'd just given her brother.

A few minutes later, Marta arrived. Jennifer instantly realized that Marta had been wearing her working garb in Watch Hill—faded jeans, an old sweatshirt and a quilted parka that had seen better days. Now she was dressed like a fashion model in a deep red dress that did marvelous things for her coloring. Her black curls, such a wild mess in Watch Hill, were arranged in a trendy style held together by an elaborate gold clip. Intricate gold earrings dangled almost to her shoulders, and, with the right makeup, her dark eyes were downright sultry. Jennifer didn't blame Josh for losing his voice when he saw her.

The dinner went well. The first snow of the season fell beyond the picture window looking out over the Hudson. The winter weather outside and the warm candlelit ambience inside set a scene of delightful intimacy.

They decided to skip playing a game in favor of conversation in the living room, accompanied by demitasses of strong black coffee and slender liqueur glasses of Benedictine. Marta sat on the couch next to Josh. Soon they were chatting in low voices, prompting Kerry to push his armchair closer to Jennifer's.

"I'd say they get along well," he observed quietly, nodding discreetly in Josh and Marta's direction.

"This is a first for them, as far as meeting strictly socially is concerned," Jennifer confided in a whisper.

"Looks promising," Kerry whispered back.

"I hope so. I really hope so. I think Josh is very much attracted to her, and vice versa. But Josh is so . . ."

"Did I hear my name being spoken?" Josh called out.

"Kerry and I were saying that you should come up to Watch Hill and take a look at the mansion yourself," Jennifer ad-libbed.

"Well, maybe I will. Matter of fact, Marta was just suggesting the same thing," Josh admitted.

A moment later, speaking sotto voce, Kerry asked, "Jenny, do you always recoup so quickly?"

"Recoup?"

"Recover, whatever. You fibbed to Josh without even blinking an eyelash."

"I wouldn't exactly call that a fib," she objected.

"Okay, don't get excited. Sometimes I think you have the world's thinnest skin," he teased.

"You're a fine one to talk."

He flushed slightly but said only, "I've been told it's socially taboo to talk about religion or politics. Maybe, with the two of us, we should say religion, politics, or each other." He glanced toward the window. "The snow's coming down heavier. I think we'd better wait till morning to set our hour of departure for points north. Give them a chance to plow the highways."

"That sounds reasonable to me."

"Why don't I call you around nine, and we'll make a decision then."

"Fine."

An hour later Marta rose reluctantly and said, "I hate to break this up, but I should get going."

"So should I," Kerry said quickly. "Did you drive, Marta?"

"No, I took the subway. And I neglected to wear boots, of course. But no one warned me it was going to snow."

"I left my car in the hotel garage and came over in a cab," Kerry said. "I'll drop you off, if you like."

Marta laughed infectiously. "Well, I share a loft down in Soho with another photographer," she told Kerry. "The Essex House is miles closer, so I'd say I'll be dropping you off. Anyway, cabs are probably going to be hard to come by in this weather, so I'd be happy to share one with you."

There was laughter in parting and thanks for a marvelous dinner and evening. Kerry pressed Jennifer's hand but didn't kiss her, not even her cheek.

When the door closed behind their guests, Jennifer and Josh looked at each other. Jennifer couldn't believe the feelings that had come over her, watching Kerry go off with Marta. Not jealousy—it wasn't that—but definitely a very disquieting sensation.

Josh exhaled forcibly, then said, "So much for that."

Jennifer matched his frown. "What's that supposed to mean?"

"Nothing. They make a good-looking couple, don't they? He's so fair; she's so dark. They could pose for one of those TV ads for expensive cars," Josh added, giving his sister a wicked smile.

"Oh, shut up," she murmured crossly, then took out her frustrations on the kitchen clean-up.

In the morning, Kerry reported that a television advisory had said the roads were in pretty good shape, and he suggested they leave by ten if she could be ready.

Not only was Jennifer ready, she was waiting at the curb when Kerry pulled up in front of Josh's apartment building.

He looked tired; she felt tired. Fortunately, they were in equally uncommunicative moods. Somewhere between New Haven and New London, Kerry, said, "Hungry?"

"A bit."

He pulled off the highway and drove to a Chinese restaurant. Jennifer thought of the Chinese restaurant they'd eaten in the first time they'd driven from Providence to Watch Hill.

Over lunch another memory nagged her. She sipped her jasmine tea as she pinpointed it. Then she asked, "What did you ever do with your fortune?"

"My fortune?"

"The last time we ate in a Chinese place, the fortune in my cookie said that romance would move me in a new direction. But you wouldn't tell me what yours said. You folded it up and put it in your pocket."

"So I did," Kerry recalled.

"Do you remember what it said?"

"Every word of it."

"Well, what did it say?"

"That's classified."

"Come on!"

He shook his head. "I can't tell you. Maybe someday, but not now."

Jennifer sat back, narrowing her eyes as she surveyed him. "I don't believe you!" she said finally. "Certainly you're not that superstitious, are you?"

"About some things . . . maybe I am."

"What could that fortune possibly have said that you'd want to keep such a deep, dark secret?" she persisted.

"The only way I could answer that is by reading it to you."

"Reading it to me? You mean you still have it?"

He patted his breast pocket. "Right in here." He added tantalizingly, "I keep it close to my heart."

"Kerry!"

"Yes, Jennifer?"

"It's that important to you, but you can't tell me what it says?"

"No."

He softened the negative with a smile, but Jennifer still felt hurt. She tried to tell herself she was being silly, but it didn't work.

When they were outside again, the wintry landscape was white and smooth and beautiful, but the whole scene made Jennifer feel bleak and cold. Probably, she conceded silently, because she felt so bleak and cold inside.

Kerry seemed preoccupied, too, for the balance of their trip. As they approached Westerly, he said, "I'll drop you off and head on to Providence, if you don't mind. I'm running late."

"Oh?"

"George and I have a meeting at four with a client who's interested in having us design a large enclosed mall up in New Hampshire."

He didn't elaborate, and Jennifer didn't ask any questions, though it did occur to her that if Kerry started trekking to New Hampshire on a regular basis, it would interfere with the time he put in at Watch Hill. But that might be for the best, she mused. A long-distance separation would be a surefire way of reinstating and keeping their pledge.

"If we accept the commission, we won't get into it until spring," Kerry said, his words slicing across her thoughts. "Preliminary plans, of course, but nothing final until we've thoroughly researched a number of different aspects. Zoning laws, utilities, ground studies—things like that, most of which will fall within George's province."

Was he implying that he would be free to spend as much time as he wanted at Watch Hill, regardless of the New Hampshire venture? Jennifer didn't ask.

In Westerly, Kerry insisted on carrying her suitcase upstairs for her. He set it at the top of the landing, then said, "I'll call you in the morning."

"I was going to drive over to Watch Hill first thing," she told him. "Why don't I call you tomorrow afternoon, when I've finalized my thoughts about the kitchen colors. Then you could go ahead and order the appliances, and perhaps by the middle of the week your contractor can get started."

"Harry's already started," Kerry informed her.

"He has? I didn't know that." She was miffed, and she made no attempt to hide it. "You might have told me."

"I thought I had. I'm sorry I wasn't more specific. Anyway, Harry's crew started in the kitchen today."

Jennifer had agreed with Kerry's idea about converting the pantry into a walk-in refrigerator area, and with his plan to combine the two small storage rooms into the new pantry. To do that, a wall had to come down. Also, there was the business of opening up the large window over the sink. Kerry had thought that notion terrific and had quickly done a design, which he'd mailed to the contractor last week.

"If you like," he said, "I'll meet you at Watch Hill tomorrow morning so I can introduce you to Harry."

"Thanks," she murmured, "but I think I can handle that myself."

Kerry had started down the stairs, but he turned back and looked up at her. "Okay," he said evenly. "Why don't you call me at the office when you make your final decisions on the colors? I'd like you to go with me to select the appliances, or at least to choose them from catalogs. I have a patchwork sense of color."

Jennifer nodded her agreement. Kerry smiled briefly, gave her a quick wave and then was gone. She stared at the front door as it closed behind him and felt a sharp pang of loss, a brooding sense of dissatisfaction. She and Kerry simply had not been on the same wavelength today, not for a minute during their trip up from New York.

She unpacked, then decided she might as well face the music Kerry had orchestrated for her by driving over to Watch Hill and introducing herself to Harry Kominsky, the contractor.

She was getting into her car when the inn's red station wagon pulled into the space beside her. The lovely old hostel was owned by Cora and Ben Madison, with whom Jennifer had spoken only briefly. Now Cora climbed out of the station wagon and quickly approached Jennifer.

"I'm glad to have caught you before you went off," she said breathlessly. "Ben and I would like it if you'd have dinner with us one night."

"That would be very nice," Jennifer replied, surprised and pleased by the invitation. She'd immediately taken to Ben and Cora, both of whom hailed from Maine originally.

"How about tomorrow night?" Cora suggested.

"That would be great."

It was with a renewed sense of optimism that Jennifer started out for Watch Hill. She'd been feeling rather adrift, a shade lonely. Cora's invitation did much toward dissipating that feeling.

She felt even better after she'd met and talked with Harry Kominsky. He was an enormous man who looked as if he should have been a professional football player. Though not much over forty, he was almost totally bald, with twinkling blue eyes and a captivating smile. He introduced her to his crew, all young and weathered and healthy looking, and their greetings gave her a warm feeling, too.

This hadn't always been the case in Jennifer's dealings with construction workers on a job. Sometimes the men tended to disdain the "lady decorator." Occasionally she'd been treated like someone who was always in the way. But Kominsky and his crew made her feel like an important member of the team.

In less than a full day of work they'd already made strides. Harry explained each step he'd taken in detail and seemed eager for her approval. Jennifer gave it freely and knew she was going to enjoy working with the man.

That night she returned to Westerly feeling considerably more hopeful about the project. With work underway, there wouldn't be so much time for Kerry and her to worry about their personal relationship. She'd be free to devote herself to the mansion, free to supervise its conversion into the home of Kerry's dreams so he'd no longer have second thoughts about playing "lord of the manor," as he'd put it.

When that place was finished, Jennifer vowed to herself, he'd want to live there for a long, long time.

Dinner with the Madisons proved to be a very interesting experience. Jennifer discovered that she had more in common with Ben and Cora than she would have guessed. Cora was quite an artist and put her talent into wallpaper designs for a New Haven specialty shop. When Jennifer asked to see a sample of her work, the older woman rather shyly brought forth some absolutely beautiful selections with swatches of matching or contrasting fabrics. Though Jennifer was careful not to commit herself on the spot, she was delighted with what she was seeing and sure that some of Cora's creations would find their way into the decor of Kerry's home.

Ben was the chef in the family. He prepared a dinner with surprising nuances of flavor. Though only an experienced gourmet could achieve such taste subtleties, Ben modestly insisted it was "nothing."

As they lingered at the table drinking coffee, Jennifer's hosts confessed they were realizing a dream come true with this inn at Westerly.

"We'd been wanting to run a country inn ever since I can remember," said Cora, who was on the plump side, with a pretty, open face and curly, prematurely gray hair. Ben, in contrast, was tall and rawboned thin, with a prototypical "Down East" New England face.

"Ben's uncle left him a windfall, so we started scouting around," Cora continued. "We wanted someplace a mite warmer than Maine in winter, but we didn't want to go too far south, either. Coastal Rhode Island seemed like a perfect compromise for us, and I think other folks are drawn here for the same reasons we were. This past summer was our first season, and we did pretty well for newcomers to the scene."

"If you serve people dinners like the one you just gave me, you're going to be internationally famous." Jennifer groaned, having eaten more than her share of Ben's delicious meal.

A little later, she said good-night to Ben and Cora and trudged up the stairs to her suite. It was barely nine o'clock. As she opened the door to the parlor, she heard the phone ringing, and it was only then that she realized she'd forgotten to call Kerry about the kitchen colors.

He was annoyed. Disproportionately annoyed, Jennifer decided defensively. She wished the two of them didn't always have this beyond-the-norm effect on each other.

"I was beginning to wonder if you'd gone out on the town with Harry," Kerry accused.

"You are kidding, I presume," she countered.

"Only half kidding. I was about to call Harry, but I'd already told him I'd catch up with him in the morning."

"What actually happened," Jennifer said sedately, "was that the Madisons asked me to have dinner with them." She immediately wondered why she felt she owed Kerry an explanation for her whereabouts. "Anyway," she continued, trying to shine light on the small morass between them, "I assumed that Harry was the ultimate family man, so I doubt he'd try to date me."

"What makes you think Harry's the ultimate family man?"

"He certainly looks the part."

"Didn't anyone ever warn you that you can't judge a book by its cover?" Kerry asked impatiently, throwing her earlier words back up to her. "In fact, Harry's a bachelor."

"You're kidding!" Jennifer blurted, honestly surprised. She'd pictured the contractor living in a sturdy New England home with a wife who was a full-time homemaker and at least four cherubic youngsters.

"Why would I kid? I've known Harry for a couple of years. He's never been married and lives with an old aunt. I guess you'd never think this, either, but as I hear it, despite that girth, Harry cuts a mean swath on the dance floor. Fortunately, he finishes whatever job he's working on before he goes out and paints the town red. But I wouldn't be at all surprised if he suggested the two of you dabble around a bit together in the interim."

Jennifer muttered something unladylike under her breath, and Kerry chuckled. "I didn't know generals' daughters ever said things like that," he observed innocently.

"From your performance record, I'd say there's a lot you don't know about generals' daughters," Jennifer informed him coldly.

"I'll go along with that. But I guess it's going to be a while before I find out all these things I don't know." Hearing silence at the end of the line, he cleared his throat. "The pledge," he reminded her. "I think we did say it would go into effect once the job started, didn't we?"

"We should have put it into effect the first time we looked at each other," Jennifer sputtered.

"I can't believe you mean that, Jenny," he told her softly.

She didn't, of course. She would never regret what had happened between them that night in his apartment, though their long hours of incredible rapture had taken an odd kind of toll. There'd been a strain between them ever since, an edginess that wouldn't go away.

She heard Kerry saying, "Can you meet me in Providence tomorrow afternoon, say around two-thirty? If you'll come to my office, I'll have the appliance catalogs there so you can go over the colors. I'd suggest lunch or dinner, but unfortunately I'm tied up."

He sounded distressingly like an employer. And he acted the same way when Jennifer met with him the next afternoon and selected the things she wanted for the kitchen. He approved of all her choices with little more than a glance at what she was suggesting. She had the feeling, in fact, that his mind was on something else entirely.

From that point on, Jennifer became more and more involved with working directly on the house. She dug up tidbits of the home's history by interviewing a clerk at the town hall, an old-timer who remembered the previous owners very well. She researched period furniture and sought out area antique shops where potential pieces might be acquired. She shopped for paints, papers, artwork and bric-a-brac to enhance the various rooms. The list of things to be done seemed never ending, and the reasons to consult Kerry increasingly apparent.

"I told you right at the beginning that you have license to do whatever you want, buy whatever you wish," he reminded her one afternoon on the phone.

She'd found a spectacular cherry refectory table with twelve matching chairs at an exclusive Westerly antique shop. The set was perfect for the dining room but very expensive. Still, Kerry approved the choice and the price without even wanting to see it.

Normally, such a vote of confidence from a client would have given Jennifer a real ego boost. But hearing Kerry reaffirm this position was a letdown. Jennifer admitted to herself that she wanted him to participate more in what she was doing at Watch Hill. She wanted to see more of him personally. She knew all about the dangers involved, but that knowledge didn't obliterate her desire for him.

It was a relief when Marta came to Westerly the week before Thanksgiving. She planned to stay a few days and finish up her "before" photos of areas in the house where work had yet to start. Then she could turn her attention to "progress" photos of the kitchen and elsewhere.

Jennifer again fixed supper for them on Marta's first night at the inn, but when the meal was ready, Marta pleaded, "Do you suppose we could have another glass of wine before we eat?"

"Of course," Jennifer said agreeably. She was tired, as was Marta. It had been a busy day, first at Watch Hill and later here in the corner of the living room that she'd set up as her office. She was thankful that Kerry had had a private phone line installed for her. Otherwise, with the increasing number of calls relating to the project, she would have overtaxed the Madisons' small switchboard by now.

She poured a full glass of wine for Marta and half a glass for herself. Marta immediately took a long sip. Then her eloquent dark eyes filled with tears.

She set the glass down as the tears began rolling down her cheeks. "I'm sorry," she said, digging a Kleenex from her purse and dabbing furiously. "I guess all it took was a little juice of the grape to relax me enough to let go. That and being with you. The minute I met you I felt I'd found a friend."

"What is it, Marta?" Jennifer demanded automatically. "What's wrong?"

"Not what, but who," Marta said, her sobs subsiding. "It's Josh. After that dinner at his apartment, I thought maybe he was beginning to melt a little bit. But I was so wrong. Before, he was just cool to me. Now, whenever I stop by his office, he's absolutely aloof. Yesterday I got up my nerve and asked him if he'd like to go out for a drink when he was through for the day. I even intimated I had some things about the Watch Hill assignment I wanted to discuss with him.''

"What did he say?" Jennifer prodded.

"I've never been turned down flatter!" Marta wailed. "I mean, why does your brother have to act like that? I know it's crazy, but I have this weird feeling that deep down he's as attracted to me as I am to him. Why does he have to pretend he's carved out of stone?"

Jennifer listened silently as Marta poured out her tale of woe. She knew the answer, and Marta was right. It was indeed crazy. She and her new friend were both in love with men who were as strong as rocks—and just as immovable. Men who, for all their strengths, were incredibly vulnerable and labored under complexes that seemed unshakable. Totally different complexes, to be sure, but with the same result: they undermined the basic self-esteem necessary for a successful relationship.

As she contemplated this depressing concept, Jennifer decided that Marta, though currently stymied, probably had a better chance of winning Josh over than she did of ever having Kerry take her fully into his life.

Chapter Ten

"My mother still lives in Maine, and she's nearly ninety," Cora Madison said.

"Does she ever come to visit you?" Jennifer asked.

They were having a cold snap, and Cora had come upstairs to make sure Jennifer had enough heat in her suite. Jennifer had asked her to stay for tea.

Cora shook her head as she reached for another of the chocolate chip cookies Jennifer had baked the night before. Kerry hadn't called, and she desperately needed something to keep herself occupied. "No," she said. "Mum's arthritis keeps her down these days. Everyone in the family—my four brothers and sisters and I—is willing to pitch in and buy a mobile home for her in Florida. We've been trying to convince her she'd be more comfortable in a warmer climate, but she won't hear of making such a move. She's committed to Maine. Says too much hot weather addles the brain."

Jennifer chuckled. "Your mother sounds great."

"She is great," Cora agreed. "That's what makes me sad about Thanksgiving. Ben and I haven't told her we won't be able to make it up to Maine." She stopped abruptly and slanted a guilty glance at Jennifer.

"Do you mean to say that you and Ben aren't going to Maine because you've rented these suites to Marta and me?" Jennifer asked. She knew there were no other guests at the inn at the moment.

"Please, Jennifer," Cora implored, "I didn't mean it to sound like that, and you shouldn't take it that way."

"Well, it's true, isn't it?"

Cora thought for a second, then insisted, "When Mr. Gundersen got in touch with us and wanted to book the suites for six months, we were really happy about it. It was our decision, so don't you fret."

Six months! Kerry had booked these suites for a full six months and then nearly backed out of the project.

Even if he *had* backed out, he would have paid the Madisons in full, Jennifer conceded silently. Kerry was that kind of person. Also, he obviously had money to spare. He never talked about money—except to tell her she could spend whatever she wanted. He'd even given her a stack of signed checks for that purpose. Other than that, he'd once mentioned that he and his partner, George Sonntag, invested a percentage of their profits in markets George had faith in. Obviously, they paid off!

Cora was looking at her anxiously. "Please, Jennifer," she repeated. "Ben and I are delighted to have you here, and I don't mean just because we can use the rental income through the winter months. We both really *like* having you here. Marta, too. We took to Marta right away, just as we did to you."

The Madisons had entertained Jennifer and Marta twice at dinner since Marta had started commuting from New York to Westerly, updating her photographic diary of the progress being made at the mansion. That day Marta was in New York, not due to arrive back in Westerly until either late evening or first thing in the morning, so Jennifer had no opportunity to consult with her about the idea that suddenly struck her.

She plunged in anyway and said, "I have a suggestion. In fact, it's more than a suggestion. It's a request. You and Ben go to Maine over Thanksgiving, and let Marta and me inn-sit for you."

Cora started to protest, but Jennifer held up her hands to stop her. "Please, Cora, hear me out first, okay? I'm not suggesting this merely out of the kindness of my heart. I have a bargain to strike with you."

"A bargain?"

"Yes, exactly that. We'll keep an eye on the inn if you'll let us—if you'll let me, that is—use your kitchen to cook a Thanksgiving dinner."

When Cora looked slightly skeptical, Jennifer's words came in a rush. "Cora, this is something I really want to do," she insisted. "The more I think about it, the more I want to do it. It's been years since I've had an old-fashioned American Thanksgiving dinner. And your inn would be such a perfect setting for one. I'd like to ask my brother to come up from New York . . . which would mean I'd like to use one of your downstairs guest rooms. If any cleaning is needed, I'll be happy to do it myself."

"Honestly, Jennifer."

"Cora, I'm serious. You don't know how much it would mean to me to do this. I'd ask Kerry Gundersen, too. So there would be the four of us—Marta, Josh, Kerry and me. The reason I'd need a downstairs room is because my brother has a bad leg. He'd have a difficult time handling the stairs." She paused, out of breath.

After a moment of reflection, Cora said, "Ben would be more than happy to cook Thanksgiving dinner for you, Jennifer. What about the four of you sharing our Thanksgiving dinner with us? How would that suit you?"

"Well, to be honest, it wouldn't," Jennifer said frankly, softening her reply with a smile. "I've grown very fond of both you and Ben, Cora—I already consider you my friends. Maybe that's why I can admit to you that I want to play house this Thanksgiving. I've never really had a home all my own. My father was a career army officer, and we were always moving from place to place. We lived in some very lovely locations, but I was always aware that in a couple of years we'd be moving on."

"What about when you were married?" Cora asked, for she knew by now that Jennifer had been married to a Frenchman and had lived in Europe for years.

"Thanksgiving isn't a French holiday," Jennifer said dryly. "Anyway, most of the time Andre and I lived in an apartment in Paris."

The older woman smiled. "You *are* a surprise," she professed. "When you first came here...well, I would have said you were a high-powered career woman who didn't know how to boil an egg."

"Thanks a lot," Jennifer objected mildly.

Cora giggled. "Well, it's true," she said. "I wouldn't have expected that you'd give a fig about something like cooking Thanksgiving dinner."

"I'd give a whole crate of figs!"

With a smile, Cora promised, "I'll speak to Ben."

Jennifer suspected she'd won Cora over and guessed Ben would go along with his wife. She was right. As she was leaving for Watch Hill the next morning, Cora waylaid her to say that if she wanted to "mind the inn" and cook Thanksgiving dinner, it was fine with Ben.

Only then did Jennifer pause to wonder whether Kerry might have other plans for the holiday.

He'd been keeping his distance. He showed up unexpectedly at Watch Hill two or three times a week, sometimes when Jennifer was on the scene, sometimes when she wasn't, as Harry Kominsky would inform her later.

"The boss was here," he'd say.

Kerry had been right about Harry. The contractor did make a few good-natured attempts to get Jennifer to go out with him, but he took her diplomatic refusals in stride. Evidently, he'd gotten her message and wasn't bothered by it. Several days had passed since he'd come up with any suggestions, but he still worked closely with her, still smiled affably, still treated her like the important member of the team she was. Jennifer hoped Harry would leave things that way. She enjoyed working with him.

The day Cora told her she could have the inn for Thanksgiving, Jennifer spent more time than usual at the mansion, hoping Kerry would appear. Marta was photographing the upstairs, still in the "before" stage, while the downstairs rooms gradually took shape.

She'd spent the last week concentrating on the huge drawing room. The walls were now a pale shade of gold, the high ceiling just a tone darker. She had dared to attend an art auction one weekend and had purchased two magnificent seascapes, which now flanked that room's large brick hearth. They were illuminated by recessed ceiling spotlights, a suggestion of Harry's.

Kerry showed up one day with an incredible acquisition of his own—a full-size concert grand piano that had once belonged to the house during its golden era. It was an early vintage, the workmanship on the wooden cabinet exquisite. Every time she looked at the instrument, Jennifer commended Kerry's good fortune, not to mention his good taste. Whatever he might think, he had excellent taste. She discovered that anew whenever they got down to the details of decorating and furnishing. If only Kerry believed in himself.

The piano was featured in one corner of the huge room. To balance it, Jennifer carefully positioned her purchases from an estate sale in Connecticut: two tapestry-covered sofas, plus a number of parlor chairs, all in excellent condition, their original upholstery beautifully preserved. Pale oak end tables and coffee tables completed the setting, providing a nice contrast to the burnished dark wood floor.

The result was that while the drawing room was formal, it had a lived-in look. The soft, warm colors of the furniture she'd chosen invited guests to sit down and relax. When the floor-to-ceiling dusty-rose drapes were hung, the room sparked to life.

Only one more thing was needed, Jennifer thought, admiring the results of her work from the wide doorway that led in from the foyer. An Aubusson rug she'd seen not long ago in a New York gallery. It was outrageously expensive, but she'd actually cut corners by her careful estate-sale shopping.

Maybe, she decided, I should splurge. Then she wryly reminded herself that it was Kerry's money she'd be splurging with, not her own.

That afternoon, she hung around while Marta photographed the drawing room from numerous angles. The two had decided to go out for dinner before heading back to the inn, and Jennifer kept hoping that Kerry would appear. He didn't.

The letdown was terrible. By the time they reached the pub-style restaurant they wanted to try, Jennifer was feeling downright morose. She ordered Scotch on the rocks, downed it with uncharacteristic haste and ordered another. At that, Marta cast a skeptical glance at her.

"What's bugging you?" she demanded.

"What do you mean?"

"You don't usually go for two stiff drinks in a row," Marta pointed out. "That's more my style when the problems seem overwhelming. Still, two drinks is my limit." She added, "Fortunately, I'm learning to live with my present problem, or I'd be a candidate for AA."

"Josh, you mean?"

"Your dear brother, yes. I think he's decided to become a human glacier. But let's not talk about me. Not, at least, until we've done some talking about you. What is it, Jennifer?"

"Kerry," she admitted bleakly.

"Aha!" Marta exclaimed in triumph. "I wondered when you'd drop his name. I'm not a nosy person, generally speaking, but I have been wondering why the great man so seldom looms up at Watch Hill when you're around."

Jennifer stared at the ice cubes in her nearly empty glass. "I guess you could say he doesn't want to run into me," she muttered.

Marta snorted. "That's crazy. Whenever I'm around the two of you, I'm afraid I'll be electrocuted, the current's so strong! I mean, there's more than an obvious attraction going on here, Jennifer. Anyone could see that. Maybe I'm telling tales out of school in saying this about your eminent client, but Kerry's so plainly crazy about you that he lights up every time he sees you."

Jennifer laughed weakly, polished off her drink and beckoned the waitress to bring her another. Alarmed, Marta cautioned, "Hey! You're driving, remember?"

"I'll drink a lot of black coffee."

"That's no cure for too much alcohol, dummy," Marta pointed out affectionately. "You know, I'd like to think that one day you'll be my sister-in-law...."

Jennifer's eyes widened. "You're *that* serious about Josh?"

"Yes, I'm that serious. But I realize I may have to climb a range of mountains higher than the Himalayas before I can get through to him." Marta drew a deep breath. "Okay, I'll risk the question. You're equally crazy about Kerry, aren't you?"

"God, yes." Jennifer nodded, her eyes suddenly filling with tears.

"Then what's the problem? I asked Josh if Kerry was married. He said he's pretty sure he never has been. You've been free for years, and Kerry's eligible. He's also about the world's handsomest man—except for Josh. Great sense of humor. Fun to be with. Rich in the bargain." Marta spread her hands wide. "What more could a girl ask for?"

"Nothing," Jennifer said shortly. "But you neglected the all-important fly in the ointment."

"Oh?"

"Kerry's not in the marriage market. You've heard of confirmed bachelors. Kerry's worse. He's taken a private vow to stay single until the sun freezes."

Marta shrugged. "A lot of men try that route," she stated diffidently. "All it takes is the right woman to make them change course."

"Not in Kerry's case. This is something...deep with him." For a treacherous moment, Jennifer nearly told Marta about Kerry's problem—an identity crisis that could never be resolved. She bit back the revelation. Even too much Scotch, she vowed, wouldn't loosen her tongue to that extent.

And, she had had too much Scotch. She was barely into her third drink but realized she was fuzzy. Worse, she was afraid that if she ate anything, it would make her sick. She picked up her handbag and mumbled apologetically, "I don't think I can manage dinner, Marta, so I'd better be getting along. I don't like to leave you like this, but . . ."

Marta picked up her own handbag and placed a bill on the table to cover their tab. "You're crazy if you think I'm going to let you drive home," she said. "I'll speak to the manager about leaving your car in the parking lot overnight. He can ask the local cops to keep an eye on it, and we'll pick it up on our way back to Watch Hill in the morning."

Jennifer was not in the mood to argue. She subsided meekly into the front seat of Marta's car and, at Marta's insistence, kept the window partially open. The cold November air was like a slap in the face. By the time they reached the inn, she felt considerably restored.

Nevertheless, she was glad they didn't encounter either Ben or Cora on their way in. Marta kept a steadying hand on her arm all the way up the stairs. Jennifer started to protest but decided to let well enough alone. She fumbled for her key, then let Marta open the door of the suite for her.

On cue, the phone rang. Marta crossed the room and picked up the receiver. "Hello?" she said. "Yes, she's here. But I think it might be better if you talk to her a little later on. Or maybe tomorrow."

Jennifer knew it was Kerry, started to say that she could talk to him right now, then collapsed into the nearest armchair and stared helplessly at Marta.

After hanging up, Marta said briskly, "I think we'd better get you into bed. Then I'm going to make you some hot soup."

Jennifer wouldn't have believed she could handle soup. But with the warm food in her stomach, she began to feel better.

Marta placed their empty dishes in the sink, then came back and perched on the foot of the bed. "Well," she observed with satisfaction, "you're beginning to look a bit more human. For a while there, you looked more like wax."

"Thanks a lot . . . for everything," Jennifer told her.

"Well, tell Josh what a great Florence Nightingale I am," Marta suggested. "No, on second thought, don't tell him. He probably hates nurses."

"Marta?"

"Yes?"

"Did Kerry want me to call him back?"

"He didn't say to, so I imagine he'll get in touch with you tomorrow."

"What did he want, do you know?"

"He didn't say. Look, Jennifer, try to get some sleep. One reason the whiskey hit you was because you're exhausted. You haven't been eating properly, you run around all over the place doing eight jobs at once, you don't get enough sleep, you worry too much . . ."

"You sound like my mother," Jennifer complained.

"Never mind that. What I'm saying is true. Give yourself a break, huh? Kerry's house is getting more beautiful every day. That's what you're worried about, isn't it? Well, stop worrying! When you get through with that house, it's going to be perfect. The only thing Kerry Gundersen will need in it is you!"

Jennifer felt in her bones that Kerry would come to Watch Hill the next day. She was on the phone, talking with the gallery in New York where she'd seen the Aubusson rug, when Kerry walked into the upstairs bedroom where she'd set up a temporary on-location office.

"Sorry, but that's definitely too much," she was saying as he loomed up before her.

"What's too much?" he demanded when she hung up.

"There's a rug I want for the drawing room, but they're asking top dollar for it."

"Is it worth it?"

"Yes, but—"

"Then buy it," he ordered sharply.

For a moment, there was silence. Then Jennifer said, "You gave me carte blanche to spend your money. That doesn't mean I intend to squander it."

"If you think the rug in question is the right one for the drawing room, then it's the rug we should have," Kerry stated stubbornly. "Everything you've done to that room is perfection. Each piece of furniture looks as though it's been lovingly handed down from one generation to the next." He added dryly, "I do appreciate your buying those seascapes rather than fake ancestor portraits, though. They're very beautiful paintings, incidentally."

"Thank you," Jennifer said curtly.

There were two straight-backed chairs in the room. She was sitting in one, at the card table that served as her desk. Kerry pulled up the other and sat down. Trying to busy herself with an assortment of papers, samples and folders so that she wouldn't have to look at him, she decided card tables weren't nearly as wide as she'd thought. Kerry was much too close to her.

"Will you buy the rug?" he asked abruptly.

"I think if I wait a couple of days they'll lower the price by a few hundred dollars."

"Suppose someone else buys it in the meantime?"

"That's a chance you take."

"Buy the rug," he commanded.

"Is that an order, Mr. Gundersen?"

She did look up at him now, a surge of temper jolting her like a shot of adrenaline.

"Maybe you need a few orders," he growled.

She bristled. "Are you implying you don't like the work I'm doing here?"

He shook his head, his intense blue eyes centered squarely on her face. "Now, why would I say that when every time I discover something new you've done, it takes my breath away? I knew the house had potential, but I didn't envision things the way you have. What you've done here has exceeded all my expectations."

"Would you care to elaborate on that?" She was still tired, still upset with both herself and him.

"Not particularly, unless you really want me to," Kerry rebuked gently. "You're giving me a home, a background. You're even coming damned close to making me feel I belong here. That's what I'd hoped could happen, but I didn't honestly expect it would. Anyway," he added rather grimly, "that isn't why I came over here this morning."

"Oh? Then what is?"

"I wanted to find out what was wrong with you last night. Marta's working in the kitchen again. I stopped and talked with her for a couple of minutes. I'd say you've found a real friend there. She's pretty closemouthed where you're concerned, but she admitted the problem last night was that you'd had too much to drink."

Jennifer's temper flared again. "Marta told you that?"

"Not in so many words. I read between the lines, and it worried me like hell. Don't you know better than to drink and drive?"

She glared at him. "I didn't drink and drive. Marta drove me home. And I don't like the implication that I was drunk. If that's what Marta said . . ."

"Marta didn't say that," Kerry corrected. "She said you were dead tired, you had a couple of drinks and they hit you. That can happen to anyone, Jenny. No one's condemning you for anything. She didn't come out and say what I'm about to get into, either. I figured it out for myself. Obviously, you were upset about something. You were discouraged . . . which makes me feel you've been holding out on me. If anyone's been giving you any grief, you should come to me."

Was he thinking about Harry Kominsky?

"No one's been giving me any grief," Jennifer said steadily. "You guessed right about Harry, though. He did ask me out a few times, entirely good-naturedly. I told him no, and he was very graceful in being refused."

Kerry couldn't repress a smile. "I know," he admitted. "He told me."

"Does everyone around here tell you everything?"

"Far from it," he said ruefully. "You, for example, tell me almost nothing at all."

"I haven't seen much of you lately, have I?"

"There's usually a phone close at hand. If you wanted to talk to me, or see me, all you had to do was pick it up and dial. If I haven't been here, I've been at the office or my apartment."

"Are you saying that you've been waiting to hear from me?"

"I've been hoping to hear from you," he said. "There's a difference. If you've had any problems involving this place, I wish you would have communicated them to me."

"There haven't been any problems."

"Well, I'm happy to hear that. So what's wrong?"

"Must something be wrong?"

"I'd say so. When you're running yourself to exhaustion for no reason, when you feel so low you decide to drown your sorrows in booze, something must be getting you down. It isn't Josh, is it?"

"Why should it be Josh?"

"I know you care a lot about him, and he's been awfully moody lately. I had lunch with him in New York the other day. He was . . . preoccupied, shall we say?"

"You had lunch with him?"

"I was in New York on business. Whenever I'm in New York on business, I call Josh. He wasn't his usual self, but of course he didn't say why."

"Josh needs to take a good look in the mirror," Jennifer said disgustedly. "He needs to get over this little problem he has with women," she added, looking away.

To her surprise, Kerry chuckled. "Marta's a pretty determined young lady," he observed. "I have the feeling she'll hold the mirror for him pretty soon."

And who will hold the mirror for you?

Jennifer's gaze brushed Kerry's face as she posed that silent question. Then she closed her eyes, because if she looked at him any longer, she knew she'd crumble.

"You're awfully pale, Jenny," he said abruptly. "Are you sick?"

"No," she said quickly, opening her eyes. "No, I'm not sick."

"Look, you're acting as if there's a race on to get the house finished. You've been working less than a month—accomplishing miracles, if you ask me. But will you kindly slow up the pace in the interest of your health . . . and my sanity?"

"Why your sanity?"

"Because having you miserable bugs me more than anything I've ever run across before," he admitted simply. "I...care a great deal about you, Jenny. I hate to see you like this, especially when I think I'm the one to blame. It makes me feel like an ogre. I'm not interested in having you achieve some kind of track record here. What I want to see is the end result. You could take a year to accomplish that, as far as I'm concerned. Two years. I don't care about the time involved."

Jennifer heard his words, but her mind had stopped listening when he'd said, "I *care* a great deal about you, Jenny." For a telltale instant, she'd thought he might say *love*.

Chapter Eleven

I t's a crazy idea," Kerry stated bluntly.

Jennifer's heart sank. She had expected an entirely different reaction when she invited him to Thanksgiving dinner at the inn.

"Crazy," he persisted. "Weren't we talking just this morning about your working too hard? Didn't we agree you need to take things easier, get more rest? And now you want to put on a feast and do all the work yourself. That doesn't make sense, Jenny."

Kerry had reminded her that there was always a phone nearby. He'd said that he'd always be there should she call for him. So, after returning to the inn late that afternoon, she'd dialed his office. When she'd asked for Mr. Gundersen, his secretary had politely informed her that he was in conference and could not be disturbed. When she'd identified herself, the woman had quickly asked her to hang on.

A moment later, she'd come back on the line to say, "Will you give me your number, please? Mr. Gundersen says to wait where you are, and he'll return your call as quickly as he can."

Kerry was true to his words. A minute later, he'd called back.

Now, after protesting her holiday plans, he suggested, "Why don't I take us all out to dinner somewhere on Thanksgiving?"

At least he hadn't made other plans. Chalking up a small victory, Jennifer stated resolutely, "I don't want to go out on Thanksgiving, Kerry. I want to cook dinner here. I can't think of a lovelier setting for Thanksgiving than this inn... except maybe your house at Watch Hill."

That slipped out.

"Okay, maybe next year we can have Thanksgiving at Watch Hill," Kerry said gruffly.

It was the nearest thing to a long-range commitment he'd made to her, Jennifer realized giddily. She restrained herself with the reminder that it had been a casual statement, nothing more.

"Next year's a long way off," she reminded him. "This year I want to grab a lovely opportunity. Kerry, it's been years since I've had a family Thanksgiving."

"I've *never* had a family Thanksgiving," he replied glibly. "Anyway, I'm not part of your family."

That hurt. "Marta's not part of my family, either," she said defensively.

"Well, maybe one day she will be, if she can convert Josh to her way of thinking."

But you'll never convert me. He didn't come right out and say it, but he couldn't have made himself clearer.

Jennifer fought back a wave of sorrow and frustration. She gritted her teeth. Damn it, she wasn't about to beg

Kerry Gundersen to share Thanksgiving dinner with her. Let him eat in solitary bachelor splendor, she decided vehemently.

With finishing-school politeness, she said, "I'm sorry you won't be able to join us, Kerry. Sorry I interrupted your conference, too. I won't take up any more of your time. Good luck on whatever you're working on."

Silence rang in her ears. Then Kerry growled, "That sounds like some kind of farewell speech."

"I just wanted to let you go, that's all."

"Do you want to let me go, Jenny? Is that what you want?" The chill had left his voice, but the heat that replaced it seemed tinged with anger. "When you speak in that tone," he added, "you sound exactly like the general's daughter I met ten years ago. So damned polished, so damned polite." He waited a few seconds, then said, "Well? You haven't answered my question."

"I was speaking of our hanging up," Jennifer told him, aware that her pulse was beginning to pound.

"I was speaking about something else. You baffle me, do you know that?"

"No."

"You *should* know it." His laugh was bitter. "I used to have a one-track mind, at least when it came to my work. Nothing and no one could divert me from the job at hand. Now my powers of concentration are shot. When you called... well, there was no way I could have put off calling you back. Fortunately, George has all his marbles, because at times I certainly feel I've lost a sackful of mine."

"I'm sorry I called, Kerry."

"I don't want you to be sorry you called. I told you to call me whenever you wanted me for anything. Ever since you moved to Westerly, I think I've had one ear on twenty-four-hour duty, listening for the phone to ring. But—" He broke off, then muttered something short and not at all sweet. Into the phone, he said, "Excuse me, Jennifer, I do have to go. Seems our client has a plane to catch, and there are a couple of details we have to finish before he leaves." He hesitated. "Shall I call you later?"

"No, there's no need." Jennifer had to force herself to make that statement. She added quickly, "Anyway, Marta's cooking supper in her suite tonight, so I'll be over there."

"I'm glad it's Marta, not Harry," he said quietly.

He sounded both weary and whimsical saying that, and the sudden urge to be next to the man she loved, the need to feel his warmth and strength, became so overpowering that Jennifer wanted desperately to ask him to come to her tonight.

She didn't let herself. The next move, she warned herself, had to come from him.

"I'm not going to ask you this again," she told him. "Do you or don't you want to come to the inn for Thanksgiving dinner?"

He groaned. "When you put it that way," he conceded, "what else can I say but yes? Of course I want to spend Thanksgiving with you. So much so, I wonder where I ever got the strength to say no in the first place."

"Thank you," she said softly. And as she hung up the receiver, she was smiling.

Jennifer sat at the table in the inn's big old-fashioned kitchen and went over her menu with Marta one last time.

"Cranberry-orange relish—that's done and in the fridge," she mumbled. "The sweet potatoes are ready to be candied—I can do that tonight. The creamed onions and the broccoli casserole I still have to do. I think the pumpkin pies came out well, and I also made a mince-meat pie, because that's Josh's favorite.''

"Speaking of Josh, how's he getting here?'' Marta asked.

"Kerry's going to pick him up at the Providence airport Thanksgiving morning, and they'll drive down here together.''

"Blast Kerry,'' Marta muttered.

She was sitting across from Jennifer, sipping tea and periodically asking if there wasn't something she could do in preparation for their feast. Each time she posed the question, Jennifer assured her there would be plenty for her to do the following day.

For herself, Jennifer was psyched to get up at six in the morning, stuff the enormous turkey she'd bought, then place the bird in the oven. Once the turkey was in, she could concentrate on the other dishes. Then she and Marta could set the table.

"Kerry sent a centerpiece for the table,'' she told Marta abstractedly. "I put it in the pantry. It's a blend of fall colors fashioned around three candles in amber glass holders. Really lovely.'' She paused, having finally registered her friend's comment. "Why do you want to blast Kerry?''

"Because I would have liked to pick up Josh at the airport myself.''

"But Kerry's right there in Providence.''

"I know, I know.'' Marta sighed. "Must you always be so practical?''

"I don't think I'm especially practical,'' Jennifer protested, a glint of mischief in her eyes. "I just think it would be foolish for you to drive all the way up there, given the circumstances.''

"Oh, would it?" Marta countered. She noted Jennifer's teasing glance and had to smile. "Okay, you win," she said.

"Tantalize my brother a little bit," Jennifer advised. "If he has to wait till he gets here to see you, the anticipation should make him all the more eager."

"Josh, eager to see me? That'll be the day."

Jennifer remembered Marta's glum conclusion when Josh and Kerry arrived at the inn late the next morning. Marta, she instantly decided, was wrong. Josh was very eager to see her, though he concealed it quite well. Still, knowing Josh as well as she did, Jennifer diagnosed that he was having a hard time keeping his emotions in check.

He kissed Jennifer. Then, all of a sudden, Marta was standing right in front of him, looking up at him. Josh's mouth twisted in a funny little way, Jennifer saw. But without missing a beat, he bent and kissed Marta square on the lips. Marta actually swayed, and for a minute Jennifer was afraid she was going to sink straight to the ground from shock.

Josh recouped first. He glanced around quickly and observed, "Hey, this place is great! Has it ever been used in a movie? It should be."

"Ben and Cora would be pleased to hear that," Jennifer told her brother. Then she turned toward Kerry, who was standing off to one side.

"Kerry?"

His eyes met hers, and a whole new current swirled between them as he answered huskily, "Yes?"

"Josh has room three in the west wing, right down that hall. Your room is number four, just down from Josh's. If you want to stash your bags, we can all have some coffee and quiche."

"Quiche, on Thanksgiving?" Josh queried.

"That's all you're getting until dinner," Jennifer informed him.

By then, the aroma of roasting turkey permeated the house. The dining-room table had been set with the Madisons' best china and glassware, which Cora had removed from a locked cabinet and insisted Jennifer use. Kerry's centerpiece was exactly right, the perfect touch for the soft apricot damask tablecloth.

Jennifer had placed bunches of colorful chrysanthemums all around the living room, where, during the summer season, guests mingled and enjoyed their complimentary continental breakfast, featuring Cora's homemade blueberry muffins. The copper accessories gleamed, the country-style lamps gave off a warm glow and the hearth was set up for a fire, come evening.

Kerry had been taking it all in. When Jennifer headed for the kitchen, he followed her and said, "I can't get over what you can do to a place."

"We'll have the quiche out here at the kitchen table," she murmured absently. Then she looked at him curiously. "I haven't done anything here, Kerry. Cora and Ben made the inn what it is."

He shook his head. "You've given it your special touch, with the flowers, the table setting..."

"You should get credit for that," Jennifer cut in. "Thanks for the centerpiece, by the way. It's really lovely."

"So are you," he said softly. He moved closer and rested his hands on Jennifer's shoulders. "This," he whispered in her ear, "is the hello kiss I didn't give you at the door."

His lips descended to touch hers, setting off an instant earthquake inside her. Time stood still, space lost dimension as his kiss began gently. But the taste of him, the masculine scent of his skin, excited Jennifer's passion. She returned his kiss fervently, and Kerry responded, their mutual longing threatening to build into an explosion.

Finally Jennifer forced herself to pull away from Kerry ever so slightly. He took the cue and released her. They stood mere inches apart from each other, their faces flushed, their breathing ragged.

"I...I have to organize the dinner," Jennifer managed.

Kerry flashed her a wicked grin. "So you're still insisting on playing house, huh? I said I could take us all out to dinner, you know."

"No way, mister."

Later, as she let him baste the turkey, finish the creamed onions and sample the tiniest wedge of pumpkin pie, Kerry said, "Thanks for persisting about this, Jenny. I'll never forget today."

"Come on," she chided, determined to keep them from plunging into devastating emotional depths, "the day is just beginning. The feast won't be ready for another hour."

"I've been feasting in a different way all the while I've been here with you," he told her.

He was standing a few feet away, and Jennifer looked at him and smiled. She'd tied one of Ben's big white aprons around his waist, and he was awaiting her next instruction, holding the wooden spoon with which he'd just stirred the creamed onions. She had on a floral-sprigged cotton pinafore apron that belonged to Cora and was much too big for her. But by her own admission, she wasn't the neatest of cooks, and she didn't want to spot her rust-colored wool dress.

To Kerry, no woman in the world had ever looked more beautiful, or half as desirable, and the words he'd been holding back for what seemed an eternity to him slipped out. "I love you, Jenny," he said quietly.

Jennifer had been stirring the sauce for the broccoli casserole. She promptly dropped the spoon into the pot and, in trying to fish it out, scorched her finger. Kerry heard her exclamation, saw what she'd done and quickly got an ice cube out of the fridge. He was applying it to her finger when he heard the thump of Josh's crutch. He didn't know whether to resent the interruption or welcome the reprieve.

He had never intended to tell Jennifer he loved her. Saying those words would open a door he didn't want opened. All along he'd thought of Watch Hill and the renovation of the mansion as an interlude in his life that would forever remain precious beyond all price because Jenny had been part of it. But it was an interlude, nothing more. He had never intended to fall deeply, irrevocably in love with her. He'd known deep inside from the very beginning that loving her would lead only to heartache.

He remembered feeling powerless to halt the passion that had flowed between them, first on the stairs in the mansion and later in his apartment. Then, as the memory of their magical night together swept over him, he admitted to himself that he'd been avoiding Jennifer ever since. After that night, their relationship had stopped being merely a matter of chemistry. That's when he'd started to run scared, certain that it would be best to let Jennifer go.

Now he'd slipped. Slipped badly.

He tried to cover his confusion by searching for a better way to soothe Jennifer's finger. "Anyone who cooks as much as Ben Madison does should have an aloe plant around," he proclaimed. "That'd take the sting away."

It was Josh who found a first-aid kit in the pantry behind the kitchen. Inside was a tube of ointment reputedly good for burns. Josh dabbed the ointment on his sister's finger, then topped it with a bandage.

At that, Jennifer said, "Okay, enough fussing. There's still a lot to do before we can sit down and feast."

Marta shooed both men out of the kitchen. Kerry welcomed a pre-dinner Scotch with Josh while Marta and Jennifer finished getting things ready.

The dinner was an unqualified success. The turkey, stuffing, vegetable dishes, gravy and cranberry sauce were so delicious that the pies were barely touched. Later, the four settled around the fire, sipping coffee and letting the holiday laziness take over.

For the first time in his life, Kerry began to feel that he was really part of something. Part of this scene. Part of a family setting. He listened to Josh and Jennifer quibble as only siblings can, each taunting the other with embarrassing childhood anecdotes. Marta chimed in with tales of her own childhood. She was the only girl in a family of five children and maintained that her four brothers had eternally persecuted her. "In fact, they still do," she admitted, shaking her head.

Kerry remained silent, a smile curving his lips as he sprawled contentedly on the rug before the fire. And only Jennifer knew why.

It was nearly midnight when they began talking about calling it a night. Meantime, they'd partaken of a late-night snack of turkey sandwiches, hot cocoa and pie.

Josh, snitching a last piece of turkey, observed complacently, "This is always the best part of Thanksgiving."

"My brothers used to pick off all the good stuff before my parents or I had the chance," Marta put in.

"And Josh always gets to the crispy skin before I can," Jennifer revealed. "Whenever there was hired help, Josh somehow managed to get them on his side."

Josh chuckled. "Once Dad made general, we usually had a noncom assigned as our houseman. I remember when Dad was stationed out at the Presidio in San Francisco, we had this Mexican sergeant assigned to us. He used to put hot sauce on the turkey sandwiches he fixed for himself. He gave me a taste one time, and I damned near burned the roof of my mouth!"

Jennifer flinched at her brother's reference to a noncom. She didn't dare look at Kerry, knowing how he felt about the gaps between certain military ranks.

Marta, immersed in her own reflection, said, "I used to love drumsticks, but do you think I ever got one in my house? The first thing I did once I had my own apartment was cook a turkey and eat both drumsticks. Nowadays, on those rare occasions when I cook a turkey, Stan hovers around and pesters me for the drumstick just like my brothers used to."

"Stan?" Josh inquired.

"My roommate."

"Your roommate?"

Now it was her brother Jennifer didn't dare look at. She could hear the frost edging his voice.

"Yes, Josh. Remember, I told you I share a loft in Soho with another photographer?"

"You didn't say the other photographer was a man."

"You never asked," Marta said sweetly.

"Well, I assumed it was a woman."

"Don't you know you should never assume anything about women, Josh?" Kerry interjected lightly.

"Isn't that the truth!"

"Look, this is silly," Marta said. "Stan and I share space, not lives."

"How much space?" Josh persisted.

"Seems to me I've invited you down to see for yourself," Marta recalled. "Our loft's on the third floor of what used to be an old warehouse. We've partitioned a lot of open space into rooms with screens, tapestries, beaded curtains, stuff like that." Marta deliberately grinned at Josh in a way that made him visibly grit his teeth. "In other words, it's very bohemian," she finished.

"I can imagine."

"Stan has his sleeping space, I have mine. We've set up a communal darkroom and studio. There's a small kitchenette and what passes for a bathroom. The shower leaks all the time."

"Sounds charming," Josh said, staring at the dwindling flames in the fireplace.

"You're a snob, Josh."

He snapped to. "Now just what the hell makes you say that?" he demanded.

"Kids, kids," Jennifer protested. "Look, I don't know about the rest of you, but I'm tired. Suppose we stash these dishes in the sink till morning and call it a night."

"I'm sorry, Jennifer," Marta said apologetically. "I was being a brat. Your brother deserves it, but you don't. I'll do the dishes for penance."

All of them wound up doing the dishes, then said their good-nights. But when Marta was almost at the top of the stairs, she impulsively turned back. "Excuse me, Jen. I'll be right up, but I have to talk to him first."

Looking over her shoulder, Jennifer saw Josh starting down the hallway to his room. Marta sped down the stairs and called after him. Josh slowly turned around and leaned on his crutch. Then Marta reached out an imploring hand, touched his shoulder... and Jennifer was satisfied that Josh was at least going to listen to whatever it was Marta had to say.

She was getting into bed when she heard footsteps on the stairs: then Marta's door thudded closed. Even as she wondered what Josh and Marta had talked about, she heard a soft tapping on her door. Moonlight slanted across the darkened room as Jennifer darted through the shadows. Then she paused with her hand on the doorknob.

"Yes?" she asked.

"It's Kerry," came the answer.

He was standing on the threshold, wearing dark blue pajamas. His hair, in contrast, was pure silver.

"Do you always lock your door?" he demanded irritably.

"Cora and Ben suggested it when I moved in," Jennifer told him, standing back to let him enter. "Their apartment's at the far end of your wing. They felt I was pretty much alone in the main inn, and although Westerly is a very safe town, you can't be absolutely certain of anything anywhere. They suggested that Marta lock her door, too."

"I didn't try Marta's door," Kerry said dryly. Moonlight banded his handsome face with light and shadow. "Oh, God, Jenny," he groaned. "I knew I never should have stayed here. I should have had the sense to drive back to Providence tonight. Being downstairs, knowing you're up here..."

She didn't know what to say. She, too, had been supremely conscious that he was in this same old inn, only floorboards and rafters separating them.

With obvious difficulty he said, "I'm going to leave this up to you, Jenny. If you want me to go back downstairs, I'll go. But if you feel the way I'm feeling..."

"I am, Kerry," she said softly.

She was wearing a pale yellow granny gown, but Kerry thought he had never seen anything sexier. He enfolded her in his arms, pressing her against him so that she'd soon have little doubt about the extent of his arousal. Then he swooped her up into his arms and carried her toward the bed.

Jennifer had opened the window, but Kerry didn't feel the cold. With loving tenderness, he lowered her onto the bed. Then, bathed in moonlight, he slid his pajamas off and got onto the bed next to her. His fingers were unsteady as he slowly unfastened the buttons down the front of her gown. Finally he came to the last button, and the gown fell open.

Jennifer was alabaster in the moonlight, but there the resemblance to stone ended. She was soft and yielding, her contours pure beauty, a gift of nature.

Kerry was already nearly at passion's peak. As their bodies molded together, as caresses became as intimate as caresses can be, Jennifer urged him to take his pleasure. All of his pent-up passion exploded in a burst of ecstasy, while he moaned her name over and over again.

Afterward, she was content to lie within the circle of his arms. But when his hands began to rove, when his mouth began to rain kisses on her body, when he began to touch her in ways no man had ever touched her before, Jennifer was more than ready to let him return the pleasure she'd given him. And he did, lavishing her with ardent attentions until she crested, stifling her moans against her pillow lest Marta should hear her as her world exploded.

Minutes passed. Minutes during which the silence in the room was lovely to hear, the darkness lovely to see. Then their movements became those of timeless lovers as they teased, tempted, coaxed until at last they were mutually out of control, lost within the boundless realm of their lovemaking.

This time, there followed the wonderful exhaustion, the total peace of sensuously satisfied togetherness. Jennifer's mind was off on a heavenly voyage, leaving her body to rest, leaving her heart to regain its rhythm. Kerry slipped carefully out of bed and got back into his pajamas. He stood over her and pulled the bedclothes up around her shoulders. "Want me to close the window?" he asked gently.

"No, honey. I like the fresh air."

"You're sure you won't be cold?"

"I'm sure, Kerry. But I . . ."

"What, darling?"

"I don't want you to go."

"I have to, sweetheart. It's not that I'm a stickler for appearances, but . . . well, this *is* your brother we're dealing with. And Marta."

He was right, of course.

Jennifer realized this and was only dimly aware of him bending down to kiss her forehead. Then he slipped out of her room so silently that she didn't even hear him go. But her heart knew only too well that he'd gone.

Chapter Twelve

A few days before Christmas, Kerry departed on a two-week Caribbean cruise. He hadn't mentioned the cruise until the time of departure was close at hand. Then he said only that it was something he'd booked quite a while back.

Marta was leaving Christmas Eve morning to be with her family in Pennsylvania through the New Year. Jennifer, who had been hoping to stage a repeat of Thanksgiving at the inn, was motivated to head out herself. She knew that Cora and Ben would feel obliged to remain in Westerly if she decided to stay at the inn over the holidays. She also realized they'd much rather drive up to Maine and spend Christmas with their relatives.

Finally she called Josh. "Looks as if you and I will be doing our caroling in the nation's capital," she told him.

"I have no desire to go to Washington."

"I think we owe that much to Mom and Dad, Josh."

"Since when have you started feeling noble?"

"Damn it, I love our parents."

"So do I. That doesn't mean I want to spend the holidays with them."

"They'll be hurt if we don't. If we had other plans, it would be one thing. As it is . . ."

"Okay, so we've both been abandoned," Josh conceded. "Come on down to New York, and we'll take it from there."

The weather was bad. The drive along busy Route 95 was slow and demanding, so she and Josh decided to take the train to Washington that evening.

They were both preoccupied with their own thoughts on the trip down and said very little to each other. They arrived to find the capital scene a snowy one. It took a while to snag a taxi at Union Station and twice as long as usual to reach the large Connecticut Avenue apartment hotel in which the elder Smiths lived.

As she embraced her parents, Jennifer felt guilty that she hadn't seen them since an initial visit after her return from London. Josh had lunched with them not long ago while in Washington on business for the magazines. He'd reported that it had been the usual session in the hotel's elaborate formal dining room.

"Stuffy, stuffy, stuffy," Josh had complained. "The place is wall to wall with retired generals and admirals."

That evening, parents and grown-up children again had dinner in the formal dining room. The setting was opulent—thick rugs, floor-to-ceiling draperies, glittering chandeliers. They were served by expert waiters who handled their tasks discreetly and deferentially. General Smith was a gracious host, Caroline Smith a gracious hostess.

Surveying the room, Jennifer felt sure that she and Josh were two or three decades younger than any of the other diners. The hotel catered primarily to retired, higher echelon officers. Many of those present had served with her father. Singly or in pairs, they came over to greet the Smiths and meet Jennifer and Josh. There was a touching pride in the way the elder Smiths introduced their children.

"I think they really miss us," Jennifer whispered to Josh at one point, feeling a slight lump in her throat. However, she felt Josh was overdoing it when, in the elevator on the way up to the Smiths' apartment, he said to his father, "That was an excellent dinner, sir."

The general beamed as if he'd personally supervised the preparation of the meal. "Fine cuisine they have here," he said with satisfaction.

Josh's use of *sir* prompted Jennifer to remember her brother's career in the military had been brought to a halt by his accident. Though she tried to envision Josh as a career officer, she simply couldn't. She'd known many wonderful career officers and was well aware that they weren't necessarily the regimented individuals people tended to think of them as. Still, in his own special way, Josh was a maverick. Maybe he'd become that way, she conceded, because of his handicap. After recovering from a terrible personal trauma, he'd had to work his way through a total life change. Despite the fact that they didn't see eye to eye on certain issues—like Marta, for instance—she admired her brother's fortitude and liked him exactly as he was.

For the next couple of days Jennifer lived in the style to which she had once been accustomed. It was a gracious way of living, to be sure, but a predictable one, and the sameness of it made her as restless as it always had. Hattie, the maid who'd been with the Smiths on a tour of duty in Washington some years ago, had reappeared on the scene. She was older, and her hair had turned white, but she was still the same imperious Hattie who liked to think she ruled the family roost.

She immediately told Jennifer that she should fatten up a bit. "You're getting to look like a picked chicken," she complained.

The general was at his benevolent best on Christmas. Gifts were distributed. Sherry was served before dinner. Dinner itself was in the formal dining room again.

"Hattie wanted to cook a turkey, but we thought she should have the day with her own family," Caroline confided to her daughter.

The day after Christmas, however, Hattie was back to supervise breakfast. It was a lingering meal, with the general scanning the headlines and venting his approval or disapproval of the way the nation's affairs were being handled. In an earlier era, General Smith would have then left for post headquarters, or the Pentagon, as the case might be. Now he informed Josh that he had a meeting with his stockbroker, then a luncheon scheduled at the downtown army-navy club. And he insisted Josh accompany him.

Caroline had also made plans for a luncheon, at which she could introduce Jennifer to some of her friends. It was the last thing Jennifer wanted, but she painted on a smile, remembering how many smiles she'd painted on, growing up, and turned on the kind of charm her mother expected of her.

The hotel arranged the luncheon in a small private dining room. Afterward, card tables were set up for those women who wished to play bridge. Most of them did. Fortunately, there was an odd number, so Jennifer was able to politely bow out. She returned to the apartment, got her coat and struck out for a walk in nearby Rock Creek Park.

She hoped the hour of brisk walking might clear her head of cobwebs, but it didn't. She returned to the apartment feeling physically refreshed but as woolly as ever mentally. All the while she'd thought about Kerry. This world in which she'd been brought up was so entirely different from his. Until now she'd fancied that he'd created the vast gap between their upbringings. Now she could see that he really hadn't. That gap or difference was more obvious to her suddenly, but it wasn't really important.

Kerry had set his own standards, done his own thing. Like Josh, he had become a maverick. And though the torment of not knowing about his roots had clearly taken its toll, Jennifer was confident that he could bridge any gap in the world—if he wanted to.

It was late afternoon. A beautiful mauve dusk was veiling Washington. The evening stars were starting to sparkle in the deep blue sky overhead. Wistfully, Jennifer wondered where Kerry was at that precise instant. She imagined him on a cruise liner in some tropical harbor, standing on the deck watching the sun set over the peaceful, warm waters of the Caribbean.

Jealousy twinged, because she couldn't imagine dashing, distinguished Kerry in a setting so idyllic without a beautiful woman at his side.

Jennifer and Josh headed back to New York on the morning of New Year's Eve. Someone from Josh's publishing firm was giving a party that evening, and Jennifer had agreed to accompany him. But after a couple of hours, they both agreed that it was just another noisy bash, and they quickly made an escape.

It had started snowing before they'd left Josh's apartment, and it was snowing heavily by the time they reached home. By morning they were virtually snowed in. An icy gray Hudson River knifed between Riverside Drive and the Jersey Palisades, which looked like glaciers on loan from the Arctic.

For New Year's dinner, Jennifer opened a canned ham she'd bought for Josh to have on hand, "in case you want to have someone to dinner some night." She'd been thinking of Marta, of course. Josh hadn't picked up the cue.

Jennifer planned to leave for Westerly first thing the following morning, but Josh wouldn't hear of her driving, even though she protested that the roads would be cleared by then.

"Suppose you run into ice?" he countered.

Jennifer thought Josh was being excessively cautious, but she agreed to postpone her departure for another day.

It was sunny, bright and beautiful when she finally left, and the highways were clear. Jennifer didn't encounter any problems whatsoever as she headed toward Rhode Island. She planned to stop at the inn and unpack, then drive over to Watch Hill and check on the mansion. But at the last minute, she changed her mind and drove directly to Kerry's house.

Snow had blanketed the countryside, and the winding roads around Westerly and Watch Hill were not entirely clear. Jennifer didn't want to take any chances, so she drove slowly and carefully. Still, she had an overpowering desire to view the magnificent old house in this winter-white setting.

The driveway had been plowed. Kerry, she thought appreciatively, must have prearranged that service whenever the snow cover warranted it. Perhaps Harry had a plow he hitched onto his truck.

She pulled up under the porte cochere, then gazed through her windshield in astonishment. Beyond her was a car pulled off to one side of the driveway, so heavily covered with snow that she thought for a moment it was a frosted clump of bushes. The car's shape, to say nothing of its color, wasn't really discernible under the mass of snow.

Jennifer hesitated and knew the sensible thing would be to go for the police. On second thought, she saw no particular reason not to call the police from inside the mansion. This car must have been abandoned early on in the blizzard, and the owner was obviously gone.

As if to bolster her conviction that the car had been abandoned, Jennifer discovered the mansion's wide entrance securely locked. She opened the door and stepped into surprising warmth, considering the temperature outside. A new furnace had been installed in mid-December, but she recalled setting the thermostat to marginal heat just before leaving for New York.

As far as she knew, she was the last person to have worked in the house. Harry had pretty much finished up the inside renovations and had decided to take his major holiday of the year and go off to Colorado to ski for three weeks. Thus, his crew members were on temporary leave, too. Kerry had taken off for his cruise, Marta had departed for Pennsylvania....

Frowning, Jennifer advanced across the foyer, then stopped short. The foyer was still unfurnished, but there was a heavy overcoat thrown over the newel post at the end of the curving stairway. A canvas tote bag lay on the floor beneath it.

For a few seconds Jennifer was clutched by icy fear. Then she moved closer to the coat. There was something very familiar about it. She bent over the thick wool and caught the unmistakable scent of the after-shave Kerry used. Then her eyes fell to the tote bag and to the initials K.G. stamped on the clasp.

He hadn't said exactly when he'd be back from the cruise, and somehow she hadn't expected to see him for at least a few more days. Conflicting emotions warred within her. Her anticipation at seeing Kerry was even more intense than she'd expected it to be. She'd thought so much about him while in Washington. The environment there, though her father was retired, was still very military. Spending time with generals and admirals after so many years away from the service life had brought home some of Kerry's concerns. Now more than ever Jennifer appreciated his feelings about the chasm between ranks.

She could more clearly understand that chip on his shoulder about rank and roots. She could sympathize with his feelings about his background and origins . . . or rather his lack of them.

Still, impatience with him surged. In her opinion he had actually triumphed over all of that, yet he stubbornly refused to realize it.

Maybe because she'd gone through so much introspection herself, Jennifer was oddly hesitant about facing Kerry now. She couldn't swear that he'd avoided her after their memorable Thanksgiving night—she knew he really did have his hands full with his work—yet she also felt that he could have come to Watch Hill more often than he had during December. At the very least he could have phoned regularly to check on the progress being made.

Also, she was deeply resentful of his going off on the cruise over the Christmas holiday. She'd tried to bury that emotion, but now it surfaced anew. Hadn't he guessed that she'd wanted, more than words could say, to spend Christmas with him? He had made prior plans, she realized. But he could have cancelled them if he'd wanted to.

Jennifer laughed bitterly to herself. Maybe he didn't trust her or himself to honor their pledge. Maybe, mellowed by the holiday spirit, he knew they would never be able to maintain it. But they'd both done their share of violating the pledge. She wished, in fact, that she'd never heard of the damned pledge. How could she have seriously believed they could possibly be together and resist each other?

Irresolute, she stood at the foot of the stairs and listened. Deathly silence greeted her. Thus far, the only noise had been the thud of the front door as she closed it. Kerry might have heard that, but then again, the house was so large.

Slowly Jennifer began to move through the rooms, but Kerry was nowhere to be found on the first floor. Even more slowly she ascended the stairs. At the top she looked down the long hall and listened again. Nothing.

Except for a few odd pieces, the bedrooms were unfurnished. In fact, there still was painting and papering to do in most. Why would Kerry be up here in this silent empty space? Why hadn't he heard her footsteps on the stairs?

Jennifer's answer came as she crossed the threshold into the vast master suite at the end of the hall. There, in the huge bedroom, Kerry Gundersen had set up a cot. And there he was, sprawled out, fully clothed and sound asleep.

Sunlight blazed through the curtainless windows that looked out over the dark blue North Atlantic. Golden light fell full upon his upturned face, but it didn't seem to bother him. Then, as she quietly started across the floor, Jennifer heard him groan. Nearer to him, she saw that his face was flushed.

At that instant Kerry broke into a paroxysm of coughing that wrenched him awake. He sat up, gasping for breath, unaware that Jennifer was standing only a few feet away. Nor did he see her hurry into the bathroom and bring him back a paper cup full of water.

Only when she thrust the cup at him did he look up. And only after he'd sipped the water did he shudder, then observe huskily, "Wow. I thought I was really out of it. I thought you were a vision." He paused, then asked carefully, "It really is you, isn't it, Jenny?"

Jennifer pressed her palm to his forehead. He was burning up!

"My God, Kerry!" she exclaimed. "What's happened to you?"

"I dunno," he said dully, sinking back against the pillow on the cot. "I—I didn't want to go home."

"What are you talking about?"

"I left the cruise . . . flew back from San Juan . . . rented a car in New York . . . came up here. Found the cot in a closet. Lucky. Needed a place to sleep."

His speech was punctuated with bouts of coughing. More worried by the moment, Jennifer told him, "Stop talking, Kerry. I think I get the picture."

He nodded wearily and closed his eyes. Studying his face, Jennifer noticed that dark shadows circled his eyes. "How long have you been here?" she asked.

A moment passed before he managed, "Really can't say. Since yesterday, I guess. Been asleep most of the time."

Jennifer fought the desire to wring her hands. This was no time to be helpless. She said resolutely, "You're going to have to make a real effort, Kerry. We've got to get you out of here, and you'll have to help. It's going to take all the strength we can manage to get you down the stairs."

It did. He was so tall and surprisingly heavy as he leaned on Jennifer's slim shoulder. But nature gave her a shot of added adrenaline, and she managed to edge him down the curving stairway. Only later did she wonder how they made it to the bottom without falling and breaking their necks.

Getting him out of the house and into her car wasn't much easier. Only after she'd fastened his seat belt and locked the car door did Jennifer run back inside the mansion and grab his coat and the tote bag. She spread the coat over him, said a prayer and started out for the only place she knew to take him. The inn.

With any luck, Cora and Ben would be back from Maine. Then she could put Kerry in the downstairs room he'd had at Thanksgiving. With the heater in the car on full blast, Jennifer drove as fast as safety would permit. Luckily, Watch Hill was only a few miles up the road, and it wasn't long before she was turning into the driveway. It was plowed, as was the front walk. But when she ran to the door, she found it securely locked.

Cora and Ben weren't home yet.

Fortunately, Jennifer had a key to the front door. She propped the door open, then went to get Kerry, who was asleep again, his head lolling against the window.

She got him as far as the living room, where he sank gratefully into an armchair and immediately fell back to sleep. Jennifer, becoming more and more anxious, started for the downstairs bedroom, where she planned to put him to bed. The door to that wing was locked, and she had no idea where Ben kept the keys. Nor did she want to go snooping around to find them, though she knew the Madisons wouldn't object, given the circumstances.

She squared her shoulders resolutely. She would have to get Kerry *up* a flight of stairs this time, to her own quarters.

It was perhaps the most difficult physical task Jennifer had undertaken in her entire life. By the time Kerry lay collapsed across her bed, she wondered what damage she'd done to her muscles.

She retrieved Kerry's tote bag and found a pair of pajamas. Next came the job of getting him out of his clothes. She managed his shirt and sweater and got his pajama top on, but she nearly gave up getting the pants on. Only the knowledge that he needed the extra warmth kept her trying. Finally she succeeded.

Sitting on the bed next to him, she was incredibly moved by his masculinity. The task at hand had almost blinded her to the beauty of his manly body, but not quite. She took a deep breath and pulled the covers up over his chest.

Early in the evening Ben Madison telephoned. "I was hoping I'd catch you," he said. "Called New York, and your brother said you'd gone back up to Westerly. Anyway, Cora's mother's taken sick, and she's in the hospital up here. Looks like she's going to be all right, but we thought we'd better hang around a couple of days longer to be sure she's out of the woods."

It was hardly the moment to tell Ben that he had an added guest at the inn. Answering his questions, Jennifer said convincingly, "Everything's fine, Ben. As far as I can see, there wasn't any damage from the storm, so don't worry about a thing."

As she hung up, Jennifer felt she was doing enough worrying for everyone. Her anxieties, of course, centered on Kerry. Every time she checked him, his breathing sounded more labored than before. The coughing spells were coming more frequently, too.

Obviously, she realized, Kerry needed professional help.

The Madisons had never spoken of having a doctor in the area, so Jennifer consulted the phone book. She was unfamiliar with the names of most of the small communities around Westerly and had no idea how far a doctor would have to travel. Finally, close to the end of her rope, she called the police.

A few minutes later, she discovered that there were still doctors who would make a house call in an emergency. Dr. Arthur Flynn called the inn and promised he'd be over as soon as he handled another house call first.

Within the hour, there was a knock on the front door, and Jennifer opened it anxiously. Dr. Flynn was a mild-mannered, middle-aged man with a quiet air of competence about him. Jennifer led the way up the stairs and took him to Kerry. Then she returned to pace the living room floor while awaiting the doctor's verdict.

He looked considerably more serious as she met him at the bottom of the stairs. "He's a sick man, all right," he conceded. "Bronchial pneumonia, the result of a viral infection. A virus, of course, won't respond to antibiotics, but I did give him a shot to help quiet the cough."

He opened his medical bag as he spoke and took out a number of physicians' samples. "Lucky I have these," he commented, setting the packets on a table. "It's a new medication that will help with the cough—that's about all we can do at the moment. He needs all the rest he can get. That, peace and quiet, and, needless to say, liquids. Do you have some fruit juice on hand, or chicken broth—things like that?"

"Yes. The kitchen is well-stocked."

"Good," Dr. Flynn said. With a smile, he advised, "Don't look so worried, young lady. Your friend is strong, though he'll be weak as a kitten for a few days when he comes out of this. But he's going to be fine. I'll stop by tomorrow afternoon after my office hours."

"Thank you so much," Jennifer said from the heart.

She locked the front door behind the kindly physician, then pulled her living room hassock into her bedroom, propped it in front of the armchair and made herself a makeshift bed where she could get some rest and be near Kerry.

During the night he had intermittent bouts of coughing, but they didn't seem to be taking quite the toll they had. Occasionally he'd stay awake long enough for her to give him some fruit juice. Most of the time he'd turn over and immediately fall back to sleep.

It was dawn before Jennifer finally fell asleep herself. And sunlight was peeking around the window shades when she awakened to discover that her bed was empty. Then Kerry appeared, weaving his way back from the bathroom.

Jennifer, her nerves frazzled, was already on her feet. "Why didn't you call me?" she demanded.

His grin was weak, but a grin nonetheless. "Had to answer the call of nature," he told her. He subsided onto the bed and allowed her to pull the covers over him. Then he murmured hoarsely, "Know something? No one's ever tucked me in before."

"Stop talking," Jennifer ordered.

"Jenny..." Kerry began, but a bout of coughing interrupted him. After a moment, he smiled sheepishly and said, "'Fraid you're right."

By noon he was sitting up in bed eating soup and crackers. By late afternoon, when Dr. Flynn called again, his fever had broken. "I applaud you on your strong constitution, Kerry," the doctor said.

From then on Kerry continued to improve each day. Marta had left Pennsylvania for an assignment in New York and wasn't due back in Westerly for another week. And the Madisons were still away....

This was a time when Jennifer and Kerry were alone together, and each hour became precious to her.

As Dr. Flynn had predicted, Kerry was weak once the acute stage of the illness had passed. There was no danger, just then, of violating the pledge. Because of this, other feelings began to emerge. Different, maybe even more intimate feelings.

Jennifer had always been too intensely aware of Kerry to ever feel really relaxed around him. Now, though, due to their unusual circumstances, they enjoyed a quiet camaraderie as they watched television together or played Scrabble or simply sat before the fire reading.

At night, Jennifer slept on the couch in her living room, insisting that Kerry keep her bed until he was strong enough to go back to Providence. Kerry protested at first but ultimately yielded. Right now, he needed Jennifer's care—an eye-opening switch for him. He had always been so self-sufficient, and it amazed him to realize he could actually enjoy being dependent upon this beautiful redheaded woman who sparked him to passion or fury one minute and baffled him the next.

Kerry had known he loved her. He'd even said as much aloud. Only now, though, did he realize how deep that love ran, deep to the point of need. This, Kerry realized, was what loving and caring were all about. A glimpse of how it could be. It was a dangerous glimpse, however, because the fundamental differences between Jennifer and him would always remain.

Chapter Thirteen

As the winter passed, the mansion at Watch Hill began to emerge as a showplace of exquisite beauty. Forgetting everything except her desire to create the most perfect of homes for Kerry, Jennifer threw herself totally into the effort. Every time Marta came up from New York to update her photography of the project, she marveled at the transformations that had taken place during her brief absence.

From early morning until dusk the house was a beehive of activity. Painters, carpenters, paperhangers, plumbers, electricians and cabinetmakers were simultaneously at work in the many different areas, gradually bringing together the whole Jennifer envisioned.

Experts were called in to deal with their specialties. Electronic wizards rigged the house with a computerized sound system that could direct music from a master stereo console to any or all rooms in the house. The televisions and VCRs were the latest and the best. Every appliance and convenience was state-of-the-art, balanced by a magnificent collection of antique furniture and fixtures.

Each day brought new problems to be solved. Jennifer discovered a crack in one of the medallions in the upstairs stained-glass window. With even one tiny area weakened, there was a danger of the whole window falling apart.

She didn't want to substitute a modern pane of glass. That meant a safari to find glass of the same vintage and color as the damaged piece, as well as a craftsman who could do the necessary repairs. The search led her on a telephone journey all across New England. Finally, in a small Vermont village, she located the perfect glass and the artisan who could handle the job. The glass came from an old church that had been destroyed by fire.

The landscaper, hired to brighten the grounds with flowers and shrubs, also worked under Jennifer's supervision, since she had very definite exterior effects in mind, too. Hundreds of crocus, tulip and daffodil bulbs were planted so they would bloom that spring. When they did, the result was so breathtaking that word floated back to the garden editor of the Providence newspaper. He, in turn, immediately dispatched a photographer to capture the scene for their front page.

Inevitably, the photograph aroused area attention, and each weekend brought more and more sightseers. Most people were content to slowly drive by the old mansion "gawking," to use Harry's expression. Others were more aggressive and actually parked their cars, got out and strolled around the grounds. This became such a nuisance that Kerry finally placed a security guard at the lawn's edge on Saturdays and Sundays to keep the curious at bay.

"I didn't buy the house to attract a lot of people who have nothing better to do than trespass," he grumbled over lunch one day.

He and Jennifer were at a French restaurant in the Arcade, Providence's venerable enclosed shopping center, reputedly the oldest "mall" in the country. Jennifer was on the trail of the perfect furniture for the master bedroom and had been tipped off by one of her contacts to an auction the next morning. She'd driven to Providence for a preview of the furniture and was delighted with it. Still, because this would be Kerry's bedroom, she felt he should see the exquisite set before she bought it.

She'd called him at his office, and he'd promptly invited her to lunch. Jennifer suspected that he'd juggled an appointment or two in order to arrange such a hasty date with her, but she wasn't about to quibble. She was so glad to be with him that she could hardly concentrate on the reason she'd called him in the first place.

She hadn't seen much of him since his return to Providence after his illness. He'd explained that his bout with pneumonia had put him far behind in his work and had added, rather noncommittally, that he'd get down to Watch Hill as often as he could. That had been exactly twice.

Now, Jennifer surveyed him . . . and was dismayed by what she saw. He'd lost weight during his illness, despite her attempts to keep him well fed during his convalescence. He was pale and uncharacteristically haggard, with dark circles under his eyes.

Abruptly, she asked, "Have you had a checkup since the pneumonia, Kerry?"

"No. Should I have?"

"If you'll recall," Jennifer pointed out, "Dr. Flynn mentioned that you should see your own physician once you were home again."

Kerry stirred restlessly. "I don't have a physician."

"Then you'd better get one."

"What's that supposed to mean?"

Jennifer sighed. "Do you ever look in the mirror?"

"When I shave."

"I expected that's what you'd say. All right, can you honestly tell me that you feel well?"

He shrugged. "Well enough, Jenny. I'm tired, if that's what you're getting at. But I think that's natural enough. I've had a heavy work load for the last month, and it's just now beginning to lighten up."

"Then maybe you could take a little time off, even a weekend, and get away somewhere. Someplace where you could rest and eat right and relax."

"Look, Jenny..."

"Yes?"

"I appreciate your concern, but I've never been a big fan of vacations. Most of the time I'd really rather work or just spend quiet time at home."

"Were you working on that Caribbean cruise?" she asked sarcastically.

"It's not like you to be nasty," he observed.

"Well, were you?"

"I won the cruise, Jenny."

"You what?"

"It was a fund-raising affair for a local charity," he explained. "A raffle. They held a dinner with a hefty per-plate charge, and since it was a cause I believed in, I contributed. I didn't even go to the dinner. But I did win first prize."

"What was the cause?"

He looked away but said levelly, "A home for found-lings. Anyway, I won the prize. That was last September. Later... well, I thought about cancelling out or giving the ticket to someone else, but then I decided it would be a good idea to get away over the Christmas holidays."

"Why, Kerry?" Jennifer asked quietly. "Please, tell me."

"Quite simple, really."

"Is it?" she persisted. She'd never seen him look more uncomfortable.

"Look, I knew that you and Josh and Marta... and almost everyone else I know except Harry, who wanted to escape from his aunt for a couple of weeks, would have family commitments."

Jennifer fought back the urge to throttle him. Then, when he stared at her, his blue eyes puzzled, she fought back the even stronger urge to throw her arms around him and kiss him.

"You seem angry," he mused. "You've been, well...kind of stiff every time the subject of the cruise has come up. So if it's any satisfaction to you, I didn't have a good time. That's why I cut it short. I flew back from Santa Lucia to San Juan, then directly to Boston."

"Fine."

He drew a long breath, then said, "Now, to get back to the matter of Watch Hill. As I was saying, I want a house, not a zoo. I never dreamed people would come around and gape at the house the way they have since the paper ran that front-page photo. What do you think is going to happen when Josh's magazine does that feature series?"

"Are you saying you don't want Josh to go ahead with the articles?" Jennifer asked quickly.

Kerry shook his head. "No, I'm not. I gave my word on that, and Josh and Marta are the last two people I'd go back on. But I can just imagine the added curiosity more publicity will generate. I'll have to put a gatehouse in, with guards to keep people away."

"Such is the price of fame," Jennifer replied.

"I'm not famous, Jenny."

"I disagree. You've made quite a name for yourself, Kerry Gundersen. I don't think you appreciate how well known you are. Even I'd heard about you, all the way over in London. Don't you realize you're currently listed as one of America's most sought after bachelors? It's amazing that you manage to keep the low profile you do. But that doesn't negate the facts, so stop hiding your light under a bushel of your own invention."

He glared at her. "I am not hiding my light under a bushel, Jennifer," he stated flatly. "I have no illusions about myself, nor do I have any false modesty. I'm a damned good architect, and I've earned my reputation. As far as the rest of the guff, it's a lot of rot, and you know it."

"Are you denying that you could be right in the midst of the social whirl, not just in Providence but almost anywhere where people read magazines and watch television?"

"You mean in the midst of people who issue invitations without really knowing anything about their guests?"

"That's it exactly!" Jennifer exclaimed in triumph. "You made yourself into a mystery figure."

Kerry's deep blue eyes raked her face. "You *are* out of your mind."

Jennifer laughed. All of a sudden she was enjoying this interchange. She was arousing a spark in Kerry she hadn't seen in quite a while. His righteous indignation had brought a vital gleam to his tired face, a gleam that had been missing lately.

Despite his obvious fatigue, stirring him up seemed to be doing some good, she decided. "Mystery and glamour go hand in hand," she teased. "You really are a mystery figure, you know, whether you admit it or not. Part of the mystery is that low profile you keep; the other part is your meteoric rise to success. You're sort of the man who came out of nowhere."

"I'm not 'sort of' the man who came from nowhere, Jennifer," he corrected angrily. "I *am* the man who came from nowhere."

"Ah, but no one knows that," she reminded him. Determined to knock at least one chip off those strong shoulders of his, she continued. "So your dark past only makes you all the more alluring. Women can fantasize about where you're from and what you did before you suddenly became big news. With your shadowed past and your good looks, you could write any kind of ticket you want." She was half teasing, half serious, but she consciously wanted to get a rise out of him.

Instead, he pushed back his chair and slanted her a look of pure disgust. "Let's get out of here," he said abruptly.

They hadn't even finished their entree, to say nothing of peeking at the dessert menu or ordering an espresso to round out the delicious meal. Jennifer, preceding Kerry out of the restaurant, had the uneasy feeling she'd trespassed into forbidden territory, just like the strangers who gawked at his house.

At the top of the steep steps leading from the Arcade down to the street level, Kerry said, "I'll leave you here, if you don't mind."

Jennifer suddenly felt very small and totally miserable. She sensed that she'd hurt him, which was the last thing in the world she wanted to do.

"Wait a minute," she said quickly. "The purpose of our meeting was to give you a chance to see the furniture I've found for the master bedroom. They told me at the auction gallery they'd let us in whenever we came, though they won't be open to the public for a showing until this evening."

"I don't care about seeing the furniture," he said coldly. "If you like it, buy it. I don't give a damn."

His tone completely startled Jennifer. And before she could answer him, he vaulted down the steps and disappeared around the nearest corner.

She felt ashamed, emotionally shaken. She'd goaded him when she should have known it would hurt. Though her intentions had been good, she remembered too late the old saw about the road to hell being paved with good intentions. Well, she'd laid down her share of bricks with Kerry.

Bleakly she made her way back to the auction house. She knew the furniture in question was right, but she'd wanted Kerry to see it. It was, after all, destined to occupy his most personal space.

Jennifer drove back to Westerly that afternoon; the temptation to call Kerry would have been too great if she'd stayed in Providence. She would have called him or shown up at his door. Luckily, her common sense overruled those desires and told her to get out of town.

The next morning she was up early and on the road back to Providence. She reached the auction house a few minutes before the selling began. When the bedroom set came up, she bid what she felt was a reasonable sum and was satisfied that she'd acted in Kerry's best interests.

That night, Jennifer was no sooner in her suite at the inn than Marta came knocking on the door. Since she'd thought she'd be facing a lonely, brooding evening, the prospect of company suddenly seemed very agreeable.

"Hi, there," she greeted her neighbor warmly.

Marta arched a thin dark eyebrow. "And why are you so blasted pleased about seeing me?" she demanded skeptically.

"Because I didn't expect you for a few more days," Jennifer hedged, realizing that Marta had seen right through her.

"Have you and Kerry had a fight?"

"What makes you think that?"

"Why else would you paste on a cheery face?"

"That obvious, huh?"

Marta grinned. "Come on, Jennifer. We get along, you and I. In fact, I'd call us a mutual admiration society, so I think I recognize your exuberance for what it is."

"Well, what about you?"

"Josh and I have definitely had a fight," Marta announced soberly.

"Do you want to talk about it?"

"You first," Marta insisted.

Jennifer laughed. "Why don't we have a glass of wine and cry on each other's shoulder?" she suggested.

A few minutes later, sitting cross-legged on Jennifer's couch, Marta said, "Josh is so stubborn, sometimes he totally defeats me. Actually, most of the time he does. I really want him to come up here and see the house before it's all finished and Kerry suddenly decides to sell it or something."

Jennifer's antennae went up. "Has Kerry told you he's going to do that?" she asked.

"Don't look so disconcerted, Jen. No, not in so many words. But I've gotten the impression that he doesn't want to live there, either. The few times I've talked with him, he hasn't been nearly as enthusiastic as he was in the beginning. Anyway, you've got to admit that huge house could be a pretty lonely bachelor abode. Unless, of course, he decided to start a harem."

Marta grinned at Jennifer's expression. "Don't worry. I doubt there's any harem in Kerry's future. A monastery, maybe, but not a harem."

"You picture Kerry as a monk?"

"No. But I think he's very gun-shy where women are concerned. Anyway, he's in love with you, so it doesn't really matter."

Marta spoke as if she were stating an undisputed fact, and Jennifer wished she could be that sure of Kerry's love. Passion, yes. The chemistry between them was as strong as ever. Whenever they were together they waged a constant battle to suppress their desires. Also, she knew he cared for her. He'd even said he loved her.

That, Jennifer reminded herself, was a statement he'd made only once and never repeated. An impetuously spoken phrase, she was sure, not to be taken too seriously.

"As I was saying," Marta said insistently, recapturing Jennifer's attention, "I've been trying to get Josh up here, and he keeps putting me off. So this morning I marched into his office and put the question to him."

"The question?"

"No, I didn't propose to him, idiot! Can you imagine his reaction if I had?" Marta's piquant face again turned very sober. "Jennifer," she said, "I can't even get him to come up here. He seems to think he'd be a drag."

"Why?"

"I don't know. He won't say. But I think he's worried about getting around. You know, on the stairs, for example."

"He doesn't have to climb all over the house in order to get the general concept," Jennifer blurted impatiently. "I don't blame you for being annoyed at him, Marta. Josh is as stubborn as Kerry—perhaps more so."

"Well, at least Josh has a reason. I don't happen to agree with it—meaning, his handicap—but at least it's understandable. With Kerry, though . . ."

Jennifer wanted to say, "Believe me, Kerry has a handicap, too. An invisible one, actually more difficult to deal with than Josh's." But she bit the words back out of loyalty to Kerry.

This wasn't the first time she'd wanted to confide in someone. In New York, there'd been moments when she'd longed to confide in Josh. But Kerry came first, so she'd inevitably kept his secret to herself.

"I'd still like to see the woman who burned Kerry," Marta stated. "No matter what you say, Jen, there had to be someone." When Jennifer didn't answer, Marta pleaded, "Try, will you, to get Josh up here? Maybe this weekend?"

"It'd be better if he could take a couple of days off during the week," Jennifer answered. "Weekends aren't the greatest at Watch Hill right now."

Marta hadn't been part of that particular madness yet. When Jennifer explained to her why weekends had become so difficult, she promptly asked, "How does Kerry feel about being the focus of such attention?"

"He dislikes it intensely. I made the mistake of telling him that's the price of fame, and he nearly bit my head off."

"It'll die down," Marta predicted.

"Yes, but when your features come out, it will happen all over again."

"And again it won't last, Jennifer. The mansion will undoubtedly be the focus of attention for a lot of curiosity seekers, but then they'll latch on to something else. They always do. Fame really is fleeting, you know."

"All right, philosopher. Shall we have soup here tonight or at your place?"

"Mine," Marta said. "I have some canned gourmet stuff straight from Manhattan. Just give me ten minutes to get things in order, then come on over, okay?"

"I'll call Josh in the meantime," Jennifer promised.

"The Watch Hill assignment isn't the only thing I have to keep tabs on, Jennifer."

"I thought it was important to you, Josh."

"It is important, damn it. But Marta knows what she's doing. And you're there."

"Marta's an excellent photographer, but I'm not an editor."

"You know what I mean," Josh growled.

"I'm not sure I do. Regardless, this is something I'm asking of you, Josh. Stop being so damned obdurate and get yourself up here, will you?"

"I like your choice of adjectives."

"Oh, dry up! Look, Josh . . . for personal reasons, I really wish you'd come."

"What personal reasons?" he asked suspiciously.

"Maybe if you come up and stay a few days, Kerry will deign to invade the premises," Jennifer told him.

"Kerry's been staying away, has he?"

"Very definitely."

"Why?"

"He says it's because of work pressures."

"Well, I talked to him on the phone last week, Jenny. He was hoping to come down here on business and at the same time meet me for lunch, but he had to cancel because of a priority commitment right there in Providence."

"I don't doubt he's busy, Josh. I just think that if he wanted to, he could find three hours a week to trek down to Watch Hill and see what we're doing, that's all."

"Maybe yes, maybe no."

"Maybe yes," she stated firmly. "Anyway, will you come? Frankly, if you don't, I'm going to be very, very annoyed with you."

Josh chuckled. "You terrify me," he teased. "Okay, I'll come. Can you book my room at the inn for tomorrow night?"

Jennifer hadn't expected her brother to capitulate so easily. When she told Marta that Josh was due on the scene the following day, Marta actually swayed on her feet before collapsing on her sofa.

Looking up at Jennifer, she managed, "Whew! I don't think I was ready for that."

"What are you talking about? You saw Josh only this morning, didn't you?"

"Yes, but having him at Watch Hill will be different. I . . . I'm hoping he'll sort of go around with me and suggest some photo angles I haven't thought of."

"I'm sure you've missed a lot of them," Jennifer retorted, shaking her head.

"People look at things with different eyes and react differently to what they see," Marta evaded.

"I think you just want to have Josh to yourself," Jennifer teased. Seriously she added, "Just keep an eye on him, will you? He's going to run up against some obstacles, like that long flight of steps down to the beach. Knowing Josh, he might try to navigate them to prove that he can. The same thing with the curving stairway in the foyer—''

She stopped short. That stairway reminded her of just one thing: the first time she and Kerry had kissed. The memory of that kiss made her ache with want.

Into the silence that followed, Marta said, "Believe me, I don't intend to put Josh to any endurance tests."

"It's not you, Marta," Jennifer said carefully. "It's him. We both agree that Josh is far too conscious of his handicap, but sometimes I get the feeling that you're pretending it doesn't even exist, and that's not wise. Let's face it, Josh *is* limited."

"He isn't limited at all!" Marta objected vehemently. "So he can't race up and down stairs or pole vault or enter triathlons. So what? He probably wouldn't do those things anyway. But he's not limited!" She covered her face with her hands. Then, just as Jennifer was about to speak, she looked up and smiled ruefully. "Sorry, Jen," she said, "I got carried away. I tend to do that where your brother is concerned."

"Keep right on doing what you're doing," Jennifer told her softly, feeling her heart ache for her friend.

"I hope you, Marta and Josh will be free to have dinner with me tonight," Kerry said. "I thought we might drive up to Point Judith for a real New England seafood dinner."

"We can't," Jennifer said into the telephone.

"Oh? Why not?"

"Marta's making paella. Her grandmother was Spanish, and this is a traditional family dish. Cora and Ben are going off to a Grange meeting tonight, and there are no other guests at the inn right now. They told Marta she could have the kitchen to herself, and she took them up on their offer. She's going over at noon to get things started, so she'll only have to finalize everything later. She tried to get you on the phone last night, but evidently you were out."

"That's right," Kerry said tersely.

"Well . . . I'm inviting you in her name, okay?"

"I wasn't angling for a dinner invitation when I called you, Jenny."

"Then why don't you just say you don't want to come?" she snapped irritably. She was suddenly tired of dealing with difficult men—her brother and Kerry.

"Because I'd like very much to come," he said. "May I bring the wine?"

"If you'd like to. This is Marta's dinner, not mine."

"Well, maybe I can catch Marta at the inn later. Perhaps there's a particular wine that goes best with her paella. Meantime," he went on, "Josh was going to drive up, but I persuaded him to fly. I'll be picking him up at the airport at two, so we should get to Watch Hill an hour or so later."

Hearing that, Jennifer's treacherous pulse shifted into high gear. Kerry never ceased to surprise her, that much was for sure.

"Jenny?" he asked softly.

"Yes."

"I suppose I could ask you this later, but it's something I've been wanting to know. Did you buy the furniture you wanted? The pieces for the master suite?"

"Yes."

"Well, I'm glad. Also . . . I want to apologize for behaving so badly the other day. You really got under my skin, mocking me like that."

"I wasn't mocking you, Kerry."

"I thought you were. Anyway, I'm sorry."

"I'm sorry I rubbed you the wrong way."

"Truce, then?"

"I'd like that," she said. She hesitated, then added carefully, "You sound awfully tired."

"I am tired. And before you start to lecture me, I'm going to do something about it. George recommended his physician, and I plan to make an appointment with him soon. I personally think it's a waste of time, but George has been hassling me, too. So I'll go get a checkup to satisfy both of you."

"Tell George I bless him," Jennifer said.

"He'll be glad to hear that. Speaking of which, the two of you really must meet each other one of these days. I've told him a lot about you. Maybe the next time you and I have lunch together..."

So, there would be a next time. With Kerry, Jennifer was never entirely sure.

The sun was just beginning its western descent when Kerry and Josh arrived at Watch Hill that afternoon. It was still high enough in the sky to burnish the mansion's numerous windows and sprinkle gold dust on the flowers and shrubs.

Josh got out of Kerry's car slowly, then stood leaning on his crutch as he gazed in awe at the magnificent house and the beautiful sweep of grounds.

"Only Marta's photography could possibly do this place justice," he said finally.

Marta, already at his side, grinned. "That's going to cost you, Mr. Editor. My rates just went up."

"So scare me," Josh replied, smiling.

Marta clapped a firm hand on his free arm and tugged. "Come on," she urged. "I have a lot I want to show you before it gets dark."

Jennifer shot her a slightly alarmed glance, but Marta winked knowingly. Then she was unobtrusively matching her pace to Josh's, chattering all the while so he wouldn't realize what she was doing.

Left alone with Kerry, Jennifer decided he looked even more haggard and tense than he had in Providence just a few days ago.

"Have you made that doctor's appointment yet?" she blurted.

"That's a hell of a greeting," he answered, frowning.

"Sorry, but have you?"

"I'm not going to get into that now," he warned.

"Fine," she conceded easily. Inadvertently, she tugged at his sleeve, just as Marta had done with Josh. "Follow me into the house, if you will," she said. "The rest of the dining room furniture arrived this morning, and we just finished putting everything into place a little while ago."

Kerry did as she asked, a faint smile curving his lips. When Jennifer was excited about something, she was like a little girl with a new doll. That touched him. In fact, *she* touched him . . . more than anything else in his life.

When they reached the dining room, all Kerry could do was stop and stare. The transformation Jennifer had effected was nothing less than amazing. The walls were pale gold, with wainscoting in deep gold panels of brocaded tapestry. The antique cherry refectory table she'd acquired before Thanksgiving was polished to perfection, its twelve matching chairs all in position. An enormous sideboard, done in the same wood and style, highlighted one wall. And the chandelier, the magnificent chandelier that had been there all along, dulled with cobwebs and grime, sparkled like a collection of gemstones suspended in space.

"Well?" she asked expectantly. "What do you think? Will twelve chairs be enough, or should we add a couple of leaves to the table and scout around for a few more?"

"I'm absolutely flabbergasted," Kerry admitted, his voice hoarse. He cleared his throat and added, "Just what kind of entertaining do you think I'll be doing here? I mean, the thought of putting on a formal dinner for twelve is overwhelming to me."

He nearly said, "Of course, if you were my hostess, it would be different." But Jennifer was already tugging him over to the lovely old sideboard, so the words remained unspoken.

Chapter Fourteen

Josh stayed for two days. Then Kerry drove him back to Providence to catch a plane to New York. At the last minute, Kerry decided to fly to New York with Josh to attend to the business he'd had to postpone.

"So, here we are," Marta observed as she and Jennifer sat on the terrace at Watch Hill, sipping coffee.

Marta was brooding as she gazed out over the ocean, absorbed in thought, while Jennifer was trying in vain to push the memory of last night out of her mind.

Kerry had taken them all out for an early dinner; then they'd returned to the inn. After just a few minutes he'd declared that he had to get back to Providence. "A bit of unfinished business at the office" was how he'd explained it. Jennifer had walked him to the door, baffled at why he was leaving so suddenly.

The spring night beckoned, sweet scented with lilacs. She'd walked with him to where his car was parked. He'd

opened the car door, then looked down at her. Hesitant for
a second, he'd whispered huskily, "Jenny, later...may I
come back? Will you leave the doors open for me?"

So, like a schoolgirl bent on a forbidden caper, she'd
sneaked down the stairs after everyone else was asleep,
unlocked the inn's front door, left the door to her suite
unlocked, then climbed back into bed. There, she'd drawn
the sheets up around her shoulders and waited for him.

Kerry tiptoed into her room late that night...and they'd
found each other in the pale moonlight. Found each other
and made love. Freely and uninhibitedly made love until
they finally fell asleep in each other's arms.

When she'd awakened in the morning, Kerry was gone.
Not even the imprint of his head on the pillow remained.
She'd had the crazy feeling he'd never been there at all,
except...he most definitely had been. Once again they'd
broken the pledge. Once again their desire for each other
had overwhelmed them to the point of no return. Jennifer, certainly, had thrown caution to the wind anew. She'd
jeopardized the already shaky state of her heart by becoming more involved with the man she loved.

Now she told herself that she'd damned well better get
her act together with respect to loving Kerry Gundersen.
The aftermath of this game she and Kerry were playing was
too painful, the emptiness in the wake of passion too deep
and dark a chasm. She didn't think she could stand much
more of it.

She and Marta finished their coffee, then began on the
work they'd set for themselves for that day. They both had
plenty to do. Nevertheless, the hours dragged. After two
wonderful days with Kerry and Josh, concentration was
extremely difficult.

At the inn that night, Marta said, "I think I'll head back
to New York tomorrow, Jennifer. I don't know about you,
but I'm up to my neck with Watch Hill for the moment. I

have another assignment that'll only take a couple of days. I think I'll go with it and clear my palate before I come back here.''

Marta left early the next morning, and Jennifer drove over to Watch Hill by herself. Again she had a hard time keeping her mind on her work. This wasn't like her at all, but then, this wonderful home was like no other she'd ever created. Everything about the place spelled Kerry—it was as simple as that.

When the noon hour approached, Jennifer admitted that she'd had enough for the day. Rarely before had she felt so unable to concentrate on her work, so ''up to her neck,'' as Marta had put it, that she wanted a respite. Yet that was definitely true now. She desperately needed a change of scene.

A valid excuse to get away came that evening in the form of a phone call from Josh. Josh informed her that Nigel Evans, an old friend from London, was in town and had called several times, hoping to connect with her.

''He's only going to be in the States for a few days, Jenny,'' Josh drawled, ''and he seems to have a super yen to see you.''

Nigel was a friend. She had dated him in London, but their relationship had been completely platonic. Nigel owned a very successful antiques business. They had a lot in common, and they enjoyed each other's company. He'd be just the tonic she needed right now, Jennifer realized, her desire to see him mounting by the second.

Matters at Watch Hill were going along very well. She knew she could take two or three days off without causing any noticeable delays. She reluctantly conceded that she should call Kerry and tell him she was taking the time off. And she was actually relieved when she dialed his office and was told he was in New Hampshire for the day. Just now she needed distance from Kerry, a respite even from the sound of his voice.

She called Harry Kominsky and told him that she was going away for a couple of days. Harry immediately made a great mock protest. "I won't be able to work without your pretty face around giving me that added transfusion when my energy gets low," he kidded. Jennifer was laughing as they concluded the conversation. Harry was a great guy to work with.

Spring had come to New York. The air was soft and tantalizing. Central Park was speckled in green. It was that special time of year for lovers, when the new warm air whisked away the toll of winter.

Nigel was certainly not a lover, but it was good to see him. He and Jennifer spent most of the next three days together, walking in the park, taking in the museums, dining in little out-of-the-way restaurants they discovered. On her last night in town Jennifer invited him to Josh's apartment for dinner. She tried to reach Marta but only got her answering machine.

She, Josh and Nigel enjoyed a pleasant evening together. The company was good, the food terrific, the conversation fun. Time passed quickly, and then Jennifer and Nigel were saying goodbye, indulging in a last hug and farewell kiss while Josh looked on, masking his curiosity.

When the door closed behind Nigel, Jennifer trailed after her brother into the living room. "Well," she asked, "how did you like him?"

"Nigel? He's a good guy," Josh admitted. "Why do you ask? Is there something I don't know that I should know?"

"Come on, Josh," Jennifer protested.

"Seriously, Jenny. Nigel obviously dotes on you, or haven't you noticed? He can't keep his eyes off you. And he acted like a drowning man when the two of you were wrapped up in that final embrace."

"I hope you don't allow that kind of hyperbole in your magazine copy," Jennifer told him testily.

"I'm only stating facts," Josh taunted with a lopsided grin. "It strikes me as odd, that's all."

"What's that supposed to mean?"

"I never thought you were the type who enjoyed keeping men dangling."

Jennifer sat down opposite her brother and gritted her teeth. After a moment of silent anger she said tightly, "Out with it, will you? I never thought you were the type to hide behind stupid phrases."

"Fine. I thought you and Kerry had something going, that's all. So you threw me a curve when this suave, good-looking Englishman—who appears to know you very well, I might add—suddenly walked into the picture."

Jennifer wanted to explode. "How well do you know Kerry Gundersen?" she demanded.

"Pretty well, I think."

"Then you must realize he's essentially a loner. Matter of fact, if I recall correctly, you pointed that out to me yourself at some stage of this game."

"I might have said that."

"You did. I remember I thought maybe you were trying to warn me off of him. Maybe you were actually worried about the possibility of my being hurt."

"That could be." He nodded thoughtfully.

"Then why this sudden need to protect Kerry's alleged interests? That *is* what this is all about, isn't it?"

Josh considered his sister's point, then said, "In a way, yes. Whatever I said to you about Kerry was way back, Jenny. The picture has definitely changed since then, in my estimation. I've seen a lot more of Kerry, we've all spent time together in Westerly and Watch Hill, I've watched him watching you." Josh grinned. "A guy can give an awful lot away when he's looking at a woman and doesn't think anyone's looking at him."

"Tell me about it," Jennifer taunted.

Josh's cool gray eyes met hers levelly. "Do I detect a bit of sarcasm in that comment, little sister?" he queried.

"You should see yourself looking at Marta."

To Jennifer's surprise, Josh actually blushed.

"Well? What about Marta?" she persisted.

"What about her?"

"I tried to get her for tonight. I left two messages on her answering machine. I would have thought she'd have called back by now."

"Marta isn't in New York."

That came as a surprise. "Then where is she?" Jennifer asked.

"How the hell do I know?" Josh answered irritably. "I believe she went off on an assignment for another magazine. She's independent as hell, in case you haven't noticed. She told me Watch Hill can sit there a little while longer, that she won't miss anything if she's away for a week. And, I suppose she's right. She's taken literally hundreds of photographs, of which we'll use only a small percentage. Still, it makes me angry when she just ups and leaves. I wanted her to cover the whole scope, that's all."

Josh subsided into a grouchy silence. Obviously, Marta's actions bothered him, though Jennifer wasn't sure whether her brother's objection was personal or professional. Perhaps the reason Josh wanted Marta at Watch Hill so much of the time was because his sister was there to keep an eye on the lively young photographer.

Jennifer, on the verge of teasing Josh about that, took a long look at his averted profile and decided not to.

When Jennifer returned to Watch Hill after four days in the city, she discovered she'd been right. Everything had gone along very well in her absence.

Harry greeted her exuberantly, wrapping her in a huge bear hug. To her surprise, she discovered that Harry and his men had embarked on a new project. They were adding a fairly large ell adjoining the two studios beyond the kitchen. "Kerry says he wants it for a workroom," Harry explained.

In a way, it was heartening to hear that. It implied that Kerry intended to stick to his bargain and move into the mansion for at least a year. On the other hand, it irked Jennifer that he hadn't consulted her about the addition before telling Harry to go ahead with the construction.

She plunged back into her own work and tried not to think about what Harry and company were doing out back. Still, she couldn't help but brood. She wondered if Kerry would consult her about the decor of his "workroom," or if he'd handle it himself. Maybe, she thought snidely, he decided he wanted one corner of the mansion to look as gray and sterile as his office.

Kerry appeared that afternoon. A tight-lipped Kerry who accosted her upstairs as she was consulting the painters over border colors she wanted in two of the guest bedrooms.

"May I speak to you?" he asked curtly.

Jennifer swung around, startled. His tone was disconcerting. She stared up into his deep blue eyes and had never seen them look so cold. Why? she wondered. Curbing both her curiosity and her instinct to rise to the bait, she said politely, "Certainly."

She led the way down the curving stairway, heading toward the drawing room, but Kerry stopped her short.

"Not in there," he commanded angrily. "I'd suffocate, trying to talk in there. Let's get out of here."

"I . . . I thought you loved that room," she managed, shaken.

He didn't comment. Staring after him, she asked, "Where do you want to go? The kitchen?"

They could hear distant hammering—Harry's men working on the addition. Then an electrician came by, greeting them pleasantly as he started up the stairs with a roll of heavy-gauge wire.

"When I said out," Kerry said irritably, "I meant out. Do you have a sweater or something? You might need it."

Jennifer picked up the jacket she'd draped over a lovely Hitchcock chair she'd bought just before going to New York. Normally, Kerry would have noticed something like that. Today he didn't even give the antique a passing glance.

Jennifer was brimming with resentment as he held open the passenger door of his car for her. Neither of them spoke as he gunned the motor and roared down the driveway. She made no comment as he headed over to the shore road and turned east. He drove fast, not his habit ordinarily, but his repressed ire didn't seem to affect his excellent driving skills.

Finally his silence was too much for her. She felt her head would explode from the tension if she didn't say something. She had absolutely no idea why he was acting like this.

"What is it with you?" she demanded, flinging the question at him abruptly. "You come roaring upstairs while I'm talking with the painters, looking as if you're going to drag me out by the hair if I don't come along peaceably. Now you're sitting there like a block of ice, speeding down a narrow road like a madman on a mission. I mean, what exactly is your problem?"

"You infuriated me," Kerry hissed between clenched teeth.

"*I* infuriated you?" Jennifer asked, incredulous. "What have *I* done, Mr. Gundersen?"

"You took off from your job without a single word to me. You leave for New York and spend three days with your lover—"

"Are you out of your mind?" Jennifer shouted. "Three passionate nights with a former flame—is that what you think?" She would have laughed if she hadn't been so angry. Nigel had never been her lover, for one thing. But what grated the most was that Kerry must have heard all this from Josh.

What could Josh have said to him? Though she and her brother had their share of sibling disagreements, Jennifer couldn't imagine Josh ever saying anything concerning her that would come under the heading of downright sabotage.

Kerry was staring straight ahead at the road, his profile carved from granite. "You think you're so high and mighty, don't you, Jennifer Smith? You think you can do any damned thing you please and get away with it because you've been spoiled rotten all your life by those doting parents of yours. Well, supposedly you're a professional now. Out in the working world, where you have to compete like the rest of us. Let me tell you, sweetheart, the rules aren't the same. I'm amazed to think you've evidently never discovered that. But it's time you did. Let me tell you right now, if it were anyone else employing you, he'd fire you!"

Jennifer looked at Kerry in total disbelief, and very quickly her temper reached the boiling point. "You don't have to fire me," she yelled at him. "I quit! Do you hear me? I quit!"

Suddenly she wanted nothing more than to get away from him. Without even realizing it, she grasped the door handle.

A strong hand instantly grabbed her wrist. "Don't be a damned fool!" Kerry gritted. "What do you think would happen if you tumbled out onto the pavement at this speed?"

"Then stop the car!" she demanded imperiously.

"I got out of the army a long time ago," he informed her. "I no longer take orders."

"I have a right to know where you're taking me."

"Someplace where we can talk without interruption," he stated. Wearily he added, "So meanwhile, shut up, will you?"

No man had ever talked to her like that before... except Josh. Still, the few serious arguments she'd had with Josh had been tempered by the fact that he was her brother.

With Kerry, it was different. Jennifer subsided into an infuriated silence. She hated this. And she would have hated him, except that she loved him so very, very much.

The miles passed. At last there was a major fork in the road and a sign with directions. Jennifer glanced at Kerry, puzzled. "Point Judith?" she asked, her tone more normal. "Why have we come here?"

"You'll see," he promised grimly.

She soon saw, all right. Kerry parked the car by the town dock. A minute later he was helping her aboard the small vessel that served as an auxiliary ferry and mail carrier between the mainland and Block Island.

He gripped her arm firmly and didn't let go until the crew cast off the mooring lines. Only when they were underway did he say, "Now, if you can't bear being in my presence, Jennifer, you can swim for it."

It was her turn to snap, "Oh, shut up!"

A slight smile twisted his lips. "How about showing a little respect for your employer?" he taunted.

"You're no longer my employer, remember?" she taunted back. "I quit before you fired me."

Kerry clasped his hands in his lap as they took seats in the passenger lounge. Jennifer tried not to look at them; they aroused too many memories. Tender caresses she'd never forget. They were wonderful hands, gentle yet strong. As she watched, unwillingly, she saw those fingers tighten until his knuckles were white. Only then did she fully appreciate the strain he was laboring under.

He said roughly, "I went off the handle, okay? I don't do it often. Almost never, in fact, regardless of the provocation. Anyone who knows me will tell you that. But you...you seem to have a way of getting under my skin like nobody else ever has. I admit I saw red, crimson, whatever the hell you want to call the color, when I found out you'd taken off for New York without even bothering to tell me."

"I tried to reach you, Kerry. Your secretary said you were in New Hampshire for the day."

"Working on plans for the mall, yes. Anyway, you could have given her the message."

"It was a spur-of-the-moment decision," she told him. "I told Harry."

"And you expect me to believe that your man from London just happened to travel all the way across the Atlantic to see you?"

"London to New York is a relatively short trip these days," she pointed out calmly. "And Nigel didn't cross the Atlantic just to see me."

"Nigel, is it? Josh didn't mention his name."

"Just what did Josh say?"

Kerry faced her squarely as she posed that question, and Jennifer received yet another shock. With the flush of anger gone from his handsome face, he looked almost as pale as when he'd had pneumonia. She was instantly worried.

Here it was late spring, with summer just a few weeks away and every day warmer and lovelier than the one before, yet Kerry looked as if he hadn't seen the sun in months.

"Oh, Kerry," she said, unable to keep the caring out of her voice or the worry out of her eyes.

He had been about to answer her question, about to admit that Josh hadn't told him much at all, save that Jennifer had come to New York to see an old friend from London. Josh had revealed that the friend was a man, and that had started it.

Kerry had been shocked by the bolt of pure jealousy that shot through him. That was a first for him, and it thoroughly rocked him. At the same time, it possessed him with its insidious fire.

Anger had followed. Anger because Jennifer had gone off without saying a word to him. The resulting brew had been potent enough to start with and became stronger as Kerry simmered through the hours, waiting for her to return. He'd taken off from Providence in perhaps the worst fit of temper of his life. He'd acted, he realized now, like some dim-witted caveman.

On the drive down he'd tried to decide on a place where he and Jennifer could be alone, and he'd come up with the idea of Block Island. There, for a while at least, he'd have her to himself. They could find a place on the island for lunch, and maybe, just maybe, before the return trip to the mainland they could manage to thrash out their differences—such as what place this Englishman from her past had in her present.

He hadn't meant to blurt that stupid statement about firing her. The thought of her someday leaving the mansion was so painful that he simply didn't permit himself to dwell on it. He liked to imagine that there'd always be a few more things to do, so her job at Watch Hill would go on and on. Now, though...

Was she serious about quitting? he wondered grimly, knowing how desperate he'd feel if she was.

She was staring at him, her face a mask. But the impact of her topaz eyes brushed away his wrath and melted his resentment, replacing them with entirely different emotions. Desire filled him with an actual, physical pain. He wanted her so badly that it took all his self-control to sit still and not reach out for her.

"Don't blame Josh," he said suddenly.

Jennifer, still absorbed with worry, asked, "Don't blame Josh about what?"

"You wondered what Josh had told me. He only said you were coming to the city to meet a friend of yours from London. He mentioned the friend was a man and said he would be in town for a couple of days. I painted the rest of the picture myself."

"I see."

She knew Kerry wanted her to say more, but she didn't feel he deserved an explanation. He'd jumped to conclusions and would have to live with his misconceptions. She wouldn't let him off the hook so easily.

Block Island was only beginning to ready itself for the forthcoming summer season. Most places in the tiny resort were still closed or in various stages of preseason disarray. Finally, Kerry and Jennifer found a coffee shop that served chowder and sandwiches. They ate the tasty food hungrily and in tension-filled silence.

From the coffee shop they wandered until they came upon a path that struck out toward the sand cliffs edging the island. From a high vantage point they gazed out over Block Island Sound and the cloudless sky.

"It's like looking at eternity," Jennifer murmured, thinking about forever, a concept of time beyond human comprehension. In contrast, the need to deal with now, with the present, with this very moment, suddenly seemed overwhelming. She'd tried to ease those chips off Kerry's shoulders. She hadn't succeeded in budging them an inch. The only choice left was to knock them off, she decided.

Impetuously, crazily, she asked, "What would you do if you knew I was pregnant?" She meant it as a rhetorical question, but it hadn't come out like that.

Kerry swung around to confront her, his blue eyes ablaze. "Are you?" he demanded.

Appalled, she wished she'd never gotten into this. "I...I just asked you..." She fumbled, couldn't finish and saw at once that he'd misinterpreted her hesitation.

"My God," he said hoarsely. "Is that why you went to New York? You didn't..."

Seeing the horror that etched his face, Jennifer felt like a fool. Quickly, she told him, "No, Kerry. I didn't do anything of the sort. I never would."

"I don't know what I'd have done, Jenny."

"Kerry, you're way ahead of yourself. All I did was ask you what you would do, that's all."

His face was stern. "What do you think I'd do, Jenny? I'm surprised you have any doubts."

"I really have no idea," she said sadly. Turning away from him, she added, "You told me at the very beginning that you don't want children."

"I never said that," he contradicted sharply. "Not in that way, not with that meaning. You know why I felt I should never have children. I have no idea, absolutely no idea, of what kind of genetic inheritance I'd be passing on. That seemed wrong to me. But...my God, Jenny, if you're pregnant, that's something else entirely."

That statement struck home to Jennifer, and she began to think maybe it hadn't been such a bad idea after all to explore this avenue with Kerry.

"We both took chances," she said evenly. "You certainly weren't protected."

"I...I suppose I assumed you were," he admitted haltingly. "I thought most women today..."

"Well, you thought wrong."

And that was so. They had taken chances. She'd been so overwhelmed by him, she'd barely given the risks a passing thought.

"You're saying you'd give my child a name, because that would be the right thing to do. Is that it?" she asked.

He shook his head. "No. If you *are* carrying my child, Jenny, I would dare to do something I'd never have done otherwise. I would dare to ask you to marry me, to share my life, to share our child. I would consider your pregnancy something of a divine sign." He shook his head, emotion overcoming him.

Watching him, listening to his words, Jennifer felt sick to her stomach. How could she have gotten into something like this, something of such supreme importance, just to jolt him? She turned away, wondering how she could ever look at him again, ever meet his candid eyes.

He grabbed her shoulders with a pressure that hurt. "What is it?" he demanded. "You're thinking something, and I want to know what it is."

She shook her head, scalding tears filling her eyes. "Nothing, Kerry. It's nothing," she said brokenly.

"Look at me, Jennifer. Damn it, look at me! You're holding out on me. Why? *Did* you go to New York to have an abortion? Is that what you did?"

"No," she moaned. "No, no, no! There is no baby, Kerry. I'm not pregnant."

"What?"

"I—I just wondered what you'd say. What you'd do."

Blue fire scorched her. For several long seconds Kerry looked at her like a coldhearted stranger. Then, his tone flat, he said, "That...was unspeakable."

He turned on his heel and walked away, leaving Jennifer standing alone at the cliff's edge. She watched him start down the path, heading for the town and the dock. She wanted to run after him; she wanted to tug at his coat sleeve; she wanted to beg him to forgive her. Instead, she stood still as a statue until Kerry was a small figure in the distance.

Time passed. The wind blew gently off the sea. Gulls soared over the water. And Jennifer was numb to it all.

Finally she slowly made her way back toward town, wondering with each step how she could possibly face him again. How she could ever regain his love.

On the ferry trip back to Point Judith, Kerry stood at the bow rail by himself, staring ahead. Jennifer huddled inside the passenger lounge, pretending to read a newspaper someone had tossed onto the seat. She looked up at Kerry every so often, and her heart began to break.

Driving back to Watch Hill, Kerry was as distant as if he'd moved to another planet. Only when they reached the mansion and Jennifer started to let herself out of the car did she turn to him.

"Do you want me to leave?" she asked quietly.

His face was bleak. "Suit yourself," he said.

Chapter Fifteen

Cora Madison called up the stairs, "Your brother is here to see you, Jennifer."

Jennifer had just taken a suitcase out of her closet, placed it in the middle of the bed and was about to start packing her clothes. For a moment she thought Cora must be mistaken. Josh wasn't apt to trek up from New York without announcing himself, especially on a weekday. But if it wasn't Josh, who was it?

Puzzled, she went to the top of the stairs and peered down at the front hall. Sure enough, Josh was standing there.

As she slowly came down the stairs, pasting a smile on her face, Josh said pleasantly, "Thanks, Mrs. Madison." But his gray eyes were fixed on his sister, and they were gleaming in a way she didn't like.

"My pleasure, Mr. Smith," Cora fluttered.

Josh was getting to her, Jennifer saw. Josh, with his quiet charm, got to most women. He was so incredibly unaware of his charisma, she thought for perhaps the thousandth time.

"Make yourself at home in the living room," Cora suggested. "There's no one using it right now."

The inn was swinging into its season. That morning Cora had happily reported that they were booked solid from the middle of June right through July, and reservations were piling in for August. Now, addressing Josh primarily, she asked, "Would you like some coffee?"

"Thank you, yes," he said, flashing her a smile. But the smile quickly disappeared once he and Jennifer were alone.

"Will you kindly tell me what is going on?" he demanded.

"Did you have something specific in mind?"

"Don't be funny, Jenny."

"I'm not trying to be," she assured him. "How did you get here, anyway? And why did you come?"

"My, what a welcome," he observed sardonically.

"Well, you might have let me know you were coming," she snapped back. Then she silently berated herself for taking out her frustrations on her brother.

A week had passed since her trip to Block Island with Kerry. She hadn't heard from him since, and she also hadn't had a decent night's sleep. She'd lost five pounds she really didn't need to lose. She was miserable and acutely ashamed of the way she'd duped Kerry into worrying about a hypothetical situation.

She amended that. She hadn't really duped him. She'd just wanted to blast him out of that shell he took refuge in so often. Well, she thought grimly, she'd succeeded—and wrecked her life in the process.

Jennifer's face crumpled in pain. She turned away from her brother, but not quickly enough.

"What the devil!" Josh observed, taken aback. "Are you telling me the iron maiden is crying?"

Jennifer turned tear-filled eyes upon him. "Don't you ever let up?" she accused.

"Jenny, please," he implored quickly. He moved to her and touched her shoulder. "I didn't mean to upset you," he said sincerely. "At least, not that much." He fumbled in his pocket for a handkerchief, then handed it to her. "Come on," he pleaded, "cut out the tears, will you? I can't remember seeing you cry since you fell down that lava slope in Hawaii when Dad was stationed at Schofield. You scraped those knobby knees up pretty good, remember?"

She remembered the incident vividly. Josh, older and supposedly wiser, had carried her back to the cottage where the Smiths were having a brief mountain vacation. Their parents had been out, and Josh had applied his own first aid, beginning with a disinfectant that burned terribly. Jennifer had screamed, but her skinned knees had healed in record time.

Jennifer wished her brother could deal as well with her torn feelings now. Had he seen Kerry? What had Kerry said to him? The questions tumbled out of their own accord.

"Look," Josh urged, "let's sit down and pretend we're having a pleasant family reunion—for Mrs. Madison's sake, okay? She'll be along any minute with the coffee."

He was right. Jennifer had barely composed herself when Cora appeared with coffee and a plate of her famous blueberry muffins. Josh took one bite and was so lavish in his praise that Cora left the room looking as if she'd just been through a second Christmas.

When their hostess was out of earshot, Jennifer stated, "You're quite the con artist, aren't you?"

"I am not," Josh protested. "Those muffins are delicious. She ought to patent the recipe."

"She probably got it out of an already patented cookbook."

"Cynic!" Josh teased, taking another bite.

The coffee was hot and bracing. Exactly what she needed to stir up a little courage, Jennifer conceded. She began again with her original questions. "How did you get up here?" she asked first.

"I drove. Next?"

"Why did you come?"

"Marta called me, that's why."

"Marta?" That was a surprise.

"Yes, Marta," Josh repeated "You thought it was Kerry, didn't you?"

"I thought you might have talked to Kerry, yes."

"I don't think anyone's talked to Kerry for a week," Josh reported. "I know Marta hasn't. And she was pretty sure you hadn't. Also, she asked Harry Kominsky, and he said he hadn't. I don't suppose anyone's bothered to call Kerry's office or his apartment to find out whether he's dead or alive."

"Josh!"

She sat up straight, icicles pricking her spine. Kerry *had* looked terrible the last time she'd seen him. She'd left him on a dreadful note. Suppose he really had been sick?

She moaned softly, and Josh frowned. "Marta said you'd started to pack your suitcases. I gather you've quit the Watch Hill job, and that's why I'm here. I have a professional interest in seeing you finish what you started, remember? A major feature for *Living, American Style* is at stake here."

"I might have known it was your vested interest, not mine, you had at heart," she muttered bitterly.

"Come off it, Jenny," Josh retorted. "I always have your interests at heart. You know that. But Kerry Gundersen's a pretty decent guy. If you don't mind a casual observer making a couple of astute observations, he's also crazy about you, and you're equally insane about him. So can you blame me for wondering what's going on here? Marta told me she's going to run out of things to photograph unless you finish what you've started."

"I can't finish what I started," Jennifer mumbled.

"What was that?"

"I can't finish what I started. Nor do I wish to explain why. And please . . . don't take that personally."

Suddenly, Jennifer wished she *were* pregnant. Wished she were carrying Kerry's child. Wished that she'd had a valid reason for asking him that treacherous question out on Block Island. But her wishing was a little too late. Nature, during the past week, had taken pains to assure her she was not pregnant. Now she would never have Kerry's child. She would never have Kerry.

"When you come out of your trance," Josh told her gently, "maybe we can talk about this."

As the afternoon passed, Jennifer wanted to talk to her brother about the impasse she'd created between Kerry and herself. She wanted to, but she couldn't. She'd already done enough blabbing to Marta without saying very much. That was undoubtedly one reason Marta had alerted Josh to a potential problem.

Finally Josh conceded that he was getting nowhere with her and said, "I think I'll trek over to Watch Hill and check with Marta. Maybe she's heard something from Kerry by now, or maybe Harry Kominsky has."

Jennifer nearly told Josh he could reach the mansion by phone, but she bit back the words. It dawned on her that maybe Josh actually wanted to see Marta, and she wasn't about to interfere with that kind of whim.

Once Josh had left, she felt incredibly lonely. Then a nagging headache began pressing against her temples.

Upstairs again, her eyes fell on the open suitcase. Marta had seen the suitcase earlier, she knew, and evidently had misread her intentions. Now Josh was misreading them, too.

She was going to pack her winter clothes, take them down to New York and exchange them for the lighter summer clothes she'd stored in Josh's apartment, that was all.

It surprised her that Marta hadn't mentioned that she'd showed up for work each day at Watch Hill during this past week when Kerry had been so conspicuously absent. Shouldn't that have indicated that she didn't plan to walk out until the job was finished?

The problem was, the job almost was done. Only a few of the guest bedrooms and the master suite remained. In two more weeks at the most, they would be done, too. There were, Jennifer admitted, many optional finishing touches—more furniture here and there, some additional curios, maybe three or four more paintings to acquire and hang. But those were tasks Kerry could take on himself at some later date. At that point, there would really be no need for her to linger at Watch Hill.

As soon as Josh got back to the inn, Jennifer decided, she'd ask if she could return to New York with him. She could switch clothes, then take a bus back in a day or two and ask Marta or Harry to meet her in Providence.

Josh did not drive to Watch Hill after leaving the inn. He went directly to Kerry's office in Providence. Kerry was at his desk, dismally surveying a stack of papers, when his secretary announced that there was a Mr. Joshua Smith to see him.

Astonished, Kerry strode into the reception area. "Josh!" he exclaimed. "It really is you!"

"Did you think there were two of us?" Josh asked, a slight smile curving his mouth.

Kerry had never realized what a family resemblance there was between Josh and Jennifer, despite the differences in their coloring. But he noticed it now and quickly tried to camouflage the surge of emotion that came over him.

"Come in," he urged.

Josh followed him into the glass-walled office and whistled softly. "Well," he observed, "you do go from one extreme to the other, don't you?"

"Why do you say that?"

"The contrast, Kerry. Between this and Watch Hill."

"I suppose it could strike you that way."

He took his place behind his desk. When Josh had settled in across from him, he asked lightly, "So, what brings you to Providence?"

Josh grinned. "You do," he said bluntly.

"Me? Why?"

"No one around Watch Hill has seen or heard from you for a week," Josh reported. "Marta called me last night, and I drove up this morning. Things seemed to be a bit...mixed up, shall we say? I wanted to check it out for myself. You see, Kerry, we're getting into the final lap, as far as the magazine is concerned. I didn't want to take any chances with it at this point."

"Don't you have just about everything you need, Josh?"

"Not really." He leaned back and surveyed his friend deliberately. "I'd like to know considerably more about the architect," he admitted.

Kerry chose to misunderstand him. "The architect who designed the Watch Hill house died a long time ago, Josh. He was very well known in his day, though. Did a couple of the mansions in Newport and several of the estates out on Long Island, as well. Gatsby-era stuff, you know. There shouldn't be any problem getting some biographical material about him.''

Josh shook his head and chuckled. ''You know I'm not talking about him,'' he remonstrated. ''I'm talking about you.''

''Why do you need to know anything about me? Beyond what's already been touted far too publicly for my taste,'' Kerry told him.

''Simply because my readers will be curious,'' Josh stated. ''Your name will be familiar, I assure you, thanks to the publicity you've already earned. I'd say this is your big opportunity to negate the image that's been built up about you.''

''What image?'' Kerry asked suspiciously.

''Rich bachelor playboy who appeared on the scene as suddenly as Superman descended from Krypton.''

''That's a lot of rot, Josh. You haven't decided to publish a scandal sheet, have you?''

''No. And that's all the more reason to know something of the truth about you, Kerry. For my readers' sake, and for my own, I might add. We've been friends for a couple of years now, and during the last few months I think we've gotten to know each other quite well. Yet when I think back on all the conversations we've had, it strikes me that you've said virtually nothing about yourself. Remember that night we went to that boring dinner in Manhattan? Some investors' group thing that we were both invited to?''

''Yes, I remember. We had a little more than our share of Scotch, I recall.''

''Quite true. Anyway, I went back to the Essex House with you, and we sat in the bar. And while I was somewhat in my cups I told you about something I rarely, if

ever, discuss. My accident, and the effect it had on my
life.''

Kerry nodded gravely.

"I'm not saying that confidences should always be tit for
tat,'' Josh went on. "But I've gotten very little 'tat' from
you. I don't mean to come on like an interrogator, Kerry,
but I am curious as to why you're so reticent when it comes
to talking about anything that happened beyond yesterday.''

"Maybe there's not much beyond yesterday to talk
about,'' Kerry suggested.

"Come on! You don't strike me as an amnesia victim.''

That, Kerry thought ruefully, wouldn't be a bad cover,
except he couldn't be that deceptive with someone he liked
as much as he did Josh Smith.

"I'm not an amnesia victim,'' he allowed. "It's just
that . . . well, I shut the door on my past a long time ago,
and I'd prefer not to reopen it. There's nothing sinister involved, Josh, if that's what you're wondering. I've never
committed any felonies, I've never been in prison, I've
never disappeared. . . .''

"Where've you been for the past week?''

Josh shot out the question abruptly, but Kerry didn't
hedge. "I've been in the hospital,'' he said quietly.

Josh's eyes narrowed. "In the hospital . . . and no one
found out about it?'' he queried.

"I don't blame you for sounding skeptical. I asked my
partner, George Sonntag, to keep it under wraps.''

"What happened, Kerry?''

"Well, a week ago yesterday I was driving back to
Providence from Watch Hill. I stopped at a beach along
the way. I needed to walk awhile. I needed to sort out several rather chaotic thoughts. It was dusk when I started out
on the road again. I was pretty damned exhausted, Josh,
to tell you the truth. I'd been working hard, and I'd had

my share of problems. And I guess I was so bleary-eyed I wasn't seeing straight. Anyway, I didn't make one particular bend, and I wound up smack in the middle of a stone wall. I woke up in the hospital. Nothing too serious, just a slight concussion. But I guess the doctors took one look at me and decided I needed some checking out."

"So they kept you a week?"

Kerry nodded. "Six days, actually. Tests and all the rest of it. I was willing. By then I had the sense to know that what I needed was an enforced rest. Staying in a hospital is a pretty effective way of accomplishing that."

"I know, Kerry. Believe me, I know. Did they find anything?"

"Nothing serious, no. Mostly exhaustion."

"And the prescription?"

"Rest," Kerry admitted. He glanced around his office. "They said I should get away from all of this for a while. Take a real holiday somewhere. George agrees. He insists I've been carrying a major part of the load, and he thinks we should hire someone right out of college who could take care of the basics for us. I suppose he's right. We get so busy sometimes...well, I guess I didn't realize what a workaholic I've become. Lately, I admit it's been sort of a refuge."

"Has my sister been one of those problems you were talking about, Kerry?"

"Why do you ask?"

"Why? Isn't that obvious?"

"I don't know," Kerry said stubbornly.

"May I ask a question that's none of my business?"

Kerry smiled wryly. "I can't keep you from asking it, Josh, but I can't promise I'll answer it, either."

"Jenny was married to a wretch of a man when she was just a kid," Josh said. "A fortune hunter, an imposter—call him whatever you want. I wouldn't want to see her go through anything like that again. In fact, I'd do a great deal to prevent it," he said, his quiet strength unmistakably asserting itself. "That's why I'm asking you, where do you really stand with Jenny? When the two of you are together, anyone with half a brain can see you're crazy about each other."

"The same might be said about you and Marta Brennan," Kerry pointed out.

Josh waved his hand impatiently. "I'm not about to get into that," he said.

"Then what makes you think I'm about to discuss anything that involves Jenny?" Kerry countered.

Josh shrugged. "All right," he said. "You've made your point. Nevertheless, I have one last request."

"What's that?"

"She's leaving, you know. She was about to pack her suitcase when I left the inn a while ago. I tried to talk to her about it, tried to tell her she has an obligation to see your job through. But I think she feels she's done all she needs to do. That's between the two of you, Kerry. All I ask is that you don't hurt her."

Before Kerry could rally, Josh got up and moved toward the door. On the threshold, he fired his parting shot. "By the way," he said lightly, "Jenny told me that you were the soldier who rescued her from the artillery range at McKettrick ten years ago. Tell me about your days in the army sometime, will you?"

Kerry had no idea what he said in answer to Josh Smith that afternoon. He hadn't known that Jennifer was leaving, and the shock of hearing the news was profound. True, she'd told him she quit. But that was during a fit of anger, wasn't it? A moment when she hadn't been thinking straight.

Even when he considered that ruse she pulled, which had ed to their falling out, he couldn't believe that she'd leave without finishing her commission. After all, she loved the Watch Hill home. Of that, he was certain.

More and more he'd envisioned the mansion as Jennifer's setting rather than his. In that direction, he'd already taken an action she'd have to know about before much longer. The ell he'd designed was her studio, sort of a personal thank-you for putting her heart and soul into the project. But there was something more.

Kerry muddled through the rest of the day and somehow made it through the night. He had an important meeting at ten the following morning with his client from San Francisco. George could handle it for him, he decided.

He called Watch Hill and got Marta, who promptly told him that Jennifer had gone off to New York with Josh last night. That hit him even harder than he'd expected it would. And, though he knew what he had to do, he couldn't bring himself to drive down to Watch Hill and do it.

Then George was called up to New Hampshire to consult on the progress of the mall, so Kerry had a valid excuse for not leaving the office. But with George's return, there really was no reason not to take a day and head down to the mansion.

Kerry drove along the road to Westerly on a gray day late in June when it looked as if the summer sun had been drained out of the sky. He was ready to stop the project where it stood, ready to dismiss the workers and close up the house. He was personally convinced that Josh and Marta had more than enough material for their magazine. Any gaps, he decided, could only be minor ones, and easily corrected.

As for himself... it was no longer his house, anyway.

Simple as that, he told himself wryly as he parked in hi.
usual spot beyond the porte cochere. He noted a couple of
workers' trucks and Marta's sleek little blue car also
parked along the drive.

It was difficult to walk into the foyer and look up at the
curved stairway. It reminded him so intensely of Jenny, o
the first time they'd embraced. Shaking himself, Kerry
briefly wondered whom to approach first—Marta o
Harry.

Marta settled the matter for him. She appeared at the
top of the stairs and came bounding down. "Welcome
back, stranger," she greeted him. "It's about time we saw
your face around here."

Marta, her camera slung on her shoulder, was ob
viously intent on going after more photographs. "I wan
to catch Harry before he takes off," she explained. "H
has to go to Providence to get some stuff, and I promised
I'd take a shot of him working in the ell. He's a real ham
that man." Over her shoulder she added, "Jennifer's in the
master suite. Why don't you go up and surprise her?"

Kerry's feet suddenly felt as if they each weighed at leas
a thousand pounds. He couldn't budge. Then he heard
familiar voice asking, "Did you want something, Marta
I thought I heard you—" And Jennifer appeared at the top
of the stairs.

Kerry stared up at her, his heart brimming over. And he
did what was, perhaps, the most eloquent thing he coul
have done. He reached out his arms, his gesture and hi
incredible blue eyes conveying all the messages he couldn'
say.

Jennifer didn't hesitate. She came to him, moving down
the stairs with swift grace. Then he was clutching he
against him and burying his face in the softness of her hair

He felt her tension slowly ebbing away, and in a muf
fled voice she murmured, "I didn't think you'd ever wan

to speak to me again after what I did out on Block Island. When you didn't call, didn't come ..."

Kerry realized that Josh hadn't told her about his stay in the hospital. Nor was he going to tell her now. That could come later, if there was any reason to speak of it at all. Because he knew, much as it hurt, that these might be his last private moments with Jennifer.

He said very softly, "This is the first chance I've had to get down here, Jennifer. Really, it is." Slowly, reluctantly, he let go of her. "I have to talk to you," he said. "Is the drawing room all right?"

Her lovely mouth curved in a sad smile. "Aren't you afraid you'll suffocate?" she asked him shakily.

"I'm sorry I ever said that, Jenny. I was in a rotten mood that day. I admit the drawing room isn't my idea of a cozy place for a fireside chat, but it's the most beautiful room I've ever seen."

"Well, why don't we go into your private study, instead? It's ready and waiting for you."

This was a room she'd saved as a surprise for him, managing to steer him away from it every time he'd come to Watch Hill and enlisting Harry and Marta to do the same when she wasn't there. She'd had it panelled in soft walnut, and the walls were lined with bookshelves. The couch and chairs were leather, soft and comfortable. The desk was large but not massive. Across from it, in an antique gilt frame, was a beautiful oil painting of a Connecticut farm at harvesttime. She'd left room for more artwork and the personal things that would make the room entirely Kerry's.

Kerry was completely speechless for more than a minute. Then, summoning all the resolve he possessed, he guided Jennifer to one end of the couch and took the other end himself.

In a hoarse voice he said, "It was my understanding that you'd gone back to New York."

"I was going to ride down with Josh, but I decided to wait till the weekend," she told him. "The weather turned a bit cooler, so I didn't need my summer things. Marta's heading down on the weekend, anyway. Josh actually asked her to a play Saturday night."

Jennifer stopped short. Kerry was staring at her in an odd way. He was looking at her as if...

Suddenly, she realized what he'd thought.

"Did you think I'd gone for good?" she managed.

"Yes."

"You really believed I'd do that? You have that little faith in me, Kerry? Do you really think I'd walk out on a commitment?"

"I didn't know," he confessed. "You did quit as we were driving to Point Judith."

"After you'd inferred anyone in his right mind would fire me," she reminded him. "But that was just my temper, Kerry. I never meant it."

"I wasn't sure, Jenny. But that's past," he stated. He took a deep breath and added, "Anyway, I can't begin to tell you how glad I am to find you here today. As I said, I couldn't get here any sooner. But I have managed to make some legal arrangements."

"What legal arrangements?"

"Well, I won't be turning this place into a halfway house after all," he began.

"What about your promise to live here for a year?" Jennifer asked, her heart suddenly pounding.

He shook his head. "I can't do that. It isn't my house any longer."

"What are you saying?"

"It's your house, Jenny. My lawyers have worked out the details, and the deed should be finalized any day now."

"What!"

"Don't look like that, Jennifer. What I've done with this place is the right thing to do. I'm convinced of that."

"What have you done?" she demanded.

Kerry stared at her and said, "I've deeded it to you."

Jennifer got to her feet without even realizing she'd stood up. "What?" she thundered.

"You belong here, Jenny," he said simply. "I don't. It was crazy of me to think I could fabricate a past for myself by having you decorate an empty building. That can't be done—I know that now."

"You really *are* out of your mind, Kerry Gundersen."

"I don't think so."

"I can't simply take a house from you. No way. It's the most ridiculous thing I've ever heard of."

"Why?"

Jennifer's topaz eyes sparked. "Maybe because I don't want it, okay? Did that ever occur to you? Yes, I love this house. But why do you think I love it? Because I've made it yours—the home you've always dreamed about."

"I already explained—"

"You haven't explained a damned thing!" Jennifer cut in. "I'm tired of all your complexes, Kerry. You're the most wonderful man I've ever met, but you're so blind to things sometimes. I'd love to live here, but only if I could live here with you. Don't you understand that? I don't want your house. I want you!" Jennifer finished, her chest heaving.

"You don't know what you're saying, Jenny."

"That's what you think," she said defiantly. "Actually, I know exactly what I'm saying. You just don't listen to me, that's all. If you had, you'd have long ago gotten the message that I don't give a damn about your past. All I'm interested in is your future. If we were lucky enough to have kids, that's what they'd be a part of!"

Kerry suddenly looked pale, and his eyes seemed very dark. But Jennifer managed a smile as she continued. "Way back in Georgia, I did some fantasizing about you, Kerry Gundersen. I thought you'd be a great person to be shipwrecked on a desert island with. I figured you'd be resourceful. You'd find the best coconuts and know how to make a fire. And on those languid tropical nights, with the sea shimmering beneath an enormous golden moon..."

Her voice softened as she spoke, and by the time she finished her speech, Jennifer was choked with emotion. Then she held her breath, waiting for Kerry's response. Waiting and wondering if he could possibly see how much she wanted him forever. How much she wanted to love him through eternity.

He sat very still. He didn't say a word. Then, slowly, he reached into his pocket and drew out his billfold. He searched through its compartments and carefully withdrew a small slip of paper.

"Remember the Chinese restaurant and the fortune cookie?" he asked, holding it out to her.

Jennifer swallowed hard, almost afraid to see the message. "Conquer your fear, take destiny in your hands and claim the mate of your soul," she read.

She looked up into Kerry's wonderful face and saw the love shining in his eyes. And her tears came.

"Do you believe in fortunes, Jenny?" he whispered huskily.

She reached out to pull him against her and said softly, "Implicitly. Oh, Kerry, I love you so much."

They sank back, wrapped in each other's arms, reveling in the wonderful knowledge that finally—finally—they were together. Ten long years after that hot and dusty Georgia afternoon, the angry young sergeant and the haughty, confused army daughter had finally found that love was a glorious common meeting ground.

After a time Kerry asked, "Have there been any twins in your family?"

"Not that I know of," Jennifer murmured contentedly.

"Then if we ever have twins, we'll know they're from my side."

Fourteen months later, Jennifer Gundersen gave birth to twins.

*   *   *   *   *

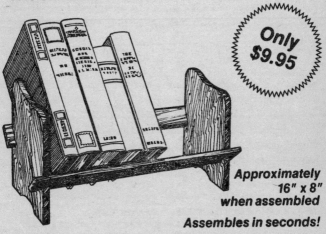

COMING NEXT MONTH

#433 ALL THE RIGHT REASONS—Emilie Richards
Crack attorney Brett Terrill wasn't looking for love—just an obedient wife who'd bear his children. Meek, maternal Olivia LeBlanc seemed the perfect match . . . till she developed her own case of ambition.

#434 HEART OF THE TIGER—Lindsay McKenna
After her marriage failed, Layne Hamilton vowed never to get involved with a CIA man again. But agent Matt Talbot had a mission . . . and enough charisma to hijack Layne's heart.

#435 ONCE BURNED . . .—Karen Keast
Morning Skye Farenthall and Brandon Bear Hunter had once pledged eternal love . . . then betrayed their youthful vows. Now a raging forest fire reunited them, and their burning passion—and blistering pride—threatened to consume them.

#436 SAY HELLO AGAIN—Barbara Faith
When Miguel Rivas met his high school heartthrob, Brianna Petersen, at their fifteen-year reunion, the old feeling was back. And this time he wasn't looking for a prom date, but a partner for always.

#437 CANDLES IN THE NIGHT—Kathleen Eagle
For practical Morgan Kramer, falling in love with idealistic dreamer Mikal Romanov was sheer insanity. Driven by his humanitarian causes, would he ever notice *her* very human needs?

#438 SHADY LADY—Patricia Coughlin
On Diamond Cay, Kara McFarland found the privacy her past demanded. Celebrity Max Ellis sought precious solitude himself. But as they trespassed on each other's turf, proximity led to dangerous passion.

Silhouette Romance ™

Legendary Lovers Trilogy

BY DEBBIE MACOMBER....

ONCE UPON A TIME, in a land not so far away, there lived a girl, Debbie Macomber, who grew up dreaming of castles, white knights and princes on fiery steeds. Her family was an ordinary one with a mother and father and one wicked brother, who sold copies of her diary to all the boys in her junior high class.

One day, when Debbie was only nineteen, a handsome electrician drove by in a shiny black convertible. Now Debbie knew a prince when she saw one, and before long they lived in a two-bedroom cottage surrounded by a white picket fence.

As often happens when a damsel fair meets her prince charming, children followed, and soon the two-bedroom cottage became a four-bedroom castle. The kingdom flourished and prospered, and between soccer games and car pools, ballet classes and clarinet lessons, Debbie thought about love and enchantment and the magic of romance.

One day Debbie said, "What this country needs is a good fairy tale." She remembered how well her diary had sold and she dreamed again of castles, white knights and princes on fiery steeds. And so the stories of Cinderella, Beauty and the Beast, and Snow White were reborn....

Look for Debbie Macomber's *Legendary Lovers* trilogy from Silhouette Romance: *Cindy and the Prince* (January, 1988); *Some Kind of Wonderful* (March, 1988); *Almost Paradise* (May, 1988). Don't miss them!